praise for Chris Rober

"This mash-up of 1930s pulp fiction with dreams of a secret heritage accessible only to the chosen is far more self-aware and entertaining than *The Da Vinci Code*. Born of Roberson's deep affection for radio serials, comic strips and writers like Michael Moorcock and Gray Morrow, this affectionate look at finding oneself and finally coming to terms with one's roots is accessible [and] entertaining."

Death Ray

"Roberson is another author to watch."

Charles De Lint

"It's quick, witty, and spell-binding. I couldn't put this down."

Random Musings

"*Book of Secrets* is... unique, refreshing, breezy, and fun."

Red Book Review

"An exciting new writer."

Jonathan Strahan

"Chris Roberson is one of that bold band of young writers who are taking the stuff of genre fiction and turning it into a whole new literary form – a form for the 21st century. A talented storyteller, he has a unique ear, a clever eye, an eloquence all too rare in modern fiction."

Michael Moorcock

Also by Chris Roberson

The Bonaventure-Carmody Sequence

Here, There & Everywhere

Paragaea: A Planetary Romance

Set the Seas on Fire

End of the Century

The Celestial Empire

The Dragon's Nine Sons

Three Unbroken

Iron Jaw and Hummingbird

The Voyage of Night Shining White

Others

Shark Boy & Lava Girl Adventures

X-Men: The Return

Star Trek: Myriad Universes – Echoes & Refractions

Star Trek: Myriad Universes – Brave New World

Warhammer 40,000: Dawn of War II

Warhammer 40,000: Sons of Dorn

CHRIS ROBERSON

Book of Secrets

ANGRY ROBOT
A member of the Osprey Group

Lace Market House,
54-56 High Pavement,
Nottingham
NG1 1HW, UK

www.angryrobotbooks.com
La Mano Negra lives!

Originally self-published in the US by Chris Roberson 2001
This substantially revised edition first published in the UK
by Angry Robot 2009
First American paperback printing 2010

Cover by Argh! Nottingham

Distributed in the United States by Random House, Inc., New York.

ISBN 978-0-85766-010-7

Printed in the United States of America

9 8 7 6 5 4 3 2 1

For Fran Striker, Lee Falk, Gray Morrow, Matt Wagner and Tim Truman

My brother and I once met at a bar, and fell to talking about family. Parents, kids, relatives, the whole sick crew. He took issue with the idea about children being some link to the future, our bid at immortality. Parents, he says, are our true link to eternity. In each of us is a little bit of each of our parents, literally and figuratively, and in each of our parents a bit of theirs, and so on and so forth. All the way back to the Garden of Eden or the Primordial Ooze, depending upon your politics. Looking at our parents reminds us of eternity, he went on, because in them we can see everything that came before. Our parents remind us of the steaming piles of history it took to get to the present moment – in our case, the two of us in that bar on that night at that particular moment.

Considering we hadn't looked at our parents since my brother and I were both five years old, watching their caskets being lowered into the ground, shuffling our feet and wishing it would stop raining, it was somewhat surprising. But that's my brother for you.

What that has to do with anything I'm not sure, except to say that it concerns family and eternity, two things that factor greatly into the events of the past week. It began in the bleary eyed hours of the morning, with a phone in one hand and a telegram in the other, and ended with me watching the setting sun, the secret history of mankind clutched to my chest.

The FIRST DAY

The phone rang insistently, again and again, and as I struggled out of a restless sleep I stared in its direction, an unfrozen caveman trying unsuccessfully to fathom the purpose of this strange, clanging thing. Finally, inspiration struck and I seized up the receiver, maneuvering it with only a hint of difficulty to my ear. Listening to the faint buzz on the line, satisfied by the sudden cessation of the ringing, I stood dumbly for a long moment, trying to remember what to do next. Finally it came to me.

"Hullo?" I managed.

"Is this Spencer Finch?"

"Um... yeah?"

"Spencer Finch, the reporter?"

"Yeah." I was slowly beginning to remember what this phone business was all about, and realized that under normal circumstances I usually had some idea who was on the other end of the line before launching into conversation.

Then I remembered that the landline seldom ever rang, and that hardly anyone had the number. I'd lost my cellphone the week before somewhere on a bender, and had been reduced to using payphones ever since.

"Am I to understand that you are still interested in pursuing your investigation of J. Nathan Pierce?" The voice, now that it occurred to me to notice, sounded cultured and refined, if somewhat breathy. An educated and somewhat fey man, or a slightly masculine woman.

"Who is this?"

"That is not important at the moment, Mr. Finch." I caught a trace of an accent, but I couldn't place it. "I'll repeat my question. Are you still pursuing your investigation of J. Nathan Pierce?"

"Possibly," I answered, reserved. "What's it to you, Mystery Caller?"

"I have some information that may be of use to you, should you be interested."

"Uh huh."

"I'd simply like to suggest that you question one David Stiles of Houston. He is a private detective, and his services were recently retained by your Mr. Pierce."

I grabbed a yellow slip of paper I'd pulled off the door as I'd stumbled in the night before, and scribbled down the name.

"And why would Pierce need to hire a detective?"

"I'm afraid I don't know. I've told you all I can. Do with it what you will." The voice paused for a beat, and then added, "My condolences on your loss."

"Yeah, well..." I began, and then the line went dead.

"What loss?" I muttered, and then absently turned over the yellow paper in my hand. It was a telegram, signed for by my next door neighbor and dated two weeks before.

My grandfather was dead.

Unable to sleep again after that, I shrugged into my suit coat and drove over to Trudy's North Star. The restaurant was farther away than I really needed to go, but the drive gave me a chance to wake up, and it's one of the few places left in Austin where you can still smoke indoors. I found a parking spot near the door, and settled into a booth before the waitress even noticed I was there. She brought over a cup of coffee without question, and went back to a table in the far corner to finish her own cigarette. She knew me on sight. I'd shown up often enough early in the morning and ordered nothing more than a bottomless cup of coffee for her to give me any special attention.

Lighting my first cigarette of the day, I dumped half the contents of the jar of sugar into my coffee, and then pulled the telegram from my pocket. After glancing briefly at the name scrawled across the back, I turned it over and read the contents more closely. It mentioned a funeral, and an address and date. In San Antonio, at a church not far from my grandfather's house, where my brother and I had lived from the age of five on. I'd missed the ceremony, and was disappointed only in that it would have marked the first time that I would have seen the old man in a church. It went on to request my attendance at the reading of the will at an attorney's office in Houston. I'd missed that as well. There was some mention made of material inheritance, but I didn't spend too much time on that.

I turned the slip of paper back over. I hadn't seen my grandfather in a decade, and was somewhat surprised he hadn't died years before. The name I'd written on the reverse, though, was sufficiently curious.

I'd been working on the piece about Pierce on and off for a while now, in between paying gigs. Since *Wide Open*, the left-leaning magazine that had kept me on staff for three years, went under, I'd returned to Austin and started doing freelance work. *Wired, Rolling Stone, Spin*. Mindless fluff to fill up the spaces between pictures and ads. I'd been getting regular work from *Logion*, an online magazine based in Austin, and they had commissioned me to do a piece on Texas millionaire and philanthropist J. Nathan Pierce. The money wasn't much, but I had a thing for the lady publisher, and if done right the story might give me a much needed sense of self-esteem. There was only one problem: there was no story.

J. Nathan Pierce, "Nez" to his friends, retired colonel USMC, successful businessman and millionaire benefactor of the University of Texas. This withered old nut was stuck in more pies than he had fingers, but the ones that interested *Logion* were some shady land deals he'd rigged in South Texas. The back-story of his generous donations to the University was rumored to involve the extortion, harassment, and perhaps outright murder of Mexican farmers, but I had yet to come up with a single bit of verifiable evidence. The *Logion* piece was intended to coincide with Pierce's official recognition for his humanitarian efforts by the University and the state of Texas. There was to be a gala ceremony in his honor on his seventieth birthday, and ground broken at a new university library that was to bear his name. If I wanted to cast a long enough shadow to sour the birthday carnival, I'd need something more than rumors and allegations. I needed proof.

But after a few months spent digging, both in Austin and around Pierce's home offices in Houston, I'd come up with exactly nothing. He had covered his tracks well, or at least his friends had, and I was left without a story. Pierce was well connected enough that his people in the Justice Department, the Texas Land Office, and the state and federal governments could simply make any evidence disappear. All of which made the name written on the back of the telegram so curious.

If Pierce had hired a private detective – and I stressed the "if," not ready to trust an anonymous call in the middle of the night; that sort of spirit in the machine only came out of the woodwork in mystery novels and bad TV, and I wasn't hanging any kind of hope on it – *if* Pierce had hired a detective, the question was why? Any business he needed taken care of, any bit of information he needed or person he wanted found, his friends with the badges and the government pensions could have handled easily. Unless – and this was the big flashing sign – he didn't want them to know about it.

The only reason someone like Pierce would step outside the good old boy club was if he had done something, or found something, that he didn't want being passed around the clubhouse. And something like that, just maybe, could mean a story.

Leaving Magnolia and my bottomless coffee behind, I was home by sunrise, and saw my place in daylight for the first time in a month. I'd been away in Chicago working on a story for Rolling Stone, and hadn't returned until late the night before. After two too many drinks on the plane and in airport bars, I barely looked at the place as I stumbled up the drive. A little two-bedroom house, with sagging wooden floors and wide gaps in the walls, it probably looked a hell of a lot better during World War II than it did now. But it was cheap, and large enough for all my crap, and I could come and go as I liked.

Once inside, I fired up my ancient computer and pulled down David Stiles's home and office number. There was no answer at his home, and I caught a machine at his office, so I sat at my desk, working my way through a pack of cigarettes and thinking it over. By the time the ashtray was full I had it worked out. I put in a call to the publisher of *Logion,* leaving a message that I might have a story for her after all, and started shoving a few things in a suitcase. By the time my neighbors were up and on their way to work, I was back in the car, heading to Houston.

The drive to Houston was three hours, down a straight and wide road, and since the radio in the car was only picking up Christian Country, Christian Contemporary, and Christian Classical, I shut it off. I began thinking in that roaming, everywhere-at-once way that you do on long car trips, and eventually, without meaning to, began to remember my grandfather.

He had always been old, as long as I could remember, but I didn't ever notice him aging. He was simply an ancient old man in the beginning, and stayed that way, untouched further by the passage of time. Towering over us, smelling of cigar smoke and bourbon, always immaculately dressed and expertly shaved. He spoke seldom, in a loud booming voice, but when angry would spit out his words in a barely audible hiss. We first saw him, my brother and I, at our parents' funeral. He simply walked over to us, where we stood next to the twin open graves, a moving wall in a black wool suit, and announced that we were going to live with him from now on. Then he turned around and walked away to his car. We weren't sure for a long time just who he was, and it wasn't until we actually reached San Antonio that we were sure.

He was not a friendly man, and had little time for social niceties, either with company or with family, and I think that neither my brother nor myself received anything resembling affection from him in all our years there. We were raised, such as we were, by his housekeeper, Maria, who was the closest thing either of us had to a parent after the death of our own.

I thought then, and still do, that the old man resented having to take us in, but as he was the only living relative available – our father's brother being the only other candidate, and at that time living in Europe – he had no choice. To turn us over to the state to be raised or adopted out would simply be bad form, and an insult to the few pleasant feelings he had left for his departed daughter. Besides, he trusted the authorities, "No farther than I could draw a bead on them," he always said, and didn't want his only descendants entrusted to their care.

I remember talking to my grandfather very seldom, if at all. I remember him talking to me, vividly, or rather issuing orders, but he had no time for the customary conversations which go on between children and adults in a family household. He left that to Maria, and spent his waking hours in his study. He had been involved in some sort of business, years before I was born, but for as long as I can remember had been retired. His energies were devoted solely to his researches, or writings, or whatever it was he did in that large room.

Once, when we were twelve, my brother dared me to sneak into the study, to see what was inside. Neither of us had ever been in there, and had only caught glimpses through the half-open door as our grandfather came in and out. He was upstairs in the bath, and we had scant moments until he would be back downstairs and at work. I don't think my brother expected that I would take the dare, but I was simply too curious not to. Stealing a quick peek up the stairs to make sure he wasn't coming, I slipped down the hallway to the study door, and then inside.

It was dark and cool, even in the middle of the summer, and as my eyes adjusted to the gloom I began to make out my surroundings. There was a wide Persian rug on the hardwood floor, and dark wood paneling on the walls, a stone fireplace built into one side. Other than a broad wooden desk and a high-backed chair upholstered in leather, the only furniture in the room consisted of bookshelves and glassed-in cases. There were framed paintings and prints on the wall, knights on crusades and pirates on windblown ships, and several posters that were advertisements for adventure serial films of the forties. There was a long glass case along one wall filled with what looked like thick, glossy comic books, but which I later decided were pulp magazines. Strewn over the desk, and laying in heaping piles on the tops of bookshelves and on the floor, were papers and books. A cartographer's nightmare of mountains and valleys, all mapped out in typewritten pages and hardcover volumes. Moving further into the room, stepping gingerly around the piles, I saw a case set on the mantle of the fireplace. In it was a pair of jet black Colt .45s, mounted on a field of black velvet. I stood looking at them a long moment, entranced in that strange spell weapons hold over boys, and almost too late heard the heavy footsteps in the hallway.

I wheeled around, sure that at that very moment the old man was regarding me evilly from the doorway, but he hadn't yet reached the door. I looked around in a panic, desperate for someplace to hide, but saw nothing, only books and paper. Standing there by the fireplace, I was sure it was all over. Then a fit of inspiration struck, and I turned and ducked into the fireplace. My back against one of the stone walls, my feet on the other, I pushed myself up off the ground like a rock climber in a tight crevasse, and by the time I heard the door swing wide was just out of sight, jammed into the narrow chimney a few feet above the ground.

I heard the footsteps enter the room and walk across the floor to the desk. I groaned slightly under the strain, and counted the heartbeats until my muscles would buckle and I would fall out onto the floor. I hadn't got to ten when the footsteps sounded again, heading back towards the door. I heard them pass to the hallway, and then the heavy door closed shut behind them. With a grunt I let my feet slip from the chimney wall, and collapsed onto the fireplace's base, shoulders first. Staggering to my feet, I dusted myself off, and limped towards the door. I leaned into the wood and listened, but could hear no one on the other side. Pulling it open cautiously, I edged my way out and into the hall.

Not even bothering to glance around, I bolted for the stairs and bounded up the flight to my bedroom. I was through the door and inside before I'd even drawn a breath. I slid down the floor and landed with a thud on the thick carpet, surrounded by my toys and comics. I closed my eyes, feeling the pain in my every muscle, and smiled. At that moment, I knew just wanted to do with my life, just what I wanted to be.

A cat burglar.

* * *

I pulled into Houston just before noon, and with only a bit of trouble found the address of Stiles's office. It was in a squat, three-story building just off of downtown, in what once must have been a fashionable neighborhood. The sprawl and urban flight had left it behind like an abandoned toy in a warzone, though, and I thought twice about leaving my car parked on the street. Figuring *Logion* would pick up the tab for any incidental damage, I walked in the front door.

In the small main lobby, there was an elevator with an out-of-order sign on it older than I was, an open door to a stairway, and a directory with little plastic letters spelling out the names of bail bondsmen and repo services on black felt. I found Stiles's name near the bottom, misspelled, and a room number on the third floor. Putting on my game face, I made for the stairs and headed up.

Stiles's office was at the end of a long hallway, most of the lightbulbs along the way burned out and the tiles on the floor warped and ill-fitting. There was a light on inside the office, visible through the pebbled glass of the doorway, and I pushed my way in without knocking.

I'm not sure what I expected to find inside, but an attractive black woman in her late twenties packing things up in a cardboard box was not high on the list of possibilities. Aside from her and the box, and a few sad pieces of furniture, the room was empty.

"Yeah," she asked, obviously not pleased by the company, "can I help you?"

"Yes, I'm looking for David Stiles."

She straightened, and put her hands on her hips.

"You're a bit late, honey." She said the word as a reflex, without any warmth, like a waitress who just got a lousy tip. "He's dead."

"But..." I stuttered, taken aback. "When..."

"Night before last," she answered. "Stupid son of a bitch fell out of his bedroom window, down six stories." She paused, shaking her head. "Wasn't just a whole lot an ambulance coulda done for him, even if they hadn't taken thirty minutes to get there."

I glanced around the room, taking a quick inventory.

"And you would be?" I asked.

"Funny, I don't remember hearing your name when you came in," she said, her eyes narrowed.

"My name is Spencer Finch," I answered, remembering to smile. I offered my hand. "I'm a reporter, and I'm working on a story I thought Mr. Stiles could help me with."

Warily, she took my hand, her long nails grazing the back of my wrist.

"Talitha Cummings," she said. "I worked for Stiles these past couple of years. He didn't pay much, but then he wasn't really around all that much either."

"I see," I answered, but didn't really. "So you were his... secretary."

Talitha yanked her hand back like it had been burned, and glared at me.

"I am not a goddamned secretary." She straightened, her chin up. "I'm a research assistant. I did go to college, you know."

I didn't, but nodded all the same.

"Then maybe you could help me," I went on. "Would you happen to know what cases Mr. Stiles was working on before he... well..."

"Went pavement diving?" she asked. "Yeah, I suppose I would know at that." She crossed her arms, and looked hard at me. "Why should I tell you?"

I smiled broadly, and gestured towards the door.

"Ms. Cummings, could we discuss this over lunch?"

Without a word she grabbed her purse and was out in the hallway. As she headed towards the stairs, she called back over her shoulder.

"You can spend all the money on me you want," she said, "but that doesn't mean I've got to tell you anything."

Talitha directed me to a Thai place on the north side of downtown, and once there worked her way through two helpings of some sort of chicken and noodle dish, while I picked my way through a plate of ground beef and rice. While eating we talked, or rather she talked and I listened. I had overheard enough conversations between women to know what they are like, and women tend to bring the same rules to bear when talking to men. By the time we had finished the main course, I knew where she had grown up, where she had gone to school, how many siblings she had, and just what her relationship with her parents was like. That, and the fact that she found me "very easy to talk to," which I accepted as a compliment. I hear it from people a lot, women especially for some reason, but in my line of work I could hardly complain.

From me she got my name, the name of my magazine, and the fact that I seldom, if ever, ate Thai food. If she was expecting any girl-talk out of me, I'm sorry to say she was disappointed. Men play by different rules. Women talk about themselves; men talk about *stuff.*

Once the check came, and we finished off our drinks, I diverted the conversation to the proper order of business.

"So," I asked, clinking the last ice cubes around in my now empty glass, "do you think you can tell me about the cases Stiles was working on?"

Talitha daubed at the corners of her mouth with a broad cloth napkin, and regarded me with an amused look.

"Well," she said, "since you asked so nicely..." She leaned forward, conspiratorially. "David had closed most of his cases in the last month. The usual, run of the mill stuff. Following some guy's wife, tracking down a runaway kid, shit like that. The only case still open when he died was a new one that came into the office last week. Some kinda snoop job for a high roller."

"What high roller?"

"I dunno, some big-money, land-and-oil, ten-gallon-hat cracker. Name of Price, something like that."

"J. Nathan Pierce?" I asked.

She straightened, and looked at me with a grudging respect. I got the impression she had been playing dumb, and wasn't expecting me to know even that much.

"Yeah, that's the one. He called the office early last week – himself, mind you, not some flunky – and asked to speak to David. The next thing I know David's bustin' out of the office trying to slick his hair back and put on a tie all at once, and didn't come back till late in the afternoon. From then on he was working on the case, day and night, weekends too, until…"

She paused, in what I took to be an uncharacteristic display of emotion.

"Until he fell," I finished for her.

"Exactly."

"What was the case, if you don't mind me asking?"

"I'm not sure if I should," she said. "Mind, that is. But I'll tell you anyway. Don't see as it can make any difference now." She lowered her voice slightly and continued. "There was a break-in at Pierce's place over in River Oaks a while back, and something pretty valuable got stolen. Some papers, or a book, something like that. David was supposed to find it and bring it back, and the fee was going to be enough to keep him in bad haircuts and cheap cologne for a year."

"Why hire Stiles? No offense, I'm sure he was a fine detective..."

"No, he wasn't," she interrupted. "He was a shitty detective. But he was a kind man, and people liked him."

"Well, there you go. Why would someone like Pierce, a) hire a detective, and b) hire a shitty one? It doesn't make sense."

"Honey," she said, with more warmth now, "you are asking the wrong woman. I asked David that when he came back with the case, and he looked at me like I'd just shit in his yard. You see, David was always sure he was a great detective, and just ain't never had the chance."

"But you knew better."

"Shit yeah. But I didn't want to hurt his feelings, so I let it go."

I sat quietly for a moment, rolling a bad thought around in my head for a while before letting it out. Finally, I had no choice.

"Talitha, do you think there's any chance that Stiles didn't just fall out of that window? Do you think maybe he was pushed?"

"Mr. Finch, since we're being all open and honest here…" She paused slightly, and drew a breath. "Yes, that is *exactly* what I think."

Talitha agreed to let me take a look at Stiles's notes on the case, but explained that they were already boxed up, and it would take her a little while to find them. With a sly grin she suggested she could probably have them together by, say, dinner time. I swung back by the office, and dropped her off outside, arranging to pick her up there at about six. Without another word, she walked off and disappeared into the building.

The car idling, I glanced at my watch. It was only one o'clock, which left me with five hours to kill before I knew anything more. I figured I could do a drive by of Pierce's place in town, to see what I could see, but would still have ample opportunity to get stunningly bored. I would have to think of something.

Stopping at a Texaco, I picked up a couple of packs of Camels, a liter of Pepsi, and an enormous bag of CornNuts. I decided that if the opportunity to stake out Pierce's house presented itself, I wanted to be prepared. As it turned out, I needn't have bothered.

The house wasn't all that far from Stiles's office, but it might as well have been on another planet. Contrasted with the cramped streets and urban blight of that area of downtown, River Oaks was like a national park, with mansions airlifted in. The streets were wide and winding, and the houses positioned artfully on plots of land the size of football fields. Pierce's was on Lazy Lane, where the largest and most opulent of the houses could be found. They were so far above the rest that you couldn't even see them, perfectly hidden by high walls, or by hedges taller than the entire line-up of the Houston Rockets combined.

There was a manned security guard-post at the entrance to Pierce's place, making it looking even more like a fortress than it already did. Cruising by slowly, I got a glimpse of a manicured lawn and white pillars in the distance, but nothing else. The security guard caught my eye, and in the subtlest of body language let me know it would be a good idea to move along. I eyed the pistol at his hip, and dropped my foot on the accelerator.

Following the winding roads out of the neighborhood and back to civilization, I wondered just what I would do with the rest of the afternoon. I could find a bar and hole up somewhere, but then I would risk forgetting about my appointment all together. I could check into a hotel and catch up on some much needed rest, but then I might sleep straight through the night. As I drove, I fished around in my coat pocket for my lighter, and came up with a crumpled piece of paper. Glancing at the telegram, I figured what the hell? There were worse ways to spend the time than picking up my inheritance, though at that moment I was having trouble deciding just what they were.

The law offices of O'Connor, Riley, and Vasquez were located in a high rise in the heart of downtown, a glass and steel obelisk rising some thirty stories into the smog. I had visited the offices only once, during high school, when the venerable R.M. O'Connor represented me against charges of breaking and entering as a favor to my grandfather. I ended up with a suspended sentence from the court, a stony silence from my grandfather, and a two hour lecture on my failure to meet expectations from R.M. O'Connor. I had seen him only twice after that, when he had come to our house on business, and I learned quickly to be elsewhere when he was around.

O'Connor was the antithesis of my grandfather, and I was always amazed they had continued their association as long as they had. Crude where my grandfather was refined, loud where my grandfather was reserved, O'Connor was an old school Texan lawyer, who played the good-old-boy angle for all it was worth. I decided there must have been something in their past that bound the two old men together, some secret thing each saw in the other that earned their respect. For my part, I never saw it, and only and ever saw O'Connor as a swaggering old ass with a weakness for cheap scotch and western wear.

I arrived in the offices unannounced, and found everything just as I remembered it. The height of oil boom opulence, with over-stuffed chairs and cheap reproductions of Remington paintings hanging on the wall, the requisite bronze cowboy frozen forever in the saddle, and a pair of Longhorn steer horns mounted on the wall. The wizened old receptionist, for all I knew, had not moved since I had been marched into the office by my grandfather fifteen years before.

"Can I help you?" she drawled, looking at me over her oversized glasses.

"I'm here to see R.M. O'Connor," I answered, stepping up to her desk.

"Is Mister O'Connor expecting you?" she asked. She gave me an appraising look and, apparently, I came up short.

"I wouldn't hazard a guess, ma'am," I said. "Could you just tell the old buzzard that Richmond Taylor's grandson is here to see him?"

Her eyebrows shot up at the mention of my grandfather's name, and her hand reached for the phone. I heard her repeat my message to someone on the other end, and then set the phone back down on its receiver.

"If you'd just have a seat, sir, he'll be with you in a moment."

I was still trying to get comfortable on the squeaking leather when O'Connor burst into the lobby a few minutes later.

"Patrick," he boomed, advancing on me. "How the hell are you, son? Didn't expect to see ya again so soon. You change your hair?"

He stuck out his hand, and I stood and took it. He held my hand in that over strong, overlong way that only lawyers and used car salesmen can.

"I'm not Patrick, O'Connor, I'm Spencer."

He let my hand drop like he'd just seen roaches crawl out of my sleeve, and narrowed his eyes.

"Ah," he said. "Ah. Spencer. Wasn't expecting to see you."

I leaned around him, and shouted to the old bat pretending to work on her computer.

"He wasn't expecting me, Mabel. You were right."

The old man turned and headed back towards his office.

"Come on, son," he called over his shoulder. "Let's get this over with."

In O'Connor's office, full of the expected law books and diplomas, I signed a stack of releases and waivers and statements of indemnity, all while listening to the old goat rattle on.

"I wasn't expectin' to see you at the funeral, mind, but you could have surprised me and showed up. You owed the man that much, at least, if you ask me. Just a little bit of respect, that wouldn't a been too much to ask, now would it?"

"I didn't," I said, not looking up from the papers I was signing.

"What's that?" O'Connor barked, losing his train of thought. "Didn't what?"

"Ask you."

"Well, that's a hell of thing, I don't mind tellin' you. All that man did for you and your brother, and you ain't even got the decency to see him be put in the ground. Not like your brother, now that he's been mentioned. He was there for the whole show, dressed up all nice, a real gentleman, your brother."

"Where is Patrick these days, anyway? I haven't seen him in a while."

"Oh, hell, I don't know. Flew in from Africa or some such place, he said, and was flying off again after. But he was here, all the same."

I finished with the signatures, and capping the pen tossed it across the desk at O'Connor. I stood, reaching into my pocket for a cigarette.

"Look, O'Connor," I said, "I have an excuse, or a reason, or whatever you want to call it, but I'm not going to waste it on you. If I happen to run into the old man sometime, I'll use it on him, but I'm not going to hold my breath." I snapped open my Zippo, and sucked the flame into the cigarette.

"The way I see it, the old man dying means that your business with him is done, and once you give me whatever the bastard wanted me to have, your business will be done with me, too. So if you could..." I waved my arm for him to proceed.

With a grunt and the creaking of his ancient bones, the lawyer lifted himself out of his chair and crossed the floor to a large wall safe. Shielding his right hand with his left, he spun the dial back and forth, and then with effort yanked open the door.

I had discovered, while looking over the papers, that the house at 217 Crescent Row, San Antonio had passed into the hands of Mrs. Maria Casares, our grandfather's housekeeper in long standing, along with all the belongings contained within it, with the exception of the library, which went to my brother Patrick. Patrick also inherited a stamp collection, which I had never seen and which I learned had been the possession of my grandmother, a woman I had never met. All liquid assets, savings accounts, stocks and holdings, were divided equally and distributed amongst three charities of my grandfather's choosing. All debts, public and private, past or pending, were to be handled by O'Connor's firm, and paid as was appropriate out of a small fund held for that end. As for me?

I ended up with a cardboard box, full of magazines, books and type-written pages, and a locked wooden case about a foot square and six inches tall, weighing about ten pounds, for which no one could find the key.

"Here they are," O'Connor explained, "just as Richmond left 'em. Appears he knew his time was up, and had everything boxed up and ready to go. We just had to roll in and pick 'em up."

"That was thoughtful of him," I answered, wondering idly how things would have been had the old man made that move twenty years before. "What is this shit?"

O'Connor shot me a glare, but kept his voice even.

"I'm not sure. He didn't rightly say, only that this was the only product of his life's work, and he wanted you to have it."

I was taken aback.

"His life's work? Why would he want me to have it?"

O'Connor leaned into me, and I could smell the cheap scotch on his breath.

"I have no idea in hell, you little bastard. If you ask me, which you didn't, you are and always have been an ungrateful sack a shit, and I told your granddaddy as much whenever the subject came up. But for some reason this box was important to him, and he wanted *you* to have it. So if you don't want me to throw out my back chucking you out of that there window, you're going to pick this stuff up, walk out of here, and try your damnedest to show a little respect to the dead."

I met O'Connor's eye and didn't look away, but saved the quips and comebacks bubbling up for another time. For some reason, they didn't seem appropriate. I hefted the cardboard box under one arm and the wooden case under the other. Without another word, the old lawyer turned away and walked back to his desk.

I headed for the door, the sharp edge of the wooden case cutting into my side, the dust off the ancient cardboard box drifting up and into my nose and eyes. When O'Connor spoke, my eyes were watering.

"It was the damnedest thing, Spencer, and I never knew just why, but that old man loved you."

I didn't turn around, didn't say anything, just kept walking out the door.

I decided to put in some time in a bar after all, but even after making friends with a half-dozen screw-drivers managed not only to remember my appointment, but to get there on time. Talitha was still up in the office when I arrived, with the case notes ready to go.

Great, I thought, another cardboard box.

I had expected to go over Stiles's notes there in the office, but instead Talitha just handed it to me.

"Go on," she said, "you take them. They're not doing anyone any good here."

"Are you worried that if somebody went after Stiles, they might come after you too?"

"Not with that shit out of here, they won't," she answered. "Besides, I'm not going to stick around long enough to find out. This is my last day on the job, and then I'm leaving town."

"Another job?"

"Eventually, but right now I think it's a good time to take a vacation." She smiled at me, and leaned on the desk in a way that made me think of a mechanic's wall calendar.

"Not a bad idea." I peeled open the top of the box and began rummaging inside. There was a large stack of black-and-white and color photos, handwritten pages by the dozen, and a large sheet of paper, yellowed with age and sealed in an enormous Ziploc bag. This last I held up, looking at it in the light. It was covered front and back with tiny little characters, in what might have been Hebrew, or maybe Arabic.

"What's this?" I asked.

"Not sure," Talitha answered, "and neither was David. He said he copped it from Pierce's place when the old cracker wasn't looking. It had fallen under a desk or table or something... it's all there in his notes."

"Why did he take it? Was it a clue?"

"A clue?" Talitha snorted. "What are you, Encyclopedia Brown? Evidence, honey, ev-i-dence. That's what it is. From the way it was laying there, David figured it must have been part of whatever got swiped, so he figured he'd have a closer look."

"He find out what it was?"

"Nah, didn't have a chance."

I dropped the plastic bag back into the cardboard box, and sealed it up again. I picked up the box again, and started slowly towards the door.

"Thanks for all this, Ms. Cummings," I began. "If there's anything I can ever do for you..."

"Not so fast, baby," she interrupted, grabbing her purse. "I'm not helping you just because you're so cute. You owe me a dinner."

She breezed past me into the hallway.

"I am not," she called back, "I repeat, *not* above taking a bribe."

We ate at the most expensive Italian restaurant Talitha could think of, and once we'd both had enough wine the atmosphere of the evening was like a fair first date. Talitha told me more about herself, and I was loose enough to tell her a little about me. I told her about the times I ran away from home, and about my three years as a cat burglar, subjects I rarely get into with strangers. Still, she seemed sympathetic, and maybe a little impressed, so I went on longer and farther than I normally would have. I could tell she didn't exactly believe me when I told her about breaking into the Federal Reserve Bank in San Francisco, so I let the conversation drift in other directions.

When we were done and the check paid, I drove her back to her place. I let her invitation to come upstairs fly right past, knowing that she didn't really mean it, even if she thought she did. It would only complicate what had been a pretty good night. I left her on the curb, and pulled away into the night.

It was too late to head back to Austin, much less go anywhere else, so I found a cheap motel on the interstate and checked in for the night. I pulled the box of Stiles's notes out of the trunk, and in a moment of drunken curiosity pulled the top stack of papers and magazines out of my grandfather's box as well. My bag over my shoulder and a pack of cigarettes in each of my pockets, I staggered up to my room and inside.

In the room, decorated in early denim, I lay on the vibrating bed and gave the photographs Stiles had taken of the Pierce home a cursory inspection. Wide shots of the yard, endless views of the interior rooms, tight close-ups of the motion detectors and infrared webs that had been disabled during the break in. Then pages and pages of notes in a scrawl only slightly more legible than my own, detailing Stiles's theories on how the burglar entered the grounds, crossed to the house, got inside, and on and on and on. The sheet in the Ziploc bag was last, and made no more sense to me than it had before. I left them all piled up on the other side of the bed and spent a while staring up at the acoustic ceiling tiles. By the time the timer in the vibrating bed ran out, I was starting to sober up, and climbed off the bed to find something else to entertain me.

The television in the room only picked up four stations, and with only two infomercials, Sheriff Lobo and a Chevy Chase movie to pick from, didn't take up too much of my time. I lit a cigarette and sat down on the edge of the bed, the stack from my grandfather's box in my hand. There were a few typewritten pages I couldn't quite get the meaning of, genealogies or timelines or some such, and a couple of magazines. The one on top was one of the pulp magazines I remembered seeing in my grandfather's study all those years before. *The Black Hand Mysteries*. With nothing better to do, I dragged an ashtray onto the bed and started to read.

"The Talon's Curse"
by Walter Reece

(originally appeared in the September, 1939 issue of The Black Hand Mysteries*)*

1

The blood-curdling scream tearing across the night air told Richmond Taylor one of two things: someone had just been killed, or someone was about to be. He didn't care for either option.

Coming up the stairs to the Carousel Club, the rooftop restaurant that had become the toast of the San Francisco social scene, Taylor tore through the crowds towards the source of the scream. Louise Aldridge, his Gal Friday and companion for the night, still hung on his arm, rushing alongside him with bated breath. Louise knew well Taylor's course in the face of danger.

The last of the crowd parted seeing Taylor approach. The wealthy financier was well known in upper crust social circles, and generally thought something of a fop, but his steely gaze and his whipcord muscles flexing like steel bands beneath the dark fabric of his suit would brook no delay.

There, on the tiled floor, lay the battered body of a young girl. She lay face up, an expression of terror frozen on her cold face, black blood encrusted round her lips. Where her heart should have been, where the beat of her young life once sounded like a small bird's wings, there was only a gaping chasm, a gory tunnel to the floor below. Taylor straightened himself, fixing his gaze on the inert body on the floor. Rush as he might, he would have arrived too late to save this girl. She had been dead for hours.

Next came the sound of shouts, and a gruff voice raising above the rest, calling for order. Taylor knew the voice well. It belonged to Detective Chalmers, pride of the San Francisco Police Department.

"Get outta my way, you blood-thirsty rubber neckers," he called again, shoving his way through the crowd. "Lemme do my job."

At a sign from Taylor, Louise slid her arm from under his and blended back into the crowd. She understood her duty at such a time: to canvas the onlookers nonchalantly, discovering what she could. Her report would aid Taylor in ferreting out the truth, and she cherished her responsibility. Of all Taylor's agents, only she knew the secret of his other life.

With Louise gone, Taylor made his way across the crowd to a man he'd noted on his entrance. They had been climbing the stairs together, and when the waitress who had discovered the body had screamed, this man had been the only one not to hurry to the scene to investigate. Taylor had recognized him as Peter Matthews, black sheep son of a wealthy shipping magnate.

Sidling up to Matthews, Taylor watched as Detective Chalmers surveyed the scene, and began questioning the witnesses. Taylor, feigning horror and a weak stomach, addressed Matthews.

"Terrible business," he began, only a trace of the Texas twang he had inherited along with a fortune from his father sounding in his level voice. "What could possess someone to do such a thing?"

"I wouldn't know," Matthews answered evenly, his gaze darting to Taylor. "I've only just arrived."

"Not the sort of thing you expect to see at such a place," Taylor commented, eyeing the other man.

"Oh?" Matthews answered coolly. "And where would you expect to see such a thing?" Abruptly he turned on his heel, and stalked away. Taylor watched him as he went, deep in thought.

When the police had finished their interviews, and the body had been carried out under a sheet, Taylor and Louise met on the stairs. Taylor produced a pair of cigarettes, and lit one for each of them with a silver-plated lighter, engraved with the emblem of an outstretched hand.

"Well, Miss Aldridge," he finally spoke, loud enough for passersby to hear, the smoke curling about his head, "I see little reason to remain. I'll walk you home."

They descended the stairs and went out into the dark street. Walking down the sidewalk, arm in arm, they looked the picture of the loving couple. But it was not endearments they whispered to one another. They spoke of crime.

"Miss Aldridge," Taylor said, his voice low, "your report."

Louise began simply, stating what she had learned from memory. "The hallway had been empty when the waitress last passed through it. It leads from the main dining room to a storage area. The storage area is visited throughout the night, waitresses and busboys going back and forth to get glasses, linens, and such. But sometimes half an hour can pass without anyone going that way. The waitress had been the last one to walk it, twenty minutes before, but when she went back, she found..." Despite herself, Louise found her voice breaking. She paused, trembling.

"She found the body," Taylor said, completing the thought.

"Yes," Louise answered.

"And beside the main entrance, is there any other access to that hallway?"

"Near the storeroom there's a freight elevator," she replied. "It stops on each floor, but is unmanned at this hour. It opens on the loading dock at the ground level."

"Likewise unmanned," Taylor commented.

"Yes."

Taylor quickened his pace, and Louise hurried to keep up.

"Then," Taylor concluded, "anyone might quite easily have taken the body up the elevator, left by the same route, and escaped detection."

"But why?" Louise asked. "Why leave the body there?"

"That, Miss Aldridge, we will not know until the body is identified. Only then can we begin to answer such questions."

Arriving at Louise's walkup in the North Beach, Taylor bid her a good night, saying he would see her the next morning at the office. Out of habit, Taylor waited in the street below until he saw the light in Louise's window go on. She was his most trusted aide, and he was always very protective.

As he was about to turn, and move on, he caught sight of a dark figure, prowling about the side of Louise's building. He thought it a vagrant, seeking a warm place to sleep, until the figure stepped into the light, and he saw his features were disguised with a hood. Then the moonlight glinted off the steel of the pistol in the figure's hand, and Taylor knew it was no vagrant.

Taylor, keeping his eyes fixed on the mysterious figure, stepped into the shadows of a doorway. Pulling on black leather gloves, and rolling down a close-fitting mask of black fabric from inside the brim of his fedora, he stepped back into the light. No longer Richmond Taylor, wealthy financier and gadabout, he now stood tall as that dark mystery of the night, that scourge of terror and nemesis to all evildoers: The Black Hand!

2

Stealthily slipping across the cold concrete, The Black Hand crept up behind the dark figure. As the figure mounted a trellis on the side of the building, intending to climb, The Black Hand rushed him. His own swift hand swept through the night air, knocking the pistol from the figure's grasp before he knew the attack was on him. The hooded man fell to the ground, cursing, and rolled away out of the Black Hand's reach.

"Who are you?" the Black Hand hissed though the fabric of his mask. "What evil do you work here?"

The hooded man rose to his feet, unsteady, and before the Black Hand could move flung himself at him. The pair fell to the ground in a tangle of arms and legs, each striking out at the other. The hooded man got to his feet an instant before the Black Hand, and raced off into the night. The

Black Hand flew after him, his feet sounding like gunshot against the pavement.

Across North Beach they raced, over Telegraph Hill and down to the docks, the hooded man always just out of the Black Hand's reach. Behind his mask, Taylor cursed himself for going out into the night without his twin .45s. It was a mistake he vowed never to make again.

Their pursuit had gone unnoticed, through deserted and empty streets, but at the Embarcadero the hooded man raced in front of a truck, bearing its cargo through the night. He made it past the truck only by inches, and the Black Hand found his path blocked until the mammoth vehicle had passed. By the time he himself had crossed the thoroughfare, the hooded man was nowhere in sight. He had vanished into the night air like mist, blending into the foggy sky.

On the other side, the Black Hand found only the empty piers, and the silent warehouses that lined them up and down. The hooded man must have gained entrance to one, and there hid in darkness. The Black Hand spent the better part of an hour, searching the perimeter first of one warehouse, then the next, but could find no sign of forced entry. Finally, he gave up the chase, and, returning his mask to its place, hidden under the crown of his hat, he made his way back over the hill, now simple Richmond Taylor again.

He came at last to Louise's door. Her light still burned overhead, and Taylor wanted to warn her against danger. Some unknown stalker had sought to do her harm, and might do again. Letting himself in the main door with his skeleton key, he climbed the stairs to her door. He knocked, and knocked again, and no answer. Finally, fearing the worse, he tried the door, only to find it unlocked. Pushing it open, he cautiously entered the apartment.

The furniture lay in disarray, strewn about the floor, and broken dishes and lamps were spread all over. Louise was nowhere to be found. Pinned to the inside of the door, with a steel hook, was a notice, hastily scrawled in red ink.

"Louise Aldridge is with me. If Mr. Taylor wants her return, it will cost him. I will contact with details."

Taylor ripped the note from the door and read it over. It was signed, "THE TALON." He crumpled the note in his gloved hand. Louise Aldridge was in grave danger, and there was work for the Black Hand to do!

3

Taylor hurried through the foyer of police headquarters, speeding to his appointment with Detective Chalmers. Though as the Black Hand he was wanted dead by criminals and imprisoned by the police, as Richmond Taylor he was a valuable member of the community, and the authorities were happy to rush to his aid.

On his way through the squad room, Taylor narrowly avoided colliding with Officer Joe Martenson. Martenson, a simple beat cop with an honest heart and a hatred of crime, was one of the Black Hand's trusted subordinates. But unlike Louise Aldridge, he knew nothing of the identity of the man he aided, and had never met Richmond Taylor. Taylor almost forgot himself and addressed Martenson by name. Instead, he excused himself and hurried by.

The night before he'd called Martenson from Louise's apartment, telling him only that the Black Hand had a use for him. He'd given Martenson Louise's address, and told him to hurry. Then Taylor had returned to his home on Nob Hill, and awaited the police's call. When the call came, he feigned shock. Someone kidnap his trusted assistant? The horror.

Now, the next morning, Taylor was to meet with the officer in charge of the investigation, and would learn the particulars of the case. He was eager to learn all he could. Little did the police realize that by talking to Taylor, they were aiding the mysterious Black Hand!

When all had gathered in Chalmers' office, Taylor surveyed their faces. Besides himself and the Detective, there was Police Lieutenant Jones, the

Chief of Police James Carroway, and millionaire industrialist Reginald Dupree. Taylor eyed this last longest.

Dupree was dressed in an expensively tailored gray suit, with a silver pin on his lapel, showing a four-armed spiral enclosed in a circular band. Though distressed, the man had an undeniable look of self-satisfaction about him, as though he considered the others in the room beneath him. Since the beginning of the Depression ten years before, few fortunes had escaped entirely unscathed, and those that had were usually comprised of some dirty money. There were rumors about Dupree's practices, rumors of ill-advised associations.

"Gentlemen," Chief Carroway began, "let me first say how sorry we are that we have to meet under these circumstances."

"I don't have time for your glad-handing!" Dupree shouted. "What about my wife?"

"Well then," the Chief answered, flustered. He turned to Chalmers. "Detective?"

"Sure, sure." Chalmers muttered, lighting a cigar. He rose out of his seat, and crossed the floor to stand before Taylor and Dupree. "It's like this, boys. You've had people kidnapped, and we're gonna do everything we can to see that you get 'em back in one piece."

"And without any pieces missing," Jones added under his breath.

"That's enough outta you," Chalmers shot back, glaring. "Show some tact, why don't ya. Now then, this creep what's got your people calls himself the Talon, like you already know. And he means business."

"Detective," Taylor began in a calm voice, "does this possibly have anything to do with the body found last night at the Carousel Club?"

"Yeah, right," Chalmers answered slowly, eyeing him. "I saw you there, didn't I? Well, yessir, it does. See, this Talon has a habit of taking two victims at once. For leverage, ya see. One pays, they get their people back. The other doesn't... they don't."

Dupree rose up out of his seat.

"You mean this has happened before?" he shouted. "You could have stopped my wife being kidnapped yesterday? Of all the incompetent..."

"Now, Mr. Dupree, we've done everything we can so far," the Chief answered. "And we're close to making an arrest." He turned to Chalmers, his voice grave. "Isn't that right, Detective?"

"Sure, sure. Now, Mr. Dupree, your wife was the fourth person kidnapped. The first was 'bout two weeks ago. We've managed to keep it outta the papers so far. That girl found last night, the kidnapper killed because her family wouldn't pay. They were workin' with us to get him, and we almost did, but it got fouled up. Then he was down to one bird, so he picked up your assistant,

Mr. Taylor." Chalmers paused, puffing on his cigar. "Looks like the guy's just going down the social register, hitting one millionaire after another.

"Now, so far two families have paid the kidnapper's money, and got their people back. They show up healthy enough, but they can't say who the creep was. He wore a mask the whole time, they say, like a hood, so's they can't identify him."

Taylor tensed, grasping the arm of his chair.

"I don't see how any of this is going to get my wife back," Dupree growled.

"Yes," Taylor added. "You must have a plan."

"That we do, gents," Chalmers added. "Mr. Dupree, this creep's gonna be calling you to make arrangements for his payoff. What you do is agree to pay him, let him pick a spot for the meeting, and then let us know. We show up, get him, and you get your wife and the money."

"And what about my assistant?" Taylor asked.

"Well, once we got this Talon character we find out where he's got her."

"What are we waiting for," Dupree answered, rising up. "I'm game. Anything to get back my Meribelle."

Taylor stayed stiff in his chair. He didn't trust the police to accomplish everything they'd planned. They might need help, and the Black Hand was the one to provide it!

4

Through Martenson, the Black Hand learned that the meeting between Dupree and the Talon was to take place that night, at the edge of Golden Gate Park. When the hour came, the Black Hand was in place, this time with twin .45 automatics at the ready.

Dupree was to wait in a clearing, a suitcase full of cash at his side. The police were hidden amongst the surrounding trees, waiting for the signal to close. When the Talon arrived, the police would encircle him, and cut off escape.

The Black Hand watched the officers take their positions, himself hidden in amongst the branches of a tree, some eight feet off the ground. From that vantage point he had seen a gap in the police's net, one the Talon could use to his advantage, and it was this spot he kept watch over.

At the stroke of midnight, as arranged, a hooded figure stepped into the clearing, dragging behind him a blindfolded and gagged woman. It was the Talon. In the moonlight a pistol glinted evilly in his hand.

Without a word, he motioned Dupree to throw him the case of money.

"Give me my wife first," Dupree shouted, red-faced and trembling.

Again, the Talon gestured for the case, and then turned the pistol on Dupree's whimpering wife.

"Okay, okay," Dupree answered, and threw the case across the clearing to land at the hooded figure's feet.

With one hand keeping the pistol trained on Dupree's wife, he reached with the other to retrieve the case. Then, stepping slowly behind her, he shoved her into the clearing and hurried back to the trees. In an instant, the police emerged from hiding and rushed towards him, but to no avail. By cunning, or dumb luck, the Talon was running directly towards the hole in their net. But the Black Hand stood ready.

As the hooded figure passed underneath him, the Black Hand leapt from his perch, landing on the Talon with the force of a sledgehammer. He batted the pistol from the hooded man's hand, and then brought his own guns to bear.

"This time, fiend," he hissed behind his mask, "I have my own claws with me. And now, you will tell me what you know."

Under the hood, the Talon quivered. The black hand of justice was upon him, and he felt its strength close around him!

5

The police found the man beneath the hood a short while later, whimpering and unmasked, tied to a lamppost. The Black Hand had learned what he needed from the man, and left him behind.

The man had turned out to be one Charlie Parsons, an out of work dockworker. He was a rough cut, simple man and, though not above breaking the law to suit his own needs, he was no criminal mastermind. The Black Hand had seen early that Parsons was nothing more than a pawn, a dupe. The true source of the evil at hand lay elsewhere.

Parsons, easily frightened into playing stool pigeon by the masked figure under the dark trees, had confessed that he knew nothing about the kidnappings. He had been hired by a hooded man simply to escort a bound woman into the clearing, retrieve a briefcase, and then return to the hooded man waiting in a sedan on a darkened street nearby. To Parsons this was simply a job, a strange one of course, but if a mysterious man wanted to pay him a month's salary to stand around wearing a hood and waving a gun about it was fine with him.

Of his employer, Parsons could only say that he had picked him up off the streets near the dock, where he had been looking for work. He had been driving a late model, dark-colored sedan, and had spoken only in whispers. He had never encountered the man until earlier that evening, and in his words had never broken the law in his life. This last the Black Hand doubted, but left that for the courts to determine. He was onto bigger prey.

Stepping into the shadows a short distance from the park, the mysterious avenger of the night emerged into the light in the guise of Richmond Taylor. Then he made his way across town to his home, and spent a sleepless night in his study, staring quietly into the darkness, contemplating. Morning came quickly, the sunlight streaming in through the shuttered windows, and Taylor reached for the phone.

He placed a call to police headquarters, and in the Black Hand's raspy voice asked to speak with Joe Martenson.

"Martenson here," came the reply after a short while.

"Joseph," Taylor whispered into the receiver, "the Black Hand has use for you."

"Go ahead," Martenson answered, his voice grave.

"The man known as the Talon still holds an innocent in his clutches. I would see her released."

"Well, you're not alone," Martenson replied. "She's not either, anymore."

"Explain yourself."

"The Talon's got another bird in the hand now. Another millionaire's kid. Peter Matthews."

"I see," Taylor answered. "I see." He paused. "Your service is valued, Joseph," he went on. "I shall remember your loyalty."

With that, Taylor hung up the phone. Now two lives hung in the balance. What was needed now was a visit to the docks. Then nightfall, and action!

6

Taylor spent the day up and down the wharf, talking to dock masters and ship captains from one end to the other. He played the bored investor, trying to find sound investments for his family's fortune. Were there any empty warehouses to be had, he asked, any piers on which space might be rented? His family was moving into shipping, he explained, and wanted to gain a foothold in the market. He let slip that he was looking for qualified men to run the operation, too, which went far towards loosening recalcitrant tongues.

In the end, Taylor caught a cab and returned home. Once there, he unrolled a large map of the city onto his dining room table, and in a blunt-end pencil began to mark different locations one by one. With his considerable power of recall, he traced the route the hooded man had fled by two nights before, placed a large "X" upon the spot where Parsons was hired, and then began to triangulate positions and calculate distances to the half dozen warehouses he had circled. After half an hour's work, he had his answer. He rolled up the map, and returned it to the shelf.

He dressed quickly. First the black wool suit, shoes, and leather gloves. Then he slipped various tools and devices into his pockets, and into the hollow heels of his shoes. Next he loaded his twin .45s, and slipped each into its shoulder harness. Last came the snap-brim fedora, the full-face mask ready to fall into place. Thus outfitted, he strode across the room to the phone.

The line rang four times, and then a groggy voice answered.

"Yeah, this is Nick," came the muffled voice. "Whadya want?'

"Nicholas Oliverio, the Black Hand has use for you."

"What? Oh, sure, yeah, I'm up."

"You will meet me at the following address, Nicholas," Taylor continued in whispers. "I will need your services for much of the night."

"You got it, boss," Oliverio replied eagerly. "Anything you say."

Taylor gave him an address a few blocks away, and told him to be there in fifteen minutes.

"I'll be there," Oliverio answered, almost shouting. Taylor hung up the phone, turned out the light, and left the room.

Nick Oliverio arrived on time, even considering that he'd driven from the far side of town and had been in bed when Taylor had called. Nick felt he owed his life to the Black Hand, and would do anything for him. Some aided the Black Hand out of fear, or of hope for reward. Nick assisted him out of gratitude. Months before, the cab driver had narrowly escaped death when the Black Hand had prevented a gun-crazed fiend from firing point blank in Nick's face. Ever since, whenever the Black Hand needed him, Nick was at the ready.

Nick pulled up to the curb, and from out of the shadows stepped the Black Hand. Without a word, he slipped into the backseat of the cab, closing the door silently behind him.

"Where to, boss?" Nick asked, not turning around.

"Pier 31," came the whispered answer.

"You got it."

In silence, the cabbie drove his dark passenger through the night, stopping at last a short distance away from the indicated spot. Nick knew the Black Hand used subtlety and surprise as weapons, and didn't want to interfere.

"Wait here," the low voice ordered. "I shall return with two other passengers, and possibly some cargo."

Nick shivered despite himself. He had a good idea what kind of cargo the Black Hand meant, and it would be destined only for a morgue. Still, he was happy to help.

The Black Hand slipped away from the cab, sidling up to the dark warehouse, number 2740. Going around the side, he came to a door secured with a rusted padlock. Slipping a slender tool from a pocket, he inserted it into the keyhole, and with a twist, jarred the lock open. Then he gently pulled the door open and stole inside.

The interior of the warehouse was cavernous and empty, the ceiling high overhead. Broken wooden pallets and empty boxes littered the concrete floor, and overhead swung a heavy iron hook on a rope and pulley. The only light came from a dim bulb set in the far corner wall, and beneath that light lay slumped a crumpled form. Twin .45s at the ready, the Black Hand made his way across the floor, and crept up towards the figure lying there in the dim pool of light. It was the bound form of Louise Aldridge.

"Miss Aldridge," the Black Hand whispered, his voice betraying his concern for his trusted aide. "Louise." He knelt beside her, placing a hand on her round shoulder. "Where is Matthews?"

Roused from a fitful sleep, Louise slowly opened her eyes. Her shock at seeing her rescuer was registered there in those crystal blue orbs.

"Richmond," she breathed.

"Where is Matthews?" he repeated. "I must get you both out of here."

"Who?" Louise asked.

"The other prisoner," he answered as he went to work on her binds. He wanted her away from there as quickly as possible, but could not leave the other victim to whatever fate awaited him. So intent was he on freeing her, that he noticed too late the look of horror in her eyes, and saw the shadow falling across his own hands. A blow like a jackhammer pounded into his head, and he fell into darkness!

7

When he regained consciousness, Taylor found himself unmasked, bound hands to feet, and laying on the floor next to Louise. She stared at him, wide eyed, unable to help.

He struggled into a sitting position, and surveyed his surroundings. Whoever had struck him had been waiting in the darkness when he arrived, and come up behind him unnoticed.

"Richmond," Louise whispered. "Are you alright?"

"I have been better, Miss Aldridge," Taylor answered in a low voice. "I take it you are the only prisoner here."

"I was until you arrived," she answered. "Now there are the both of us."

"How long was I out?"

"Just a few moments," Louise replied. "Just long enough for that man to get you tied up."

"Did you get a look at him?"

"No, he always keeps his face hidden under a mask, not unlike someone else I know." She paused. "But I suppose he's alone in that club now." She gestured with her chin, pointing at the hat and mask that lay tossed a few feet away.

"No time to worry about that now," Taylor answered, his voice grave. "Where has he gone?"

"I'm right here, Mr. Taylor," came a voice from out of the shadows. Then followed a mocking laugh, and a hooded figure stepped into the light, a pistol trained on the pair.

"He calls himself the Talon," Louise said, eyeing him icily.

"I would have thought he'd come up with a better name than that," Taylor replied. He turned his gaze on the hooded man. "Wouldn't you, Peter?"

The hooded man laughed again, and then drew himself up straight. Keeping his pistol pointed at the two of them, he reached up with the other and pulled the hood from his face. There, unmasked, stood Peter Matthews!

"I should have suspected," Taylor said evenly. "It was all there in front of me."

"I'm sure," Matthews hissed. "But it's rather too late now, Mr. Taylor. Or should I say, Black Hand." He laughed, mirthlessly. "It's a pity to have discovered your secret so soon before your death. It kind of takes the fun out of it."

"What are you going to do?" Louise asked at a silent signal from Taylor.

"I'm going to kill you, of course."

"But why?" she went on, stealing a glance at her silent companion.

"Why not ask your boyfriend?" Matthews taunted. "I think he's got it all figured out."

"You tell her," Taylor snarled. "I wouldn't want to spoil your fun." Taylor needed just a few moments more, and he knew that once bragging, Matthews would give them to him.

"Very well," Matthews sighed. "My father disowned me last year, Mrs. Black Hand, on account of my somewhat unsavory associates. A boy has to have a hobby, you know. In any case, I find myself in need of cash, and the old man simply won't give it to me, no matter how often I ask. He hates me, you see. A huge disappointment. That's the rub, really.

"But he doesn't want me dead. So say I were kidnapped, and his only choice was to pay up or get my severed head in the mail. That would spoil his brunch, don't you think?" Matthews walked to the wall about ten feet away, threw a switch, and from overhead came the sound of rusty gears groaning to life.

"So you staged your own kidnapping," Louise said. "But why me, and all the others? What do they have to do with it?"

"Well, I wanted daddy dearest to see I, that is the Talon, was serious, so I tried a few dry runs first. Pick up an heiress' daughter from school, milk a few bucks from the old cow, and puncture the little darling if mommy doesn't pay. Then the police are sure to tell daddy that the kidnapping is for real." He paused. "My father just doesn't trust me you see. Anyway, by kidnapping little beauties like you, I get the money too. Like a bonus. And I just pay some drunk fifty bucks to stand around in this smelly mask for the pick-ups, and I never run the risk of getting caught." He smiled grimly. "Pretty snappy, huh? But enough of my jawing." He swung the pistol around, and pointed it at one and then the other of them.

"Which one of you wants to go first?" He took a step to the side, and gestured behind them. There, four feet from the concrete floor, hung the iron hook. The gears above had lowered it into place, and now it stood ready.

He stepped forward, the gun trained on Taylor, until he was only a few feet away.

"You, I think, Mr. Hand," Matthews finally said.

"I think not," Taylor replied and, splitting his bonds, drove his feet into Matthews' knees. Matthews tottered, shooting blind, and staggered back, moaning. The bullet rushed past Taylor's ear, striking the wall behind him and sending splinters of wood flying into the back of his neck. Taylor pulled the now severed binds from his ankles and sprang to his feet. In his hand he held the slim blade he'd managed to pull from the hollow heel of his shoe, and with which he'd cut the rope wrapped round and round his arms and legs.

Matthews stood stock still, gaping, not sure what had happened, and as he brought the pistol once more level with Taylor's chest the man of mystery rushed towards him. Disoriented, Matthews shot wildly, but if any hit Taylor he didn't slow down. An unstoppable engine, he plowed into Matthews, driving him back.

Matthews, crazed, struck at his attacker with the pistol, and then flung it away. Taylor was inhuman, unstoppable, and bullets couldn't hurt him. Taylor slowed his advance. Matthews staggered back, and then turn to flee. He took only two steps into the shadows and was brought up short, screaming.

Taylor, blood dripping from the bullet wound in his shoulder, stepped forward slowly, but it was too late. Matthews, in the darkness, had run directly into the iron hook, and with the force of his movement had impaled himself there. Now he hung, lifeless, listing slowly this way and that. The Talon had met his death on his own claw!

8

After recovering his hat and mask, and freeing Louise, Taylor had returned to Nick's waiting cab. From there, he was driven to Louise's building. Nick helped the masked Taylor up the stairs to Louise's apartment, and then stayed to help her dress the Black Hand's wounds. When they were done, still masked, Taylor thanked Nick for his loyal service and asked him to depart.

"Sure, boss," the cabbie answered. "I'll let myself out. And call any time."

Once he had left, Taylor drew the mask from his face and called for Louise to bring him the phone. Dialing, he flexed his shoulder, testing the dressing.

"Good work, Miss Aldridge," he complimented. "I am always grateful I was able to lure you away from the medical profession."

"Anytime, Mr. Taylor," she answered, smiling. "And if you think being a nurse is more exciting than this, you've got another think coming."

"Yes," he replied, nodding. "I suppose you're right."

The line continued ringing, until at last came the sleeping voice at the other end of the line.

"Yes."

"Joseph," Taylor said, "I apologize for disturbing your rest, but I have information regarding the Talon. Direct your colleagues to the empty warehouse at Pier 31, and there you will find the Talon. I believe you will discover that the warehouse is in the possession of Matthews Industries, and that, with the knowledge that the man you will find was the face behind the Talon's hood, should be all you will need to know."

"Yes sir," Martenson answered. "Right away, sir."

Taylor dropped the handset back into its cradle, and then eased back onto the couch.

"Miss Aldridge," he finally spoke, his eyes half lidded. "I am afraid I will have to ask another favor of you."

"What?" Louise shot back, feigning indignation. "What could you possibly need now?"

"The use of your couch until morning," Taylor replied. "I'm afraid I'm not going anywhere."

Louise smiled, and drew a quilt over him.

"You got it, Mr. Taylor," she answered, "but I need something from you, too."

"And what is that?" Taylor asked, almost succumbing to sleep.

"You still owe me a dinner on the town," she replied, "and I mean to collect."

Taylor laughed, smiling, and then closed his eyes. Tonight, at least, justice would sleep.

The SECOND DAY

Morning came early with a spike in my head and an unpleasant taste in my mouth. I lay sprawled on top of the bed sheets and felt myself being baked by the white hot light that knifed into the stale air through the part in the curtain. I rolled off the bed and bumped the air conditioner down a couple of notches, but it gave a sad wheeze and sputter and then stopped working entirely.

Figuring this as good a time as any to get moving, I thumbed the television on to the morning news, and stripping off my clothes climbed into the shower. I got as wet as I could under the little trickle eking its way out of the shower head, and did my best with the doll-sized soap and shampoo provided for my convenience. Finishing, or rather just stopping a few moments later, I tried as much as possible to dry off using the little tissue-sized towels all cheap motels seem to come equipped with. I was used to the drill, never getting wet enough when in the shower, never getting dry enough once out.

As I rubbed the little towel against my head, I caught strains from the television in the next room. The usual stuff: stock market down, the wrath of God descending on some trailer park somewhere, some politician caught in some kind of scandal. When I heard the name "J. Nathan Pierce" my ears pricked up, and I ambled into the other room.

There was a commercial break, and then the anchor returned to pick up on the teaser he'd dropped just before.

"And in business news, sources close to land and oil magnate J. Nathan Pierce announced today that he had closed a deal to sell his interest in Vista Incorporated..."

The bobbing blow-dried hairdo dissolved and was replaced by a shot of an elderly giant of a man, dressed in an expensive suit and standing in the middle of what looked like a private library. There was a towering shelf of books behind him, a bronze bust of some dead white man to his right, and a large book with a silver disc on the cover in a glass case to his left. Along the bottom of the screen appeared the legend, "FILE FOOTAGE."

"...the company which he began out of his father's garage during the depression and which made him a billionaire – to the multinational information giant Lucetech."

The hairdo reappeared, and was soon followed by a computer graphic that hovered over his left shoulder. It showed a circle enclosing two intersecting sine waves, almost like a yin-yang symbol doubled and laid over itself at an angle. Below was the name "LUCETECH".

"The details of the arrangement at this time are still unclear, and it has yet to be announced whether Pierce will step down from his position as CEO of Vista, or whether he will be kept on in an advisory capacity. And now for a look at sports..."

I switched off the set as another, jauntier hairdo appeared, and sat down on the edge of the bed, dripping water onto the threadbare carpet. Though I doubted the vapid puppet of an anchorman had understood the importance of what he had just said, to me it was clear. Vista Incorporated, which Pierce had begun by purchasing up distressed real estate with his daddy's oil money back in the thirties, had always been the cornerstone of his financial empire. It was the parent company of all his oil production, real estate and property management, brokerage and consultation operations. With the sale of Vista, Pierce was left with a big house, a fleet of cars, a private jet and lots of money in the bank. But no financial power, and no leverage to obtain anything more. For any normal human being that would be well and good, to live out life driving a different car every day of the week and using hundred dollar bills as scratch paper, but Pierce wasn't exactly a normal human being.

I got dressed and scooped the pile of photos and notes back into the box. I had decided that the answer to a lot of the questions I kept tripping over was somewhere in that box, and I just needed to go to the man who could find it for me. And that meant a trip to New Orleans.

Back in the car, driving along the wide road to Louisiana, I found the same spectrum of religious broadcasting, but this time with Christian Hip Hop added into the mix. I switched it off and smoked one cigarette after another, the smoke drifting in a wide circuit around the interior of the car before being drawn out the cracked window.

I kept coming back to the story I'd read the night before. I wondered if my grandfather had kept the *Black Hand* magazine because the character had his same name, or whether the character had been named after him in the first place. I wasn't aware that the old man had known any writers in his life, but then I didn't know much about him at all. Still, another Texan high roller with the same name seemed an unlikely coincidence. The only major difference between the two was that, as far as I knew, my grandfather was never lunatic enough to go around playing Zorro. When I had the chance, and had nothing better to do, I figured I could check into Walter Reece, the writer of the story, and see what I could find out.

In the meantime, I was on my way to New Orleans to ask the help of the greatest man I'd ever met.

At the age of fourteen, I ran away from home. I suppose I'd had enough of living in San Antonio with the old man, and my brother was starting to get on my nerves, so I packed up a few things in a duffel bag and hit the road. I went to New Orleans, which I'd seen once in a movie, and after my money ran out in the first couple of days was reduced to eating out of dumpsters. The city lost a lot of its luster from that angle, so I decided to try a different approach. Remembering my life long dream, I decided to become a burglar.

The whole idea of sneaking into people's houses, and sneaking out with all their good things, seemed daring and romantic, like Errol Flynn in a ski mask. I half expected to meet some beautiful girl doing it, just coming out of the shower, wrapped up in a towel. She'd fall in love with me, help me mend my evil ways, and we'd take off together for Paris or somewhere like that.

As it turned out, I only broke into one place, and I didn't meet the girl of my dreams. Instead, I got a kiss in the mouth with a steel cane and lost a couple of teeth. I still rub my tongue over the gaps in my smile whenever I get too cocky, just to remind me never to let dreams run away with me. My first night on my new career as a burglar, I broke into Tan Perrin's house.

Once upon a time, Tan was the greatest cat burglar this country had ever seen. He was a legend, but nobody knew his name. The papers, the cops, they all knew his handiwork, but nobody had ever caught him. Tan was an artist. He'd break into museums just to rearrange the paintings, and come back the next morning to see how folks liked them. He once broke into the Federal Reserve Bank in San Francisco, stole the hundred dollar plates, and mailed them to the Treasury Department in Washington. Sent a note along saying they might think about hiring some girl scouts to guard the place for them.

Tan was true innovator, a pioneer, Michelangelo reborn as a thief. Twenty years at it, and he never got caught. Then time and luck caught up with him.

He was breaking into a museum where they were keeping some of Leonardo da Vinci's notebooks. He claims he didn't want to take them; he just wanted to look at them up close. I tend to believe him. He was up on the roof, on his way down, when a security guard up there sneaking in a cigarette caught a glimpse of him in the moonlight. The guard got off a lucky shot; Tan got a bad break and caught the bullet in his spine. He just laid there twitching, bleeding his life out, while the cops took their own sweet time sending an ambulance over. By the time they got him to the hospital, he was paralyzed from the waist down.

After that came the hospital, the court room, and the penitentiary, in that order. Twenty years all together, and when he was finally released he was just another withered old man in a wheelchair. He went back to New Orleans, where he'd been born, and moved into a large second story apartment. He'd socked away quite a bit of money over the years, on jobs no one even knew about, and hidden it where the feds could never find it. I think he intended to just live out his life in luxury, drinking twelve year old Irish whiskey and betting on the races. That's when I came along and he realized just how bored he'd become. He took me in and became my teacher.

"Howdy, Cachelle," I said as I stepped through the beaded curtain into the back of the palm reader's shop. The palm reader, Madame Divinity herself, was heating up a pan of fried vegetables over a hot plate, her back to the door.

She turned around, all two hundred and fifty pounds of her, the jewelry on her wrist, neck and ears ringing like the bells at the University of Texas clock tower.

"Spencer, you little bastard," she said, smiling broadly. "How long has it been?" She held her arms out wide, bracelets clattering.

"Too long, beautiful," I answered, and stepped into her arms. She hugged me like a professional wrestler, almost lifting me off the ground.

"Let me look at you," Cachelle said and held me out at arms' length. Her eyes took me in, head to foot. "Why didn't you call, let me know you're coming?"

"Well, I lost my cell, and–" I answered sheepishly, before she cut me off.

"You are eating right, aren't you?" She wagged a finger at me.

"I get by. But nothing like your cooking."

She laughed.

"Boy, are you full of shit." She glanced at my feet again. "I like the boots though."

"Thanks. A gift."

"A gift?" she asked, frowning. "You know that in the Philippines it's considered bad luck to give shoes as a gift. You got to be more careful."

"Bad luck for the person giving or the person getting?" I asked. Madame Divinity, better known to her friends as Cachelle Humphries, was the world's unacknowledged expert on crazy superstitions. I half expected that she made up most of them, but nobody ever challenged her on them.

"Aw, hell, I don't know. Who give 'em to you? Not a Filipino, I hope."

"Nope," I replied. "A beautiful Italian gal who didn't think that anyone from Texas should get to walk around wearing normal people shoes. She ended up leaving me for a painter, but she let me keep the boots."

"You are one hard luck case, aren't you?"

"Like I said, I get by." I glanced around the room. This was the backstage, where Cachelle came to relax between performances. The front room was all incense and effigies and altars to the Loa, but back here she was just a middle-aged black woman from small town Louisiana fixing her dinner. "Is the old bastard around?"

"Yeah, he's up there," she answered. "You better get on up there; he'll be wanting to see you." She paused, scowling. "You really should get by more often. That man's not going to be around forever, you know."

"I don't know about that," I replied, smiling and putting an arm around her wide shoulders. "Sometimes I think he's going to end up burying all of us."

"Not without a fight, honey," she said laughing, her mood lightening instantly. "Not without a fight."

I said my goodbyes to Cachelle, promising to stop by before I left, and went around the back to the stairs. I walked on up, silently like the old man had taught me, and let myself in the door. Before I'd taken two steps into the cloakroom I caught a steel cane in my shins.

"You still make more noise than a chorus line of fat tap dancers," a gravelly voice said, and then laughed.

"And I could smell you two miles away," I answered, not turning around. "Aren't you ever going to take a bath?"

"Why don't you kiss my boney ass?"

I turned in the doorway and saw the old man in the wheelchair. His head was shiny bald, his face clean shaven, and his sky blue eyes were buried in a spider's web of laugh lines. He wore a sleeveless white t-shirt, baggy black trousers, and rope sandals on his useless feet. His arms lay poised on the arm-rests of the chair, and even relaxed the muscles stood out like cords under the skin. In the years I'd known him, he didn't seem to have aged a day.

"You bathe," I replied, "and maybe I'd think about it." I walked over and hugged him, his arms circling my shoulders like steel cables. He pounded me on the back a few times, and then pushed me away.

"It's good to see you, boy," he said, his voice breaking only slightly. "It's been too long."

"I know, Tan," I answered, lowering my eyes. "I've been busy."

"Busy? Shit. Why don't you get a real job?"

"Ah, come on, Tan, you know me. I never had the chops to be a good thief."

"Bullshit. You were always just too lazy. You coulda been a pretty good burglar if you put your mind to it."

"Well..."

"Not like that little Mexican boy you used to bring around. Shee-it, he was good for nothing. What was his name? Elbow, Humidor–"

"His name is Amador, you old bastard," I interrupted, "as you well know." Pulling off my coat, I dropped it on a low table and then tossed my wallet, keys and knife on top. I turned, and made for the main room.

"Come on, Tan," I said. "I need a drink, and then I'm going to need your advice."

Without a word, the old man swung the wheelchair around and followed me down the hall.

Besides the cloak room, and a small bedroom on the other side, the entire second floor of the building was one large room. Two entire walls were made up of floor-to-ceiling windows, looking down on Royal and St. Peter Streets. The floor was hardwood, polished to a mirror finish, and the walls plain and unadorned. In the center of the room was a skylight, and the ceiling was covered with hooks, exposed beams, suspended ropes and ladder-looking affairs that ran from one end of the room to the other. There was no furniture in the middle of the room, and only a single table and a couple of chairs in the far corner. Along the wall near the next corner over stood a tall cabinet, dark wood with brass fittings. Otherwise the room was empty.

Tan wheeled across the floor to the cabinet and opened one of the lower drawers. He took out a bottle and a couple of glasses, and then rolled over to the table.

"Come on, boy," he called to me, "get it while it's still room temperature."

I crossed the room, pulled out a chair, and sat down opposite him. Tan spun the top off the bottle and filled the glasses. He slammed the bottle down on the table top, and then took up his glass.

"To the one that got away," he said, raising the glass to the ceiling. He'd always made the same toast, as long as I known him, but he never answered when I'd asked what it meant. After long enough I stopped asking. It made as good a toast as any.

"And to the one who never even came close," I added, like I always did. Tan didn't know what that one meant either, and I figured that was fair.

I took a drink. I got about a mouthful of the stuff down before I started coughing. Irish whiskey. It meant bad memories.

"You never could hold your liquor, could you boy?" Tan scolded. "Always had a beer in your hand, like a little kid." He poured himself another shot and killed it in one go. "You gotta learn to drink like a man."

"Listen, old man," I answered, still grimacing at the taste. "I gave up trying to keep up with you a long time ago. You drink your way, I'll drink mine."

"Alright, then," he said, "what's this all about? I know you didn't drive all the way out here just to look at my pretty face."

"Tan, I need your help."

Tan had told me once that a cat burglar's style, the technique they use, is as individual as a fingerprint, and that someone with a trained eye could look at a job and, just as if it had been signed, tell you who did it. Add to that the fact that, while there were four or five hundred cat burglars worth their salt worldwide by the old man's estimation, only a third of those were living in the United States. And only a lesser number were currently not incarcerated. Therefore the candidates for the Pierce job numbered only in the order of one hundred to one hundred fifty, and if Tan could pick out enough of the "tells" left by the thief, I would have a good idea who'd pulled it off.

I brought up the box of photos and notes from the car, and only after opening it realized I had the wrong box.

"What's with all these magazines?" the old man asked, rifling through the contents.

"Shit, that's my grandfather's stuff," I answered.

"Your grandfather?" Tan said, surprised. "You been to see him?"

"Just missed him. He's dead."

The old man's smile faded, and he shook his head solemnly.

"That's too bad," he said quietly.

"Why? The old guy was a fucker."

Tan whipped his cane around faster than I could follow and clocked me in the shins.

"You watch your mouth, boy. Don't speak ill of the dead, unless you want them tasking you after they've gone."

"Yeah, yeah."

"And you're *way* too old for all this bitterness. It's just juvenile. You're not a kid anymore, you know. That old man did right by you and your brother, whatever you think."

I just shook my head. It was like all old white guys were in a club and had to watch each other's backs. First O'Connor, now Tan. I'd had enough of it. I went back downstairs to the car and brought back up the right box.

The photos and hand-written pages spread out before him on the table, Tan seemed to forget all together that I was there. He was at work, immersed in the craft he loved, and I was just a distraction.

"Alright," I announced, not expecting an answer. "I'm going to go out for a while, and you can tell me what you got when I get back."

To my surprise, Tan lifted his hand in an almost-wave. I figured that was as good as I was going to get, and went back downstairs.

I decided I would ramble around the old neighborhood for a while, it being an off season and the tourist traffic fairly low. I headed down St. Peter towards Jackson Square, considering stopping in at a Voodoo museum run by a friend of mine. But when I cut across to that street I saw it closed down. I wasn't surprised. A lot of the New Orleans I remembered was gone, washed away by Katrina.

It was late afternoon, and there were only a few herds of tourists moving around the French Quarter, so my best bet would be to get somewhere quiet and cool. I started over to an old haunt of mine, and along the way passed a little used book store I used to steal magazines from. Realizing I had nothing better to do, I ducked in and browsed.

On a little table near the register was a book called *The Great Pulp Heroes*, by Don Hutchison. I picked it up, and glanced through it. Walter Reece's name jumped out at me from one of the pages, so I dropped a few bills on the counter, smiled at the pretty young clerk, and went back outside.

A short while later I was at the bar, a dive down on Chartres Street, becoming acquainted with my first beer of the day. There was no one in the place I knew, which was fine with me. I didn't feel up to any reunions. The bar was small, dimly lit, little more than a wooden door and a hand-painted sign from the outside, which meant that most tourists passed right on by on their way to the flashier spots. Again, that was just fine with me. I had no interest in contributing to the local color for a pair of young newlyweds from Des Moines.

I focused my attention on the book I'd bought, and with little trouble found the section on Reece.

> "Les Maxwell, one of the most unlucky figures in the history of the pulps, first made his mark with tales for *Top Notch* and *Popular* for

Street & Smith. Maxwell was prolific, writing in a solid if perhaps florid style, and from his years as a reporter in San Francisco for the local Hearst organ knew the importance of a deadline. On the strength of this and his past work, he was asked to produce a new series for the house. The writer went home, and came back the next day with the first installment of what he expected to be a long and profitable series. The series was to feature a dark avenger of the night, who would characteristically emerge from the mists to right wrongs and squelch evil, only to vanish again. The character's name and basic motif were cribbed from a western series which first debuted over twenty years before, La Mano Negra. Appearing in Athena Press' *True Western Tales*, the adventures of La Mano Negra, or "The Black Hand", were written by J. C. Reece, and ran intermittently for some three years from 1918 to 1921, at which point the magazine ceased publication. Maxwell simply updated the character for a modern setting, gave him twin automatics in the place of Colt Peacemakers, and generated a slightly above-average potboiler. The house name used for the series, Walter Reece, can charitably be seen as a nod to the true originator, and uncharitably as a sneer. Sales for the first issue of *The Black Hand Mysteries* were healthy, and

Maxwell was ordered to begin work on the follow up.

However, before the second issue went to press, S&S was presented a cease and desist order. It appeared that the fictional guise Maxwell had devised for the Black Hand's true identity, Richmond Taylor, was the name of a real life business man in San Francisco who was well connected enough to put the fear of God into the house. Whether Maxwell had known of Taylor and used his name intentionally, or whether it was simply an unlikely coincidence is unclear. In any event, Maxwell was sent back to work to revise his second installment to remove any reference to Taylor or his likeness. Then the other shoe fell. An unnamed firm had purchased the publishing rights for all of Athena Press' characters, including La Mano Negra. Street & Smith were threatened with a copyright infringement suit for the resemblance of the Black Hand to the earlier character, and quickly decided the series just wasn't a good bet. Maxwell was put to work on the aviation pulps, and *The Black Hand* was canceled, before the second issue had even reached the stands."

I skimmed through the rest of the book, but didn't find anything else of interest. I closed the book on the page I'd been reading, marking the place with a coaster, and ordered another round, half disappointed my grandfather hadn't been Zorro after all.

It was early evening when I made it back to Tan's place. He was leaning back in his wheelchair, smoking one of those rancid Mexican cigarettes of his and smiling like he'd just won the lottery.

"Well, old man," I asked, dropping in the chair across the table from him, "what'd you find?"

"Oh, I found your boy, alright," he gloated. "I had him before you even left. I just wanted to be able to study his moves without you here hovering over me."

"Alright, then." I paused, looking at him smile. "A name?"

"I've got his name, alright. He's a fair thief, but a miserable human being. Bad teeth, stringy hair, horrible table manners. This guy's an ape in a people suit, son. Gambling problem, too, as I understand."

"His name?" I repeated.

"The problem with guys like him is that you never know which way they're gonna jump. They've got the skills, but they've got no moral center. You know how I've always told you, if you're going to live outside the law you have just got to be honest. Otherwise you're just an animal."

"It was Dylan, old man. Bob Dylan said that."

"He did? He must have heard it from me. I broke into his hotel room once after I heard

'Subterranean Homesick Blues'. Nice guy. That kid was Woody Guthrie all over again. Knew how to treat a guest."

"Focus," I scolded. "The thief?"

"Calm down. It's Marconi; that's the bird you're looking for. Gian Marconi."

I sighed, and made note of the name.

"Anything else you can tell me?" I asked.

"I'm not sure I like your tone, boy."

"Alright, alright. 'Thank you, Tan.' Now, can you tell me anything else?"

The old man straightened up in his chair, smug, and smiled slightly.

"Sure can. First off, this job cost money. Real money. The gizmos and doodads Marconi used to knock out all them motion detectors and whatnot cost a pretty penny, and he was never the kind to have that kind of scratch laying around."

"So somebody put him up to it?"

"Yep, that's what I figure. And but for one thing, it would have been pretty slick job."

"One thing? What?"

"Well, your detective here mentions broken glass on the floor, and something about some torn paper..." Tan gestured meaningfully to the plastic bag containing the ancient paper, lying half hidden by a stack of photos.

"Go on," I prompted.

"Well, for all his finesse gettin' into the joint, it looks like Marconi wasn't real sure what to do once he got there. Near as I can tell, whatever he wanted was in a glass case in the library, and instead of cutting his way in it appears like he just busted it."

"So maybe he didn't know just what he was after?"

"I didn't say that," the old man corrected. "Maybe he knew, and just got all rushed right there at the end. Somebody coming, or one of his gizmos was on the blink or something. Either way, breaking the glass like that seems to have messed up whatever was inside, and that's where the paper on the floor come from. It had a few slivers of glass embedded in the edge of it."

Something struck me.

"So it was definitely a book, then," I said.

"That's what it looks like." He paused, then pulled the plastic bag out from under the photos. "Not that I can tell you what the book is though." He turned the bag over in his hands, inspecting the paper within. "Looks to be handwriting, but I couldn't tell you what language. Indian, maybe?"

"Feather or dot?"

"Hell, either one for all I know," he answered.

I climbed out of my chair and started towards the phone.

"Who you calling?" the old man asked.

"Amador. He's stationed in Houston these days."

"That scab? Shit," he spat. "Take a kid into your home, try to teach him what you know, and he ends up a fuckin' fed." Tan shook his head, and I could tell he was wondering where he'd gone wrong with that one. Where he'd gone wrong with *all* of us. He'd seen himself as a Cajun Fagin in those days, training a bunch of thieves and then sitting back while we brought him the goods. Instead, he ended up with a reporter, a computer geek, a special effects engineer, and various and sundry other young go-getters. We didn't always stay on the sunny side of the law, to be sure, but I knew that the old man was a bit disappointed.

I shrugged, gave him a "what-can-you-do" look, and then started dialing. I called collect. I figured someone on a government salary could afford it.

"Collect call from your mother," I heard the operator say. "Do you accept the charges?"

"I guess," I heard my friend answer, and then the operator clicked off the line.

"What's up, Lover?" I yelled into the receiver.

"Finch? I should have known. How the hell are you?"

"Not too bad, not too bad. I'm in Louisiana, visiting the old man."

"Tan! No way! How is the old fucker?"

"Same as always," I answered. "Only meaner."

"He's still pissed at me, isn't he?"

"Nah, nah," I lied, glancing over to see Tan giving him the bird *in absentia*. "He's over all that shit."

"Sure he is," Amador said. "So, what's up?"

"I need to you to track somebody down for me, find out what he's been up to."

"Sure," he sighed. "Not a single Christmas card in years, and you call when you need help. What's the story?"

Amador Ysquierdo, the Crooked Lover. My pal. We'd met years ago, in Louisiana, both runaways. We'd got into some rough spots together and managed to muddle through alright. A couple of kids out looking for trouble; it was amazing what we had found. Still, time has a way of cooling those angry fires, if they don't burn you up first. Even as close to the edge as we'd gotten, it was still possible to come back. Amador was a case in point.

After a childhood spent monkeying around with computers and phones, causing several business and more than one government agency their fair share of grief, Amador had decided to use his powers for good. Or for his own good, at least. Had himself legally emancipated from his family back in the Rio Grande Valley, finished up school out in Louisiana, and then had gone on to get a degree in computer engineering. Now, years and miles later, he was working for the FBI doing data retrieval. I doubted his employer knew that, under his old alias, Amador was still on the active warrant lists of the Bureau, the Treasury Department, and several more clandestine national security agencies.

I gave him Marconi's name and asked if he could hunt down his last known whereabouts, possible charges, last address, things like that. Amador said he'd find out what he could, which knowing him meant everything.

"One other thing," I added. "What can you tell me about an outfit called Lucetech?"

"Are you kidding me?" he asked. "Have you even seen a computer before?"

"Humor me."

"Well, outside of Microsoft, Adobe and Apple they're only one of the biggest software companies on the market. They handle mostly telecommunications, network architecture for large corporations, banks and such like... lately they've been making the move into consumer apps." He paused, then added, "Why do you ask?"

"You hear of them getting involved in any kind of real estate or manufacturing gigs?"

"Huh?" Amador breathed. "Not unless you count all the tech support and R&D facilities that're opening up all over the damned place. Nah, nothing I've heard of. Why?"

"Just curious."

"Well, where can I reach you?" he asked. "You gonna be sticking around with grumpy for a while?"

"Not this trip. I've got some more digging to do back in Texas, a couple of social calls to make, so I guess I'll just have to get in touch with you."

"Solid," Amador said. "Give me a day or two, and I'll see what I can do."

"Thanks, brother. I owe you."

"Shit, yeah, you do. Don't worry, I'm keeping score."

I heard the line go dead, and then dropped the phone back on its cradle. I turned to see Tan still at the table, shaking his head sadly.

"A fucking fed."

Tan agreed to let me stay at his place for the night, so I dragged some bedding out of the closet and dropped it down onto the floor. The box of my grandfather's things was still sitting near the table, so I picked up the book I'd bought and walked over to add it to the pile. When I opened the box, something caught my eye. I pulled out one of the magazines and examined the cover. The title, emblazoned on the cover in inch-high letters, was *True Western Tales*, the same I'd seen mentioned in connection with the other magazine. I flipped the front cover open and saw a listing for a La Mano Negra adventure there in the index. Curious, I tossed it over onto the bedding, and then closed up the box.

Tan came walking into the room, as only he can. Suspended from the ceiling in midair, he moved hand over hand, gripping onto the rungs of a ladder bolted horizontally onto the ceiling.

"You get your nest all straightened out, little chick?" he taunted, barely out of breath.

"Yeah," I answered. "Thanks for letting me crash here."

"Hell," he grunted, moving over towards the table where his wheelchair sat, "don't give me that shit. You can stay here anytime you like, and you know that."

"Okay, but thanks anyway."

Tan maneuvered himself right above the wheelchair, and without a second glance let go his grip on the ceiling rungs and dropped like a shot into the chair. He landed artfully, a ten point Olympic landing, and casually lit up a cigarette.

"You know," he continued, blowing out a cloud of rancid gray smoke, "I could probably find out about this bird of yours a lot quicker than Humidor can."

I let the dig slide, and crossed to the table where my own cigarettes were.

"Yeah?" I asked.

"Sure, I still got connections, you know. Just 'cause I'm retired doesn't mean I forgot everything I ever knew, or everybody, and I knew a lot of bodies when I was inside."

"Alright, then," I answered. "You want to ask around, great, I appreciate it. But don't be giving me shit for it later, like I can't do my job." I jabbed a finger at him in mock accusation. "You're not doing my job for me, you lecherous old fart, you're doing me a favor."

"Fine, fine." He waved me off. "Just stop crying about it. Come on, fix me a drink."

The old man finally gave up on the day, just before he was about to drink me under the table, and wheeled off to his bedroom. I kicked off my boots, wondering just what kind of luck I'd got from them after all, and settled onto the floor on my little nest of bedding. The western pulp magazine was at hand and, still too wired up to sleep, I dragged it over to me and flipped it open to the first page.

"Guns At Dawn: A La Mano Negra Adventure"

by J. C. Reece

(originally appeared in True Western Tales, *Sept 8th, 1918)*

1

"String him up, Lefty," shouted the swarthy rider on the seventeen-hand painted stallion. "Don't let him get away."

"I'll get him, Shorty," replied his companion, in the saddle of a high-shouldered bay. "Just keep your shirt on."

The two men, ranch hands from the state of their clothes and the easy way they sat in the saddle, were galloping through the brush, across the hard, level ground of the Rio Grande Valley, in pursuit of a man on foot. Their prey, a stocky Mexican in simple white cotton, was on foot, out of breath, and just about out of luck.

Lefty, standing high in his stirrups, let fly his lariat, and with practiced aim brought the loop down around the Mexican's shoulders. Kicking his mount to a halt, he pulled tight the rope, and brought the Mexican to the ground.

"Good eye, Lefty," Shorty admitted.

"What would you know about it, booze hound?" Lefty shot back. "If it weren't for you we'd've got him five miles back."

"I told ya, I was aiming for his horse, not for him."

"Yeah," Lefty spat, crossing his arms over the saddle horn, the rope clutched in his fist. "Well, next time you best oughta aim at me. You'd have a better chance of hitting him that way."

Shorty looked from Lefty to the Mexican, now laying dazed on the ground.

"Whatta we oughta do with him, you think?" Shorty asked. "Shoot 'im now?"

"Nah," Lefty answered. "I figure we oughta have a bit a fun with 'im, teach 'im what it means to rustle cattle from Mr. Pierce." Lefty paused, and spat out a greasy line of tobacco towards the Mexican. "Then we shoot 'im."

"Sounds good to me."

With a practiced hand, Lefty tied the end of the lariat to his saddle horn, and then turned his mount away from the Mexican. The Mexican, knowing what was coming, struggled to his feet, hoping against hope to find a way out. Lefty kicked the bay into motion, and it slowly trotted forward, bringing the line taut.

Lefty turned to Shorty.

"You ready, saddle sore?"

"I reckon," Shorty answered.

"Alright then," Lefty replied, grinning. He whistled, one long, high note, through his broken teeth, and then made to kick his horse into a gallop.

Suddenly, a shot rang out, and the taut line between the Mexican and Lefty was burst in twain.

Shaken, Lefty and Shorty turned to the sound of the gun shot, and saw a hundred yards away a pair of riders. As they watched, the two riders approached. On the left rode a man on a magnificent Arabian, nineteen hands high if it was an inch, as black as night. The man was dressed all in black, with a mask wound round his face, obscuring his eyes and nose, a wide black Stetson perched on his head. In each fist he gripped a Colt Peacemaker of burnished black steel, each trained on one of the ranch hands. At his side rode a Chinaman, dressed all in red silk, with his thick black hair falling in a queue down his muscled back. The Chinaman rode a stunning bay, and had a Winchester rifle in hand, its barrel aimed at Lefty's heart.

Both Lefty and Shorty, just barely containing their fear, knew who the two riders must be: none other than that scourge of the plains: La Mano Negra, the Black Hand, and his faithful Chinaman companion, Jin Ti.

The two riders stopped just short of Lefty and Shorty, coming to rest at either side of the Mexican, who looked from one to the other with a kind of quiet awe. La Mano Negra, each of his Peacemakers still trained on the ranch hands, was the first to break the long silence.

"What seems to be the trouble here, boys?" His voice was low, and rich, and seemed to rumble through the air like distant thunder.

Lefty was the one to answer.

"We're just taking care of justice, mister," he spoke, his voice belying his discomfort. "This here Messican stoled cattle from our boss, Mr. Buck Pierce of the Pierce Ranch. We was only doing our jobs, bringing him to justice."

"You say he stole cattle?" La Mano Negra asked, indicating the Mexican.

"I didn't steal anything," the Mexican piped up, indignant. "Those cattle were stolen from me. By Pierce. He is the thief."

La Mano Negra motioned him silent with a wave of his hand.

"We'll get your side in a minute here, mi amigo." La Mano Negra turned to the ranch hands again, and repeated his question. "I said, you say he stole cattle?"

Lefty and Shorty looked nervously to one another, and then nodded their consent.

"Yessir," Shorty answered. "He stole cattle."

"That he did," Lefty added.

La Mano Negra turned to look behind him, and then around to all sides, the pistols still on the ranch hands.

"That's funny," he finally said. "I don't see any cattle." La Mano Negra turned to Jin Ti, who sat stoically in the saddle. "Jin Ti, you see any cattle?"

"No, Heishou," the Chinaman answered. "I don't."

"Well then." La Mano Negra turned back to the ranch hands. "I'm not sure I see the problem, gentlemen."

Lefty and Shorty looked from La Mano Negra, to the Mexican, and then to one another. They sat in silence, afraid to speak.

"I'd expect," La Mano Negra added, "that you boys have got some work to do back on the ranch. Am I right?"

"Y-yeah," Lefty stammered.

"Yessir," Shorty whispered.

"Well, then," said La Mano Negra. "I expect you best get back to work, don't you?"

Without another word, Lefty and Shorty turned their horses away, and kicked them into a gallop. In moments, they had disappeared from view.

La Mano Negra holstered his jet black pistols, and swung from the saddle. His boots hitting the dusty ground, he strode over to stand beside the Mexican. Jin Ti, dropping his Winchester in a saddle holster, followed suit.

The Mexican, his gratitude writ in a wide grin across his face, extended his hand to La Mano Negra.

"Gracias," the Mexican effused. "Gracias. You have saved my life."

"Don't need to thank me," La Mano Negra answered, taking his hand. "Anyone would have done the same."

"No señor, they would not. Only the great La Mano Negra, and his faithful Chinee aid." The Mexican next took Jin Ti's hand, and pumped it with a hearty shake. "I am Alberto Cuellar," he announced, "and I would be honored if you would take your dinner with my family tonight."

"Well..." La Mano Negra answered, seeming unsure.

"And you are welcome to stay the night," Cuellar added. "As long as you like."

"I don't know, Señor Cuellar," La Mano Negra replied. "We usually don't stay too long."

"I don't know, Heishou," Jin Ti commented. "It would be nice to eat indoors for a change, and to sleep between sheets instead of rattlesnakes and scorpions."

"Well, Jin Ti," La Mano Negra joked, "why don't you just put on a dress while you're at it?"

"Please, Señor Negra," Cuellar pleaded. "I insist."

La Mano glanced from the entreating Mexican, to his weary companion, and then back again.

"Oh, alright," La Mano Negra relented. "But just for tonight."

2

Within the hour they had reached Cuellar's home, not five miles from the Rio Grande, and were now seated around a wide table. Cuellar himself was at the head, La Mano and Jin Ti at either elbow, and Cuellar's young children, two daughters and a son, seated beside them. Cuellar's wife, a plump and happy young woman, was at the stove, completing preparations for their meal.

La Mano, settling back in his straight backed chair, noted to himself that Cuellar's home was much more inviting inside than it had appeared outside. A rough structure, more stone and earth than wood, was held together more by good wishes than by design, but inside before a blazing fire it was as comfortable as any home the vigilante had seen on the range in many a year.

Jin Ti, sitting across from him, was quietly sipping water from a battered metal cup Cuellar's wife had produced from some unknown corner, but his quiet air told La Mano that his Chinaman friend was at ease.

Finally, Cuellar's wife ferried the food to the table: tamales, barbacoa, rice and beans, and flour tortillas. She set a plate before each of the guests, and invited them to tuck in.

With a glance to Jin Ti, who caught his eye, La Mano casually reached up and, with an easy gesture, removed the mask covering his face. He let it fall, revealing the features hidden behind its rough cloth. All motion ceased around the table, and all eyes turned to him, all except Jin Ti, who looked on with a quiet smile.

"Can't eat with the damned thing on," La Mano answered to their questioning stares, and then turned to Cuellar's wife. "Excuse my French, ma'am."

"De nada," Cuellar's wife answered quietly.

Without another word, La Mano forked a pile of rice and beans onto a tortilla, and fell to eating. Cuellar made a noticeable effort to relax, and motioned his family to eat.

Cuellar's oldest daughter, all of eight, kept staring at La Mano, her fork held motionless in the air above her plate.

"Señor," she finally said in a small voice, "if you are La Mano Negra with the mask on, who are you with the mask off?"

"Terese!" Cuellar barked. "Do not bother our guest!"

"Ain't no bother, amigo," La Mano calmly answered. "See, little lady, in my line of work it don't pay for everybody to know who you are, cause they might just come gunnin' for your family, or else catch you unawares in your sleep or just walkin' down the street. But when I'm with good folks like y'all, it don't really matter any more. You understand?"

"Sí," the little girl answered, and then after a moment added, "So who are you without the mask?"

"My name's Taylor, little lady. John Bunyan Taylor." He grinned at her, putting her at ease. "But you can call me Jack."

"Alright," she replied. "Jack. I'm Terese."

"Pleased to know you Terese."

After everyone had relaxed noticeably, they proceeded to clean the table of food. When the meal was done, La Mano and Jin Ti complimented Cuellar's wife on her cooking, and then as she and the children began to clean up the two of them joined Cuellar in the main room to share a pouch of tobacco.

Sitting in rude but comfortable chairs, the three passed the pouch around until each had rolled a butt of his own, and then lit them with kindling from the fire. They eased back in their chairs then, La Mano and Jin Ti just enjoying the temporary respite from their travels, Cuellar beaming at having two such notable men in his home.

After a time, Cuellar rose from his chair, and brought from the corner of the room a wooden chest, which he placed before the two men. He then knelt down beside it, his hand resting reverently on its top.

"This, señors," he began, "is the treasure of my family. Within are the things handed down by my grandfathers, and their grandfathers before them. We are a poor people, though we work hard, but to us this chest is worth all the cattle and gold in the world."

Cuellar then slowly lifted the lid of the chest, and began pulling out items for the two men to inspect. First came a muzzle-loading flintlock, a hundred years old if it was a day. It was rusted almost beyond recognition, long past an age when it was of any use, but the two men could see that it was a prized heirloom to Cuellar's family. Cuellar handed it over, and they respectfully passed it back and forth between themselves, commenting on its fine shape and obvious age. Jin Ti handed the thing back to Cuellar, who carefully returned it to the trunk.

Next came a metal helmet, shaped like a cone, with a metal fin running along the top. The metal was dented and scratched, corroded to an even green shade. Cuellar explained that his many-times great-grandfather had worn that helmet, when first he came to the New World, and that his sons and their sons after him had kept it to remind them of their origins. Again, La Mano and Jin Ti feigned interest in the relic, and then passed it back to Cuellar.

Next came a book, of indeterminate age, bound in leather with a round metal shield on the front. Cuellar explained that this had belonged to his forefather who had worn the helmet, and though he couldn't read a word, of Spanish or English, he knew that it must contain some great wisdom. La Mano took it in his hands, and gave it the same cursory inspection as the previous two items. The shield on the front of the book was of a silvery metal, which for the book's obvious age seemed hardly weathered at all. At Cuellar's prompting, he flipped through the first few pages. La Mano took it for a bible, though the pages he skimmed through weren't written in any language he could read. It looked something like the Hebrew he'd seen in New York [*During the events recounted in "La Mano Negra in the Big City"*—ED.], but it could have been hen scratching for all he knew. He handed the book back to Jin Ti, who then passed it back to Cuellar.

Cuellar went through a few other odds and ends, a few Indian arrowheads, a silver necklace, a few scraps of clothing, and when he was assured his guests were suitably impressed closed up the chest and put it away.

La Mano then motioned to Jin Ti, and the two men rose.

"We sure do appreciate your hospitality, amigo," he told Cuellar, "but we've been ridin' a long few weeks here, and we sure could use some rest. If you just point us out to your barn..."

At that Cuellar interrupted, cutting him off with a wave of his hand.

"No, you will sleep in our bed, my wife and mine," he demanded.

"Now, wait a minute," La Mano answered. "We appreciate your feedin' us and all, but we can't just kick you out of your own..."

Cuellar, his face set, refused to hear anymore. They had saved his life from Pierce's men, and he would consider it an insult if the two heroes would not allow him to show his gratitude. Not brooking any dissent, Cuellar led the two men to the bedroom, and practically ordered the two men to climb in under the quilts.

"My wife and I will sleep with the children," Cuellar concluded. "And I will not argue it."

With that he turned, and stomped back into the main room.

La Mano turned to Jin Ti, who shrugged.

"Well, Heishou," Jin Ti offered. "You heard the man. We are to be forced to sleep on a comfortable mattress, under fine sheets."

"Yep," La Mano answered.

"The next time we are to be tortured by some bandit villain, could you arrange it so that this man Cuellar is in control of the proceedings?"

"Jin," La Mano replied, "I'll see what I can do."

3

Late that night, as they lay sleeping side by side on the wide bed, La Mano and Jin Ti were startled awake by the sharp crack of gun fire. They leapt to their feet, stepping into their boots before even coming fully awake. They listened, tensed, and when the sound came again risked the time it took to shoot a look between them.

"Outside," La Mano barked, pulling his twin Colts from the holster lying draped over a chair back and checking the chambers.

Jin Ti snatched up his Winchester, and without another word the two bolted from the room and through the small house, coming at last to the front door. Cuellar and his family, huddled in the corner of the room, looked on them with wide eyes from the darkness. Only the youngest child, the boy, made any noise, whimpering slightly as his mother held him close to her breast.

"Alright, amigo," La Mano whispered in the dark. "You're with us. Your kin'll be fine if they stay put in here." Cuellar nodded, solemnly, and rose to follow.

"You got a gun?" La Mano asked. Cuellar nodded, and then walked to the far corner of the room, returning with a battered old double-bore shotgun. "Good enough."

La Mano glanced at Jin Ti, and then nodded. Without warning, the Chinaman shot his hand forward, and flung wide the door. With a quick look to Cuellar, the two bolted through the door and into the dark night beyond, their guns spitting fire out into the darkness.

A hasty survey of the grounds told them all they needed to know. The barn was afire, a man standing nearby with a torch in one hand, a revolver in the other. Two other men were horseback, a few yards off, one holding the reins to the torch-bearers mount.

"Cuellar! Fetch the horses from the barn!" La Mano barked, and the Mexican rushed to comply, pausing only momentarily to glance back to his family inside. He held the shotgun before him in one hand, and made a sign of the cross with the other.

La Mano and Jin Ti immediately divided up targets, and commenced to firing. The interlopers, startled at first, soon regrouped and returned fire. They had no doubt expected to catch the Cuellar family abed, and not to find two well-traveled gunmen waiting to repel their attack.

La Mano and his companion split up, running from the door in opposite directions, each sending an unrelenting hail of lead towards the attackers. The dirt at their feet was kicked up in clouds as the shots hit all round them, but not one struck true. La Mano found cover near a roofed well, and emptied his two Colts into the night air, while Jin Ti crouched near a wheel-less wagon, firing and reloading, firing and reloading.

One of the attackers, the one afoot, returned fire until he spun on his toes, caught by Jin Ti's shot in his chest. He fell to the ground with a sickening thud, and was still.

Cuellar appeared on the scene, leading both his dun and the two heroes' mounts behind him, guiding them to safety on the far side of the house, away from the blaze.

Seeing their cohort fall, the two men on horseback fired final rounds at the two heroes, half-heartedly, and then turned their steeds around, goading them to a gallop, racing off into the dark night. La Mano raced into the open yard to follow, but it was too late. They had disappeared into the inky darkness.

Relaxing, La Mano and Jin Ti converged in the yard, each confident that the other had escaped harm. They had faced danger together too often for each not to know the others abilities, and this evening's work had been well below either of them. The attackers were well-suited for terrorizing and murdering innocent families, women and children, but were no match for the two heroes of the high plains.

Together, they strode across the open ground to the fallen man, who even now was bleeding his life blood out onto the dry ground. They stood over him, Jin Ti knocking the hat from his head with the tip of his Winchester. They both knew the face they saw there, the eyes staring lifeless up into the night sky. They were neither surprised. It was Shorty, the swarthy ranch hand from whom they had saved Cuellar earlier that day.

With a wordless glance, the two heroes confirmed that they shared the same thought. Buck Pierce had escalated an act of cattle thievery into a full-scale range war, and only blood could follow.

4

With first light the next morning, La Mano and Jin Ti were high in the saddle, Cuellar riding between, heading from the Mexican's home north to the Pierce Ranch. Cuellar had left his shotgun with his wife, for the protection of her and their children while he was away, but now he cradled a scattergun in his arms, a sawed-off shotgun La Mano had produced from among his tackle.

They rode on through the morning, as the sun climbed up the eastern sky, hardly saying a word. It had been at La Mano's insistence that they rode, but both Jin Ti and Cuellar had quickly agreed. If Cuellar and his family were ever to know any measure of peace, the range war with Pierce would have to be finished, once and for all. They rode to take the war to Buck Pierce himself, and to put an end to it.

At the outskirts of Pierce's claimed property, coming over a slight rise, they happened upon a band of armed men. The rancher, it seemed, had expected some sort of reprisal, and had got his henchmen ready to meet it. Five they were, perched on ragged looking horses, each with a revolver or rifle in hand, each a murderous blood lust glaring in his eye.

Again the lead flew. Having no recourse to taking cover, the trio of La Mano, his Chinaman companion, and the Mexican instead chose to face the fire bravely, letting loose with their own firearms. Jin Ti, a crackshot at twice the distance, took out one of the ranch-hands early, and what La Mano lacked in finesse he easily made up in speed, emptying the chambers of his twin Peacemakers twice over before he was done. Even little Cuellar, ill-used to such action, did his best, though his scatter gun was of little use at so great a distance. Still, though, he fired and fired again, cracked the gun open and reloaded with one hand, fired with the other.

When all was said and done, four of the five ranch hands lay sprawled on the hard dirt, their horses either scattered or dead beside them. The fifth, turning tail and running, tore off into the distance, all thoughts of the fight left behind him. Jin Ti made to follow, but then La Mano motioned him still. Cuellar had been hit.

La Mano dismounted, and in long strides crossed the distance to Cuellar's bay. He helped the Mexican down from the saddle.

"Lemme see," La Mano ordered firmly, placing a gentle hand on the bloody arm Cuellar cradled close to his chest.

"It is nothing, señor," Cuellar insisted. "Let us ride on."

"The hell it is, amigo," La Mano spat, inspecting the wound. "That shot went clear through, blew out a hole on both sides of your shoulder. You try'n keep ridin', you'll pass out in a heartbeat."

"I... will... not," Cuellar replied deliberately, through clenched teeth, fighting the urge to collapse.

"Listen here," La Mano insisted. "Jin Ti here'll patch you up, and then you just head on home. We'll take things from here."

"No," the little man near shouted. "This is my fight, not yours. I appreciate your help, but it is my fight."

La Mano stepped back a bit, and looked the Mexican over from head to foot. In the end, he just shook his head and grinned.

"I'll be damned if you ain't as ornery as they come, Cuellar," he announced. He thought for a minute, tugging at the edge of his black mask with a gloved hand. As Jin Ti could attest, only when presented with a particular thorny problem did La Mano Negra ever display this little twitch.

"Alright, alright," La Mano finally said. "Jin'll patch it up fer ya, and then you'll ride along with us. But if you get yourself kil't, that's your lookout. You understand?"

Cuellar simply nodded solemnly, and then let Jin Ti to his wound.

"Bet you wish you were back in that bed now, huh Jin?" La Mano asked his Chinaman companion. Jin Ti just shot him a look, and continued work on dressing the wound.

5

The three reached Pierce's ranch house without encountering anymore interference, La Mano and Jin Ti with their guns cocked and ready, Cuellar with the loaded scattergun cradled in his good arm. As they approached the long, low ranch house, they found no sentries posted, no hands awaiting them in the yard. Instead, they saw the stout form of Buck Pierce himself, rocking peacefully on the wide porch, smoking a battered brier, a glass of lemonade in his hand.

"Howdy, gents," Pierce called out to them as they pulled their mounts to a stop at the hitching post. "I was expectin' you folks to drop by."

Warily, the trio dismounted, and lashed their reins to the post.

"Come on up, boys," Pierce went on. "I got no grudge against you. This has all been a big misunderstandin', y'see. I never meant for things to go like this."

With a wide, soft hand Pierce waved them onto the porch, and as they stepped cautiously up, their arms still in hand, he motioned them inside.

"Come on inside, fellahs," Pierce beckoned. "I'll have the wife set us up some dinner, and we can try to get this worked out. I figure we got no cause for all this scufflin', and we can sure reach some sort of agreement."

Without another word, Pierce turned, and entered the house.

Jin Ti and La Mano exchanged quick glances, and by subtle signs communicated that both thought it a trap, but that they were up to the challenge. With Cuellar between them, then, they followed the large rancher in.

Through the dog-run they followed him, into a well-appointed parlor. La Mano thought it looked like any brothel or whorehouse he might have stepped into over the years, but Pierce seemed to think it showed his civilized nature. Pierce motioned them to take seats on the couches and divans scattered around the floor, and the trio made to sit. He then offered them whisky, which they accepted, though watching for him to drink before they followed suit.

The whisky finished, Pierce began to pace back and forth in front of them, becoming increasingly animated, trying to explain his situation.

"What you gents have got to understand," and here it was understood that he was talking to the two gunmen, and not to Cuellar, "is the opportunities available to men like us in this area of the country. Land, as far as your eye can see, and nothing on it but scrub brush and Mexicans. Perfect cattle country, gentlemen, just the thing it needs. Space to graze, water not far off, and no damned dirt farmers to interfere. Well, except for the occasional Mexican, y'know, like your little friend here." At this, he gestured dismissively at Cuellar, who shot him cold looks all the while, clutching his bloodied arm.

"The Mexican, you see," Pierce lectured, "has never put the land to its proper use. They're as bad as the Indians before 'em. Hell, most of are half-Indian at least, like you couldn't tell. And everybody knows that dark folk don't have a head for this kind of work. Oh, they can work the land alright, with someone tellin' 'em what to do, but leave 'em alone and whatta they do?" Pierce paused. "Siesta," he spat. "Nappin', all the while lettin' the opportunities slip by. I tell ya, gents, only the European man has any hope of makin' anything of this country." He then turned to Jin Ti, and added apologetically, "Present company excepted, a'course. I heard nothin' but good things about your people, Chinaman. I heard you're quite handy at making walls, and we could sure as shit use one of those 'round here."

La Mano Negra stood, then, facing Pierce.

"Listen, Pierce," he began, "this here's a free country, so I reckon you got a right to any damn fool notion you like, but that don't mean that you can just ignore the law. This here man," and here he pointed to Cuellar, "tells me you been stealin' cattle all up and down the Valley, and drivin' off families that was here since your European man had his wide behind still back in Europe."

"Yes, well," Pierce answered nervously, averting his eyes. He then straightened, and met La Mano's eye. "I'll admit, that sometimes we gotta take desperate measures to tame the land, and I ain't proud of it all. But I stand by everythin' I done, and I'd do it again. You can't know the money in an outfit like this, raisin' the cattle here, drovin' em up to Colorado, comin' back down with more money in your pocket than the King of Siam."

Pierce leaned forward, conspiratorially.

"Listen," he whispered, "what I'm after is to cut you in on the deal. Hell, even your Chinaman buddy there. You come work for me, and we'll all end up dying richer'n you could imagine."

"Some of us earlier'n others," La Mano replied evenly.

"So, whatta ya say?"

Without saying a word, La Mano shook his head. Seeing Pierce's surprised look, he planted his feet firm on the ground, and spoke.

"So long as I wear this here mask, so long as I got strength enough to lift up m'head, I'll keep on fightin'. Fightin', to look out for the folks what ain't got nobody to look for 'em, and who can't look out for themselves. Fightin', to keep greedy vultures like you from snatching away the hard work of honest men like this Cuellar here. Fightin', to see that each man, woman, and child, gets ta live their life like they want ta, and not like some other fellah makes 'em." He paused, and eyed Pierce closely. "So, 'Buck', whatta you think m'answer will be?"

"That's just too bad," Pierce answered, and then turned away from the trio. He made a low whistle, and headed towards the corner.

At his signal, men rushed into the rooms from both doors, each hefting a club or pistol. It was the ambush La Mano and Jin Ti had expected. The two heroes became whirlwinds, their guns flashing in their hands, shots ringing out in staccato time. The ranch hands, still firing, their shots going wide in the confusion, were cut down like over-ripe wheat. In moments, they had all fallen, leaving only the trio, and Pierce.

Pierce was crouched on the floor some ten feet away from where La Mano stood, his hand reached out towards a revolver laying on the floor, dropped there by one of the fallen men. He lay frozen, his eyes darting from La Mano to the revolver and back again. Jin Ti took a long step forward, and stood over him, his Winchester trained at the rancher's heart.

At a signal from La Mano, Jin Ti stepped back, reluctantly, his posture relaxing.

"You two," La Mano ordered Jin Ti and Cuellar, "git." He jerked at thumb at the door.

Cuellar protested, calling Pierce a devil, and that he should be stopped.

"You don't worry none about that," La Mano answered. "We'll get Pierce taken care of."

Reluctantly, the pair left the room, leaving only Pierce still frozen in the act of reaching for the pistol, La Mano standing over him, his twin Colts drawn. Without another word, La Mano holstered his Peacemakers. He then inclined his head to Pierce, and offered him a choice.

"I don't much go in for cold blooded murder," La Mano explained, "so I ain't gonna kill ya. I'm gonna turn around right now and walk outta here. You can just sit there still, and once we're gone get this here mess cleaned up, and from now on never make any trouble for them Mexican farmers..."

Pierce snarled, his lip curled up.

"Or," La Mano continued, "you can go for that gun. And I'll lay you even odds, fifty-fifty. Either you'll kill me, or you won't."

Slowly, La Mano turned, and began to make his way towards the door.

Pierce, a grin of triumph on his face, could not believe his good fortune. He lunged forward, snatching up the gun and bringing it to bear on La Mano's broad back. He began to squeeze the trigger, and fire the shot that would forever end the adventures of that hero of the high plains.

In the split-second after Pierce first flexed his finger, and before the hammer had fallen into place, Pierce was outmatched. Often the difference between a good shot and a great shot comes down to heartbeat, and this was certainly a prime example.

As the hammer began its speedy descent, La Mano suddenly crouched, spinning, and drew one of the Peacemakers in one fluid motion, and fired off a single round, which caught Pierce in his shoulder. The shot blew a blood-red bloom into Pierce, and as he jerked spasmodically his shot went wild, missing La Mano's cheek by inches.

La Mano stood gracefully, holstered his gun, and then turned and walked from the room. Pierce, still alive, lay in agonizing pain on the hardwood floors behind him, clutching his shoulder with his other hand. Pierce would live, but he, at least, of all his kind, would not be troubling innocents again.

The THIRD DAY

I was up early the next day and, after saying my good-byes to Tan and Cachelle, was on my way. I had people I needed to see back in Texas, and with a seven hour drive ahead of me, wanted to get there while they were still up and around.

The morning's drive was long and numbing, just straight highway over bayou and through wood, with nothing much to look at and even less to do. Like a Warhol film on wheels. I think I must have nodded off at one point, but dreamt of driving with my eyes open, so it didn't really make much difference. I stopped once in Baton Rouge for cigarettes and gas, and passing a pay phone decided to make a call. It was kind of nice not having a cell phone ringing all hours of the day and night, but it was hell making outgoing calls.

The long distance operator found the number for me without too much trouble, and patched me through to the line. After only five or six rings, the line was answered, by a voice that sounded like its owner had far better things to do with his time.

"KXEN-home-of-Houston's-number-one-news-cast-three-years-in-a-row," the script came pouring over the line. "How-may-I-direct-your-call?"

"Could you give me the news desk?" I asked.

"*Who* may I ask is calling?" the voice asked, professional and the polar opposite of friendly.

"My name is Davis Miles and I'm an attorney representing Mr. J. Nathan Pierce," I spun. "I would like to speak with whomever was in charge of the segment about my client's business interests that aired yesterday morning."

"One moment, sir," the voice answered, sounding a bit more alert.

I heard the line click, and enjoyed a muzak version of "Friends in Low Places" for the next fifteen seconds.

"News desk," came another, more chipper voice. "This is Andy."

"Yes, this is Davis Miles," I droned. "Could I have your full name please?"

"Um… Andrew Morris."

"Uh huh," I breathed. "And am I to understand that you supervised the editing of the piece on J. Nathan Pierce's alleged agreement with Lucetech Incorporated yesterday?"

"Yes," he answered, and I could hear him bristling, defensively. "Was there some problem with it?"

"I have not been authorized to make any formal complaint, Mr. Morris, if that's what you are asking. But there were a couple of points that grabbed my attention. At the opening of the segment, my client was shown standing in a large room surrounded by statuary and antiquities in glass cases. Do you recall this portion of the airing?"

"Y-yes."

"It is my responsibility to ask how that footage was obtained by your organization, and by whom you were authorized to air it."

"Oh," the voice answered, sounding a bit confused. "That was just a bit we cut from last week's Barbara Walters special. We're an affiliate, you understand, and have blanket permission to rebroadcast any and all network transmissions."

"Hmm mmm," I hummed. "And where was that special filmed, if I may ask?"

"Wait a minute." I heard papers rustling in the background, frantically. "Here it is. *'Tonight, Barbara speaks with billionaire philanthropist J. Nathan Pierce from his home in Houston, Texas.'* It originally aired... almost three weeks ago. It's not currently scheduled to be rebroadcast, but we could provide you with a copy if you like–"

"Not necessary," I interrupted. "That's all for..." A thought struck. "Actually, that would be very useful. If you could just overnight it to my offices in Austin, I think we can get this straightened out without any serious difficulty."

I gave him the address of a place I knew in Austin, and got his assurance that he would send a copy out right away.

"Thank you for your time, Mr. Morris," I sang into the receiver. "You've been most helpful."

With that I dropped the phone back in its cradle and lit a cigarette. Something was coming together, I knew, but just what I couldn't say. For now I was just a blind man describing an elephant, and hadn't got any farther than the tail.

Driving across the state line into Texas, I got a sudden flash of memory, a rush of associations that started with a roadside marker and ended with me and my brother standing in short pants with blood on our hands. Snaking its way through the corridors of memory came an image so indelible I checked my hands for the stains, which I hadn't recalled in years. The flood gates of memory opened wide, and I lost the train entirely, focused entirely on the destination. This happens enough for me to recognize the signs; when I smell bleach I become uncontrollably hungry, when I see a woman in overalls I go weak. I leave my memories alone as much as possible and expect them to do the same for me.

It wasn't easy for us to adjust to living in Texas, my brother and me. We had spent our earliest years in California, the sons of an up-and-coming screenwriter, and thought it a matter of course to go to playgrounds with the children of the stars and to have Mister Spock over to dinner regularly. In those strange years before we became truly aware of the outside world, our little nucleus of mother, father, and brothers existed at the center of reality, and everything else revolved around us. The people we saw on television and in the movies were no less real than our own parents were, if for no other reason than that our parents seemed to know them all.

Looking back on it, it must have been incredibly strange, but in all honesty we were too young to notice it. We took it as a given that, if we pestered our dad long enough to introduce us to Donnie and Marie or one of the Brady kids, eventually we would pile into the car and drive off to some unimaginably large building past the hills and be presented to them. By which point, naturally, we had lost all interest, and hung at our father's pants legs, hounding him for some other treat or favor.

When our parents died, I think we both expected the television to stop, at least for a while, if only out of respect for them. It didn't, and I don't think I ever really forgave it for that.

In any case, when we arrived in Texas and were escorted to our new school, my brother and I quickly realized something distressing. The center of the world had moved; or rather, we had moved and left it behind. We found ourselves somehow on the periphery of reality, relegated off to a corner where no one really cared who we were. The marks of status among our new peers were how fast you could run, whether you wore the right kind of jeans, and how many of those little green peppers you could cram into your mouth at once. My brother and I were not much at running, our grandfather (or rather his housemaid) consistently refused to buy us the right kind of jeans, and at three peppers I was tearing up and beginning to wretch. We quickly dropped to the back of the herd.

Left to our own devices, the two of us had to find new ways to entertain ourselves. Our new favorite television shows, starring people we did not and could never know, were the cop shows. *Hawaii Five-O*, *SWAT*, even, inexplicably, *Barney Miller*. Anything and everything to do with crime fighting. After a light appetizer of Clayton Moore as *The Lone Ranger* and Adam West as *Batman*, we'd settle in for long hours of guns and badges and the letter of the law, all in full color. By the time we were eight, we could both recite the Miranda Rights from memory, though it was years before we knew what they were called.

It wasn't too long before we decided we knew everything there was to know about crime fighting, and only a short hop from there to deciding that we should fight crime on our own. Later, after my adventures in breaking and entering into our grandfather's study, I would resolve to put my lot in with the black hats, but for those brief summers, I was foursquare on the side of the angels.

Realizing early the practical difficulties presented by crime fighting on a large scale, we decided to start small, in our own back yard. In any neighborhood there is petty theft and vandalism that slides in under the radar of the authorities, but which served as more than enough to occupy the attention of two small boys looking for something to do. One neighbor "borrows" another's rake without asking, the newspaper in front of a certain house goes missing every morning, lost dogs and toilet paper-strewn trees. These were as close to larceny as we could come, and we made the most of it.

We started by putting up fliers all around the neighborhood:

FINCH TWINS
DISCREET INVESTIGATIONS
NO JOB TWO BIG
NO JOB TWO SMALL
217 CRESCENT ROW

Despite the spelling errors and the barely legible print, the fliers were noticeable, and within a few days we had our first client. A neighborhood kid had lost two months' worth of lunch money to a schoolyard bully, and wanted our help getting it back. It wasn't exactly the kind of case we were after, but it was undeniably a crime, and so we set to with all our energy. In the end, we dug up some dirt about the bully smoking in the parking lot after school and cowed him into returning the kid's money. As insurance, we wrote up a list of his offenses, made a dozen copies, and had him sign each and every one. Then we distributed a copy of the list to each of the kids he terrorized on a regular basis, with instructions to hand it to the nearest authority in the event that any of them were troubled further. The only real leverage we had, in the end, was that the bully's dad was a coach at the high school, and knew each of his teachers personally, but it proved to be enough.

It verged on extortion, and when it was all said and done, having collected a fee of one day's lunch money from our client, we were a little uncomfortable about our methods. But seeing justice done proved an admirable result, and we decided never to let the letter of the law stand in our way of the pursuit of justice.

We went on like that for several months, returning stolen bicycles, reuniting joyful little girls with lost kittens, and quelling schoolyard frauds. Then the case we had been waiting for dropped in our laps, and we were ready for it. A runaway, in our own neighborhood.

Ricky Young, who lived four houses down and across the street, was the kind of kid who gets a wide berth in any school. Overweight, in clothes that never seemed to fit and always seemed to be covered in dirt, or food, or both, always wearing a parka even in the warmest weather, he made strange noises while in the bathroom, picked his nose and ate the results. Always looking slightly dazed when peering out from under his chili-bowl hairdo, he never said two sentences running in anyone's presence, and was not a member, official or otherwise, of any of the free-floating cliques which form and reform in elementary schoolyards at alarming rates. Ricky was simply the fat kid, a constant presence, but a tolerated one. He was a troglodyte, but he was ours.

In the winter of our fifth grade year, our friendly neighborhood troglodyte went missing, and to be honest it took everyone, teachers included, a few days to notice. Always sick with something or other, Ricky was a perennial absentee, and his failure to appear was nothing out of the ordinary. Finally, though, his parents arrived in our classroom, looking so polished and presentable that I couldn't believe they had anything to do with the troll I knew. They wanted to know if anyone knew anything about where Ricky might have gone, whether anyone had seen him since Tuesday, if he had said or done anything that might have indicated he was unhappy. Greeted by a unanimous silence, they filed out of the room, red eyed and harried, and class was back in session.

It didn't take my brother and me that long to decide what had happened. The Ricky that we all knew and loathed had to be a front, a sham, covering some more secret self. The real Ricky must have suffered some trauma to hide away behind all those layers of fat and filth, and when it all proved too much for him had run away from home. He might even now be crouched somewhere in the rain, hungry and alone, shivering at the sound of wolves baying in the distance; never mind the fact that it was sunny and seventy degrees outside, and the only wolves within a hundred miles were in the San Antonio zoo.

We started our Grand Search for Ricky Young that afternoon, starting with the school grounds and fanning out from there. Ricky had last been seen leaving there Tuesday afternoon, and had not gone home. From that, we had deduced that he had made his preparations for running away before coming to school in the morning. None of our classmates remembered seeing him with a bag or sack of any kind on Tuesday, but we couldn't rely on that testimony. Few found that they could describe Ricky with any kind of certainty at all, except perhaps to mention his odor. We were beginning to suspect that maybe it was all part of his plan.

Our search that first night turned up nothing, and we retired to our grandfather's house and Maria's home-cooked dinner to plan out the next stage of our investigation. The weekend was before us, and all the hours of the day at our disposal. We couldn't leave a three block radius from our house, naturally, but we thought that more than sufficient. Ricky couldn't have gone far.

Over dinner, my brother showed more courage than I had seen him display in some time, and broached the subject of our neighbor's disappearance with our grandfather.

"Did you hear about that kid who ran away?" he said, his voice only cracking once or twice. "The... um... *big* one?"

Our grandfather speared an entire shrub's worth of salad and, pausing with it right before his face, examined it intently.

"There are many dangerous people in the world," he replied, and then guided the fork into his open mouth.

My brother and I just stared at him, and then at our plates, not sure how to respond.

We started the next phase of the investigation early the next morning. Forgoing the standard Saturday morning fare of *Scooby Doo* and *The Banana Splits,* we watched dutifully as Maria fixed peanut butter and jelly sandwiches for the two of us, and then we packed them away in matching nylon backpacks along with flashlights, pocket knives, and first aid equipment. We had never been Boy Scouts, but had read enough issues of *Boy's Life* at the doctor's office to know to be prepared.

We started at the house next door and worked our way down, notepads and Bic pens in hand. We asked the people who answered the door where they had been Tuesday afternoon and early evening, whether they had seen a fat kid in a parka, and if they had seen any suspicious persons or activity in the neighborhood recently. This last was standard operating procedure, learned from studying the moves of TV cops. It never elicited any kind of response, but it was good form, and we included it in our questioning as a matter of course.

By noon, we had canvassed the houses on both sides of our street, and half of the next block over. Our notepads were both blank except for a brief line on each, "MR. ANDERSON SAW FAT KID IN AFTERNOON, MON? TUES?" That was as far as our investigation took us. Deciding it was time for a break, but not wanting to head back home until our assignment was through, we cut between two houses and down an alley until we came to the Creek.

The Creek – really nothing more than a hint of a trickle that meandered down a slight slope and disappeared into a drainage ditch – was a favored spot for afterschool explorations, snow ball fights during the brief Texas winters, and dirt clod fights in the summers. On either side was an empty grassy area, about ten yards wide and running the length of the block, only slightly slanted and perfect for frisbees and touch football. By the end of the summer, and continuing into the first freeze, the grass had usually grown to an alarming height, and hid all the toys and bicycle parts lost there over the preceding months. This being the beginning of December, and the first real cold snap still weeks away, the grass rose to at least two feet and reached easily up to our waists.

Slogging our way through the brown, swaying grass, we made it to the edge of the water and found a dry spot to sit and eat. We munched on our sandwiches, and each opened a can of grape soda we'd secreted from the kitchen. We talked about the facts of the case as we knew them, about the plots of the comics we'd bought the week before, about the possibility of life on other planets and whether we could fly their space ships if we came upon them in the road. In the end, we decided that there was a strong possibility that Ricky had left town, that Superman could in fact beat up the Hulk, and that if the spaceship was a Viper from the Battlestar Galactica we could most likely fly it. Having concluded our important business, we figured we might as well finish up the day, and if we hadn't found Ricky by dinner time file the case under Unsolved.

Finishing off our cans of soda and lobbing them downstream at the drainage ditch, we headed back towards the street through the open field. A few yards in, my brother noticed a cloud of flies hovering in midair like a balloon. It was then that the smell hit us, and I was reminded of dog we'd found the summer before, lying half flattened in the middle of the road, caked with dirt and with *something* still moving around inside. We had touched it with a long stick, and then the something came spilling out, millions of them, squirming out blind onto the hot tarmac. It was that kind of smell.

We continued forward, cautiously now, plowing through the grass with our arms out in front of us, our eyes glued to the ground. It was six paces before we found it, before we almost walked right over it. In that first moment, I wasn't sure what it was, and I bent to pick it up. It was a little white creature, with four or five legs, and I held it for a long moment before my brother snatched it out of my grasp. We both looked at it, and as we did the legs began to resolve into fingers, the little creature into a hand.

I'd like to say that it was my brother that threw up first, and the smell and sound of it caused me to follow, but I can't say for sure. All I know is that we were running all the way home, my head turned to one side, his to the other, crying and vomiting all the way. Hanging in front of each of us, burned into our retinas, was the image of that hand, and that arm, laying all alone in the grass, and a couple of yards away, the hint of something else.

It was Maria who called the police and went down to the Creek with them while we cowered at the kitchen table, gulping down water and shivering despite the warm air. It wasn't until she got back that she noticed the blood on our hands and hurried us to the sink to scald it off. We hadn't said a word since the police had arrived, only occasionally glancing at one other, our faces blank.

It was all over the news for a few days, and Ricky Young's name was added to a short list of children who had been found mutilated and abandoned around and about central Texas over the previous three years. Reporters came around to the house once or twice, but they were quickly dismissed by our grandfather who told them there was no story. Meanwhile my brother and I hid upstairs, numbly flipping through the stations on a little black and white television. Maria sat stoically in the kitchen every night for a month, her eyes on the back door, one hand perched on a telephone, the other grasping the handle of a large kitchen knife. After a while, when there were no other child murders to report, the story was quietly dropped.

Our grandfather only mentioned the incident once that I can recall. That first night, once Maria had showered and scrubbed us both for hours and then locked us in our rooms, her weeping all the while, he came to our room long after dark.

My brother and I both sat on the floor near our beds, our knees up at our chins, staring wide-eyed at the opening door. Grandfather just stood there in the doorway, immaculately dressed in his coat and hat, and disarmingly calm. He looked at me, then my brother, and then back again, and nodded his head three times slowly.

"There are many dangerous people in the world," he said firmly, and then turned and closed the door. We later heard the front door open and close, and the car started and driven away. We didn't see him again until the next night, and he never mentioned it again.

I didn't sleep for a week. All thoughts of fighting crime were gone. I never wanted to leave my room again.

It was late afternoon when I finally pulled into a spot on Guadalupe, across from the University of Texas. I dodged the teenage kids on the street begging for change or cigarettes, and crossed the intersection to the campus.

It was finals week, if I was reading correctly the expression on every student's face I saw. Aside from a few sorority sisters rushing to the undergraduate library, an Asian couple discussing Shakespeare in low tones and an Indian engineering student asleep on his textbook, the West Mall was deserted as I made my way to the liberal arts buildings. Clustered together in a defensive fashion, like the deans and profs had circled the figurative wagons to stave of the attacks of irrelevancy from the business and engineering departments across the campus, the buildings housing the liberal arts had a certain rustic, old world charm. Like hairy armpits on women, or the Black Death. I barely ducked a flying dialectical necessity coming up the stairway to the central building, and narrowly missed being smacked in the eyes by a moral imperative as I skirted my way around the philosophy department. Like most ivory towers, it was dangerous to visitors.

The Department of Middle Eastern Studies was squirreled away in a corner on the third floor of the saddest of the buildings, just past the broken water fountain on the left. The bulletin board in the hall out front advertised guest lectures from professors who were simply ordinary on their own distant campuses, and notices about invitations for ordinary professors to lecture at distant schools. There was a film series of Socialist Feminist Cinema from Jordan, and a question-and-answer session with the Deputy Secretary of the Coalition to End Genital Mutilation in Yemen. I was sorry I'd missed that.

The wooden door creaked on its ancient hinges as I entered, and I stepped into the familiar aroma of stale air, dusty books, and a hint of patchouli. Behind the reception desk was a young woman in a tight-fitting tank top, Italian wrestler pants and more tattoos than the Ninth Fleet. She looked up at me around her eyebrow rings, and ran a hand over her close cropped scalp. I watched her take me in a single glance – the rumpled suit, the scuffed boot, the eight dollar haircut – and I could just tell she didn't approve. I might not have been the Man, but she could tell I was on a first name basis with Him.

"Yes," she snarled. "Are you lost?"

I have uncanny luck with receptionists. It never fails.

"I'm here to see Michelle Orlin," I answered.

She sneered.

"*Doctor* Orlin is grading exams," she said, "and can't be disturbed. I'm sure, *if* you have important business, she can arrange to see you some *other* time."

Behind her was a half-opened door, and before I could answer it swung wide and a flurry in faded denim and paisley came bounding into the room.

"Spencer!"

I smiled, catching the receptionist's eye.

"I thought I heard your voice!" The flurry came into focus, all five foot eight of her, her long tangled hair spinning around her like a nimbus.

"Howdy, Michelle," I said.

She hurried around a chair and came up to lock me in a bear hug. For someone so slight, she had a pretty mean grip.

"How the hell have you been?" she asked. "I haven't seen you since… New York?"

"Sounds about right," I answered, gently pushing her to arm's length and looking down into her eyes. "So you reconsider that offer yet?"

She smiled devilishly and chucked me a light tap on the chin.

"Still trying to make an honest woman of me, huh?" She stepped back and crossed her arms, cocking her head to one side. "I know I don't have to remind you of the one flaw in your master plan."

"I'm convinced I could straighten you out, baby," I replied, "just give me half a chance."

I could feel the receptionist's every orifice clench from where I stood and resisted the temptation to see for myself. I resisted, and failed. A quick glance her way and her gaze showed me the million ways she was planning on emasculating me. I had a notion, and ran with it.

"I'm not selfish, you know," I directed at the scowling tattoo, "I'll share her with you if you want."

Michelle slugged me in the arm and managed a frown for all of five seconds.

"Yeah, yeah, yeah," she scolded, "God's gift to women, scourge of the lesbian."

I just shrugged.

"Come on back."

She turned and started back for her office. I followed, pausing briefly to blow a kiss to the receptionist. She practically convulsed with rage, but kept her seat.

"Okay, Spence, what's this all about? I know you didn't just come to shoot the shit."

Michelle, one of only two people in the world I let call me "Spence", was leaning back in her chair, her knees folded up to her chin, one arm resting over them. Her free hand pulled at her tangled hair, teasing out the knots one bit at a time. On the desk in front of her were stacks of exam books, a few dozen stapled groups of paper, and a half-dozen ash trays full to capacity. Smoking had been regulated right out of state buildings years before, but since few of the University officials had any idea where the Middle Eastern department was, much less visited, Michelle figured she was safe.

I sat back in the antique wooden chair, the thing I came to show her resting on my knee. I lit up a cigarette and started in.

"Okay, okay, you got me. I need help, and I think you're the only one who can give it to me." I took a drag on the cigarette and let that sink in.

"The *only* one?" she asked. "Or the only one who's still speaking with you?"

"The only one," I answered simply. "I don't need someone to post bail, or do my laundry, or feed my cat–"

"You don't have a cat," Michelle interrupted, her eyes narrowing.

"I need help only you can give me," I finished.

She leaned forward in her chair, dropping her feet to the floor.

"This should be good," she said.

"I hope so."

Like a corny magician at a birthday party, I reached down out of her line of sight behind the desk and brought it back up with the plastic bag, which I'd kept out of her view up till now. Inside, untouched, was the ancient and yellowed paper with all the tiny markings. I dropped it unceremoniously on the desk in front of her and sat back. I watched her eyes widen.

"What is that?" she asked, her voice breathless.

"I don't know, babe," I answered. "I was hoping you would tell me."

Fifteen minutes and a half-dozen cigarettes between us later, Michelle had at least part of an answer.

"It's old," she pronounced. I was beginning to wonder if I'd come to the right place.

"And...?" I prompted.

"It's very old," she added. "Very, very old."

I sighed and stubbed out a cigarette.

"Fascinating," I drawled.

"I mean it, Spence, this is really a find. Based on the grammatical structures, the syntax, even the penmanship... I'd place it at Eighth, Ninth Century tops." She still hovered over it, a magnifying glass in hand. Her last cigarette, untouched on the ashtray, had burned to the filter.

"Yeah, but what is it?"

"Um, paper," she said, sarcasm dripping.

"Okay, short questions. Language?"

"Definitely Arabic."

"O-kay," I said. "And it says..." I paused, waiting for her to jump in.

"What, all of it?" she asked. "Do you know how long it took me to do my translation of the

Rubaiyat? And that was after two years of studying the grammar and vocabulary. This isn't a menu, Spencer; I can't just recite it to you." I watched her glasses begin to slip down her nose, but she was so worked up she didn't even notice.

"Do you have a general idea?" I asked calmly.

"Sure." She paused and held the paper up to the light, still sheathed in plastic. "Where did you get this?" she breathed.

"That's not important. What does it say?" I paused for a beat, then added, "In general terms?"

"Okay, okay, let's see." She pushed her glasses back up on her nose, brought the magnifying glass in close, and then hunched over the page. "Here's something about some scandal, some secrets revealed... some hidden order of men... something about the northern secrets, or the northern mysteries... the book of the one eye... no, 'god'... the one-eyed god.... the revels of the infidels... the god in chains... and..."

Her finger froze over a scribble, and her mouth hung slack. She slowly sat upright, her finger still frozen in place, her mouth open.

"Shit," she whispered.

"What," I asked, leaning over her. "What?!"

"Aeschylus," she said quietly. "Shit."

"What the hell are you talking about?"

She slowly drew her hands in towards her, as though not to upset the air around her, and folded them in her lap. She stared into space for a long minute, and then turned her head to look at me.

"Where. Did. You. Get. This?"

"I. Can't. Tell. You." I answered, mocking her serious tone. "What. Does. It. Say?"

She sighed heavily, her shoulders dropping. "How much do you know about ancient literature?" she asked.

"I had to read *Huck Finn* in high school," I answered.

"Ancient, you philistine," she countered. "Ancient Greek literature."

"Like the man said to the tailor, 'Eumenides?'"

"Aeschylus."

"Nah, nah, the tailor says, 'Euripides?'"

"Shut. Up." She took a deep breath. "Aeschylus, the acknowledged father of the Greek theater; only something like seven of his plays have survived. Dozens of his plays, praised by the ancient world, are totally forgotten to us." She had lapsed into lecturing, but she was a professor so I forgave her. "Of the ones we have, several survived only in translations made later by Arab scholars." Her eyes darted briefly to the paper, and then back to mine. "When discoveries like those are made, it's like... finding Atlantis, for Christ sake, or George Washington's teeth. Something everyone had read about, but which had been thought lost forever."

"Uh huh," I hummed, pretty much at sea.

"This paper," she continued, and then gestured awkwardly to it with her chin. "This paper," she repeated, "mentions Aeschylus… by name… and then starts talking about the 'revels of the chained god'. That's how they understood plays, Spencer, as 'revels'. The Muslim world had nothing of the kind, and they just thought of them as some pagan debauchery."

"Uh huh," I repeated.

"The chained god," she insisted. "Don't you know what that means?" She could tell I didn't. "Prometheus, you barbarian, Prometheus. One of the surviving plays of Aeschylus is *Prometheus Bound*, which tells how the god Prometheus was chained to a mountain for helping mankind. It's regarded as one of the true classics of the ancient world. We know… we know that Aeschylus wrote two sequels, three in all–"

"*Prometheus II: No More Mister Nice God*?"

"Shut up, I'm thinking… talking… whatever. Listen. If this is what I think it is" – and this time she didn't even bother jutting her chin at the paper; we both knew what she meant – "then this could contain a fragment of one of the lost Prometheus plays. Maybe both. And from the length… both sides… um…" She did some quick math. "It could well be more than any of the other fragments found before. Maybe even the whole fucking play! Or BOTH!"

She paused, and then seemed to calm down by will of force. She lit a cigarette and inhaled deeply, gazing over at the paper with love in her eyes.

"Shit," she finally said. "I'm going to be famous."

Fifteen minutes later I was back outside, less the page. Michelle had agreed to translate it fully, try as much as possible to identify its origins, and come up with some idea of what sort of book it was a part of. In exchange, she would get full publication and "finder's" rights for the completed text, which seemed to her more than sufficient. Before I'd even made it out the door, she was pulling dictionaries and concordances from the shelves, and had begun work on the assignment. I left quietly, pausing only to leer at the receptionist before going back outside.

On my way across campus, I passed the undergraduate library and, realizing that I had a couple of hours to kill, headed over. Something Michelle had said while doing her quick and easy translation had caught my attention and suggested someone else I might talk to, but if he was working at his regular schedule it was much too early in the day to come calling.

Once inside the library, packed to the rafters with panicky college kids trying desperately to fit a semester's worth of knowledge into a single evening, I made for the elevator and headed up to the classics section.

With the help of a very friendly and quietly attractive librarian, I ended up with a stack of books and found my way to an empty table. Spreading them out in front of me, I got to work. Having realized in the course of Michelle's lecture that I knew nothing of use about Greek myths, plays, or writers, I figured it would be useful to see what I could find out about all the names she was dropping. If the contents of that page were any indication of the nature of the book, it might give me some idea who had taken it, and what I was after.

I took a book off the pile at random and flipped it open to the index. There was nothing about Aeschylus, but a couple of listings for Prometheus, so I hunted them down. After a few lines in blank verse about the various and sundry evils of mortal man, the writer went to town:

> *"But Zeus in the anger of his heart hid the means of life, because Prometheus the crafty deceived him; therefore he planned sorrow and mischief against men. Zeus hid fire; but that the noble son of Iapetos stole again for men from Zeus, whose counsels are many. In the hollow of a fennel-stalk Prometheus slipped it away, so that Zeus who delights in thunder did not see it. But afterwards Zeus the cloud-gatherer said to him in anger:*
>
> *'Son of Iapetos, surpassing all in cunning, you are glad that you have outwitted me and stolen fire – which will be a curse to you and the generations to come. But I will give men as the price for fire an evil thing in which they may all be glad of heart while they embrace their own destruction.'*

So said the father of men and gods, and laughed aloud."

I looked over the page to make sure I hadn't missed anything, and I hadn't. Hadn't really caught anything, either, but that was to be expected. I really don't speak poetry all that well, and about the most I'd got out of it was that this Prometheus guy had given people matches, and the head honcho was concerned about how it would affect their job performance. I skimmed down for the next reference, which came a few dozen pages later:

"With shackles and inescapable fetters Zeus bound Prometheus to a pillar – Prometheus of the labyrinthine mind – and Zeus sent a long-winged eagle to swoop on him and devour his liver; but what the long-winged bird ate each day grew back and was restored to its full size."

Not much better, but I was beginning to get the picture. After stepping beyond the boundaries of his job description by giving humanity a light, Prometheus was transferred out of the home office to one of the branch locations. Not a cherry assignment, it appeared. I flipped back to the index again, but came up short. The book went back on the pile, and I started in on another.

The next selection, not a translation like the first but a kind of mythological Yellow Pages written in

English of all things, had quite a bit about our boy. I found the chapter devoted to him, and checked out what Robert Graves had to say about him:

> *"Prometheus, the creator of mankind, whom some include among the seven Titans, was the son either of the Titan Eurymedon, or of Iapetus by the nymph Clymene; and his brothers were Epimetheus, Atlas, and Menoetius."*

Then, just when it started to get good, Graves seemed to forget all about Prometheus, and started in on his big brother, Atlas. There was a whole section about him, the big fellow who broke some divine law or other and was sentenced to hold up the sky. He didn't say who'd been holding up the sky until then, and I wondered if it was really necessary, or just busy work. Then, just before he lost me all together, it turned back to Prometheus.

> *"Prometheus, being wiser than Atlas, foresaw the issue of the rebellion against Cronus, and therefore preferred to fight on Zeus's side, persuading Epimetheus to do the same. He was, indeed, the wisest of his race, and Athene, at whose birth from Zeus's head he had assisted, taught him architecture, astronomy, mathematics, navigation, medicine, metallurgy, and other useful arts, which he passed on to mankind. But Zeus, who had decided to extirpate the whole race of man, and spare them only at*

Prometheus's urgent plea, grew angry at their increasing powers and talents."

Okay, I thought, so the guy tends to side against management and with labor, and is pretty free with favors. A regular renaissance man and union boss, all rolled into one.

"One day, when a dispute took place at Sicyon, as to which portions of a sacrificial bull should be offered to the gods, and which should be reserved for men, Prometheus was invited to act as arbiter. He therefore flayed and jointed a bull, and sewed its hide to form two open-mouthed bags, filling these with what he had cut up. One bag contained all the flesh, but this he concealed beneath the stomach, which is the least appealing part of any animal; and the other contained the bones, hidden beneath a rich layer of fat. When he offered Zeus the choice of either, Zeus, easily deceived, chose the bag containing the bones and fat (which are still the divine portions); but punished Prometheus, who was laughing at him behind his back, by withholding fire from mankind. 'Let them eat their flesh raw!' he cried.

"Prometheus went at once to Athene, with a plea for a backstairs admittance to Olympus, and this she granted. On his arrival, he lighted a torch at the fiery chariot of the Sun and presently broke from it a fragment of glowing charcoal, which he thrust into the pithy hollow of a giant fennel-stalk.

Then, extinguishing his torch, he stole away undiscovered, and gave fire to mankind.

Zeus swore revenge. He had Prometheus chained naked to a pillar in the Caucasian mountains, where a greedy vulture tore at his liver all day, year in, year out; and there was no end to the pain, because every night (during which Prometheus was exposed to cruel frost and cold) his liver grew whole again."

There was still a lot in there I didn't get, but I was beginning to get a handle on it. This guy Prometheus was beginning to look better and better, if not something of a sucker, while Zeus was coming off like a real dick. There were a few end note markings on the more outré names, so I flipped ahead a couple of pages to the end of the chapter.

"Note: Prometheus's name, 'forethought', may originate in a Greek misunderstanding of the Sanskrit word pramantha, the swastika, or fire-drill, which he had supposedly invented, since Prometheus at Thurii was shown holding a fire-drill. Prometheus, the Indo-European folk-hero, became confused with the Carian hero Palamedes, the inventor or distributor of all civilized arts (under the goddess's inspiration), and with the Babylonian god Ea, who claimed to have created a splendid man from the blood of Kingu (a sort of Cronus), while the Mother-goddess Aruru created an inferior man from clay."

I finished that up and just shrugged. Sure, whatever, I thought. "Prometheus" means forethought, but also swastika, and maybe even a couple of other things besides. He gets mixed up with other deities at parties, people can't tell them apart, and he has some affinity for fire drills. He has problems with management, and is always getting into some kind of hot water. He was starting to sound like half the guys I grew up with.

I flipped through a couple of the other books, but didn't really find anything in them that wasn't in the others. I jotted down the names of the books, in case I'd need to find them again, and dropped them off with the friendly librarian. Then it was down the stairs, across the mall, and back to the car. I was starting to feel educated, and figured that as good a sign as any to get clear of the university.

It was well after dark before I was out of sight of the campus, which made it just soon enough for my next port of call. Moon & Son, a dive bar and fixture of the local live music scene. I could use a drink or two and, if luck were with me, the man behind the bar would be just the person I wanted to see.

Something Michelle had said had stuck in my head, while all the other stuff about Greek poets and Arab scholars went rolling on by. She mentioned the "northern mysteries," a term I'd heard a million times if I'd heard it a thousand, and never paid much attention to. People in my acquaintance are always rambling on about something or other, and I've learned it's best to just let them run their course and try as much as possible not to get in the way. However, despite myself, one or two things have been known to stick.

The bar was down near the north side of the river, on the last gasp edge of the old commercial district. Once little more than boarded up old warehouses and pitted streets crisscrossed with railroad lines, the area had seen a lot of change since the first time I was there. Just a few short years, and it went from being a last refuge of urban blight in the middle of high rise heaven to an up-and-coming retail and entertainment district with real growth potential. Trendy little restaurants which served food no native Texan would go near, valet parking in front of every bar, hip little "theme" clubs; it was starting to look like Los Angeles, with the addition of about a thousand more pickups and minus the celebrities. Thankfully, the darkened street that was my destination had escaped the ravages of the improvement and still looked threatening to all the yuppies so comfortable just a few blocks away.

It being a weeknight, and with no one on the bill, I was able to find a parking spot just out front with no problems. Pulling a fresh pack of cigarettes from the glove compartment, I locked up the car and headed inside.

It was exactly as it had always been, though the management was always trying to keep things new and fresh. They could move the bar from one side of the room to another all they wanted, bring in disco balls and strobe lights, but it wouldn't make any difference. It still always smelled of rotting wood and spilt beer, not that anyone in the place seemed to mind. Without a hot new act to bring in all the college kids, it was only the career alcoholics in attendance tonight. People with nowhere else to go and in no hurry to get there.

I found a stool at the bar and waited for the mound of flesh with the shaved head and the goofy grin to come my way. I didn't have to wait long; he was mopping up the bar in front of me and taking my order before I knew it.

"What'll it be?" he asked in perfect bartenderese.

"I want to accept Odin as my personal lord and savior," I answered.

The round head shot up, eyes locking onto mine.

"Spencer!" he roared. "How are you, my friend?"

"Never better, Brother Royce." I leaned in and eyed the chalk board with the evening's specials. "How 'bout a pint of Bock?"

"Done," he answered, then produced a glass as if from nowhere and proceeded to fill it. He slammed it down in front of me, and then rested both hands on the bar. "You know, you shouldn't make fun of my beliefs, Spencer. It's unkind."

"I know, I know," I answered, shrugging. "I can't help it."

Royce shook his head slowly at me, frowning.

"Your cynicism keeps you from seeing the truth," he said. "You know that. You're afraid of what you could find yourself believing."

"Of that I have no doubt."

A pair of UPS drivers appeared at the far end of the bar and motioned for the round head to come over to them. Royce turned to me, apologetically.

"I'll be right back," he said.

"Take your time," I answered. "I've got some questions to ask you when you get a chance."

"Questions?" Royce answered, pausing in mid-turn. "About?"

"About the northern mysteries."

The round face split into an enormous grin, lighting up his dark eyes. He thumped an open palm on the bar top and laughed.

"Finally!" he near shouted, and then hurried to get the drivers' orders.

Royce Crayton, to be charitable, was the oddest duck in the entire lunatic flock I'd collected over the years. Of all the unhinged and borderline individuals I'd encountered, he had the clearest, most air-tight claim on true insanity I'd found. And yet, he was pleasant, sociable and able to keep a job and maintain relative normal relations. When you got down to it, he seemed all in all a normal guy – big boned and bald, but a normal guy. Until, that is, he started talking about his divine charge. Royce Crayton was on a mission. A mission from Odin.

It always begins with Royce innocently enough. Over beers, or a meal, he'll begin talking about his life. His time in jail, the crowd he ran with as a kid. To the untrained ear he's just a normal guy sharing a hard luck story. Then, without warning, the story starts to change. He starts talking about his moment of clarity, his "epiphany" he calls it, when the heavens opened up their gates and he beheld the face of God. By this point most newcomers begin to lean back in their chairs, shifting uncomfortably and making eyes towards the doors. But it's too late. Royce is in full swing by this point, telling you exactly what God wants, and what he has in store for you if you only live by his simple precepts, and then you know. He's not talking. He's proselytizing.

I had the unique fortune to experience this rare pleasure first hand on two separate occasions. The first was soon after moving to Austin, when I'd met Michelle and her then current flame Janet, the owner of Moon & Son. Janet had given me an open tab at the bar and invited me to come by whenever I wanted. I'm sure to her that meant a beer now and again, maybe once or twice a week. What she didn't know was that I was at that time out of a job, with nothing to do and no money to do it with. My meager cupboards were bare, and my entertainment consisted entirely of watching geckos scale the outside of my screen door. I was always there, and *always* had a drink in hand.

It was there that I met Royce Crayton, who had only recently begun tending bar. He and I got to be pretty familiar over the first weeks, and since I was there almost as much as he was we fell to talking whenever things were slow. The first time he started in on his mission, I was at the end of an eight hour spree, and I wasn't listening to much of anything. The next day, when things cleared up for me, I remembered bits and pieces of our conversation the previous night, and thought for sure Royce was fucking with me. He simply had to be. So, after hosing off, I headed up to Moon & Son, figuring we'd both get a big kick out of the line of bull he'd laid on me.

I knew, as soon as I mentioned the mission to him, that I'd made a mistake. I could see in his eyes that particular zeal, that total lack of irony, that blind passionate sincerity that only the truly devoted or the truly insane possess. He was dead serious, and he meant every word. Then, without warning, he told me the whole story again, worried I might have missed something the first time around.

Royce was born a cracker, poor white trash and everything that it entailed. His father, from everything I've heard about him, was a walking stereotype: beer gut and wife-beater shirt and a mean left hook. His mother was bad hair dyes and fat ankles, a cigarette always hanging from the corner of her mouth. Neither ever had anything resembling a kind word for their only son, and Royce learned early to look for acceptance elsewhere. Unfortunately, in the poorest neighborhood in the poorest part of south Dallas, an area the rest of the city seemed to want to shut away until it atrophied and dropped off, Royce rarely saw anything but the worst in people. There was all the expected misery and depression one has come to expect after hundreds of movies of the week and after-school specials, all the deprivations that prey on men and women who have had everything taken away by the system and never once gotten anything back. All that shit.

Royce didn't know any better, didn't know anywhere was any different. He only knew what he saw around him, and that was a simple lesson. Obey the law of the jungle. Like stays to like, and anyone else is an enemy. By the age of twelve he'd fallen in with a group of white punks who delighted in roaming the neighborhood throwing rocks through windows and tagging every flat surface they could find. Inevitably someone saw a movie, or read a book, and it was bomber jackets, combat boots and shaved heads all around. The swastikas came out, and suddenly they were skinheads.

It's best not to dignify the skinhead with anything approaching a philosophy, but if they could be said to have a motto it is that White Is Right, and Everything Else Gets Stomped In The Face. By the time Royce was fifteen, he had gotten four chapters into *Mein Kampf,* and had a triskelion tattooed on his forearm. By the time he was sixteen he had moved out of his parents' house all together, and was squatting in an abandoned tenement near the Trinity with a half-dozen of his friends. By the time he was seventeen, he had killed a man.

The way Royce tells it, the murder was just a spur of the moment thing. He looks back on it with profound regret, but even now can't begin to explain why it happened. Like a scene out of a bad movie, he and a few of his bald pals had gone into a convenience store to cause some trouble; it all ended when Royce produced a gun and emptied it into the Korean clerk. When it was done, the gun warm in his hand and blood pooling at his feet, Royce had just frozen in place, unable to move. The cops had shown up a few minutes later, on their way to a topless place down the street, and hauled him off without any trouble at all.

Royce was tried as an adult, and by his eighteenth birthday had moved to Huntsville. He shared a cell with an enormous Samoan, and the two didn't exactly become the best of friends. Those first weeks were the roughest on him, I think, all alone and mixed in with every enemy of the white man he could imagine, and all of them coming after him. Then he met another skinhead in the yard and was invited to join the Church of Odin. It was all downhill from there.

As near as I've been able to tell from reading between the lines of Royce's story, groups like the Church of Odin are not all that uncommon. Some enterprising convict at some point in the recent past realized that religious groups are afforded rights and privileges not given the mass of prisoners. The simplest thing in the world, then, would be to start a religion. Soon it was all the rage. There was the Church of Wicca, the Moorish Science Temple, the Sons of Aztlan and New Nation of Islam. And there was the Church of Odin.

All these jokers would do, as Royce tells it, was to "conduct gang activity". What that means I don't know, unless it is to tattoo each other and plan how to beat other gangs senseless. Nevertheless, I guess the color television wasn't enough to hold the skinheads' interest, so it was church time and pagan prayer meetings instead.

Royce was approached like every other inmate of suitable ethnic makeup. A member of the

Church came up to him in the exercise yard and told him that his white brothers had formed a church, and that if he alerted the guards he would be escorted from his cell and to meetings at designated times. The word "Odin" was mentioned, Royce remembered, and that was about it. Young, bruised and impressionable, Royce agreed.

What happened next is, I believe, the thing that slowly turned Royce from a rather dull-minded thug to an intellectually eager lunatic. When next his cell block was taken to the library to select reading material, while the others all gravitated to lawbooks to help them bolster up their flagging appeals, Royce hit the card catalogue and looked up "ODIN". He came up with a children's book, *The Children of Odin* by Padraic Colum, which he took back to his cell and read straight through, cover to cover, over the next three days. Then he read it again. And again. And when it came time to go back to the library the following week, he checked it out again, along with a copy of *Myths of the Norsemen*, one of *The Lives of the Norse Kings*, a large picture book called *D'Aulaires' Book of Norse Myths*, and a collection of Norse Eddas. Slowly his reading speed increased, as did his comprehension, and as they did he would go back and read the books again and again.

Meanwhile the Church of Odin continued their meetings. While the guards were in ear shot, they called upon their Viking god to grant them strength, to protect them in times of torment, and to strike down their enemies, but when the guards wandered away it was back to how to smash the Mexican Mafia, or stick it to the Crips, all in hoarse, whispered tones. Royce sat quietly in the back, the Colum book in his lap, and became increasingly confused. He was starting to understand something, was stepping up to a precipice of belief, and he was beginning to feel like he was all alone.

Finally, he couldn't take it any more. When one of the more experienced Church members was instructing a newbie on the proper manufacture and care of a shiv, Royce leapt from his folding chair and held his book high in the air.

"Blasphemy," he shouted, his voice breaking. "This is blasphemy."

Slowly, as one, the others turned to look at him.

"What the fuck?" the shiv coach muttered, his eyes narrowing.

"You call yourselves sons of Odin, but you don't understand *anything* about him! Odin didn't just come for us, for the Aryan." Royce took a deep breath, and plowed on. "Odin hung himself from the World Ash for the sake of all mankind, and the runes he won were given to all the children of man. If this is really Odin's church, we should let anyone in.... We should invite them in: Mexican, black, Chinese..."

The air in the room seemed to drop ten degrees as he spoke, and the others started to climb slowly out of their chairs.

"What the fuck?" the skinhead at the front repeated.

"Odin is the All Father of All," Royce went on. "You... you're just a bunch of bigots."

There was a long pause, as Royce tells it, when they all just looked at him, over a dozen of them, their eyes wide, their mouths hanging open. Then, without a signal or sign, they all rushed forward and proceeded to beat the living shit out of him.

His remaining years in prison, Royce kept apart from the other skinheads as much as possible. Everyone else, for the most part, kept pretty much apart from him, too. They learned early on that the chance to knock his face in wasn't nearly worth having to listen to him talk about the glory of Odin while they did it. Through it all, Royce's strength in his new-found religion grew stronger and stronger, and became in the end unbreakable.

Finally, the parole board agreed that Royce had met the terms set for his early release. They glossed over his occasional outburst on the Norse gods, choosing instead to note simply that he had "undergone a religious conversion" while incarcerated. Royce Crayton was released back into society, his only possessions a battered bomber jacket, a key to a house that had burned to the ground years before, and a battered copy of *The Children of Odin* that had been given to him by the prison librarian when the cover had finally fallen off.

Older, wiser, and without a doubt nuttier than a fruitcake, Royce began his mission: to bring to the world the Good News of Odin.

The evening wore on, and all but the most committed drinkers filtered out in ones and twos, leaving in the end only a half-dozen of us in the place. After seeing that everyone's beverage needs had been seen to, Royce came around to the front of the bar and found a seat next to me. Resting his elbows on the counter-top, he fingered a little necklace he wore, a four-armed cross banded by a circle that seemed somehow familiar.

"So, Brother Spencer," he began in that loud, everywhere-at-once voice of his, "do you really want to know about the All Father, or are you just making fun of me?"

I put on my best wounded look and tried to seem offended.

"What? Me?" I gasped. "Make fun of you? You must have me confused with someone else."

Royce looked at me from under his thick eyebrows and set his mouth in a line.

"Someday," he said, "you're going to find yourself running headlong into something you'll have no choice but to believe in."

"Sure," I said. "Like a brick wall." I lit a cigarette and blew out a cloud of gray smoke that hung about his head like a halo. "No, seriously. I'm working on a story and the 'northern mysteries' came up, and I was hoping you could answer a few questions about them."

"Such as?" Royce pulled his tall beer over close, and took a long draw.

"What are they?"

He laughed, a thick, deep in the chest laugh, and clapped a hand on my shoulder.

"As many times as I've tried to make you listen to the truth, and now you come looking for it."

"Something like that."

"Well, you've come just in time. On Friday I leave for Graceland. My annual pilgrimage." Somehow Royce had managed to work Elvis into his whole cosmology, something about how he was the ideal Nordic man or some such. I tried briefly to imagine the King all done up with a spear and magic helmet, but the image just didn't take.

"You realize," Royce continued, "that you're not asking a simple question here. Suppose I were to ask you to sum up Christianity for me? How easily could you do that?"

"Old Southern guys talking too slow, and uncomfortable pews. Oh, and collection plates. How's that?"

Royce shook his head at me and took another drink of his beer.

"Okay, okay," I said. "There was also something about a one-eyed god. What's that all about?"

"I'm sorry, do I know you?" Royce said. "Have we met before? You can't be the Spencer Finch I know, because I'm sure I've told him all about this a thousand times before."

"Right, I know all about it. I've been listening. You're a self-ordained minister of Odin–"

"Gothi," Royce interrupted.

"Pardon?"

"I prefer the term Gothi. It means *priest*, more or less. The correct term of address is Gothi Royce."

"O-kay," I answered slowly. "You're a... Gothi... for Odin, which as near as I can divine means a One Man Watchtower of Norse Mythology."

"Not mythology," Royce corrected. "That's insulting. It implies a dead faith, a matter only of interest to historians and psychologists. It's a religion, pure and simple."

"Sorry."

"No offense taken," he answered, and then drew himself up straight on his stool. "The one-eyed god is Odin himself, the All Father, the Truth-Finder, the Changeable One. He plucked out his own eye to trade to the dwarf Mimir for wisdom, and then hung himself on the World Ash to gain knowledge of the runes. He created the heaven and the earth, and peopled it with man and the animals. He built the shining city of gold for the gods of the Aesir, and waits in patience for the final battle with the Giants to come. He–"

"Whoa, whoa," I interrupted, taking a note pad from my jacket pocket and uncapping my pen.

"Slow down. I didn't get anything after he pulled out his own eyeball."

"Sorry," Royce answered, a bit sheepishly. "I tend to get over-enthused. Let me try it again, more slowly this time."

And he did.

It took close to an hour and two pitchers of beer, but by the time Royce was done I had a pretty good idea what this Odin character was all about. He seemed at first the standard mythological Big Man in the Sky, close cousin to Zeus, and Jehovah, and Santa Claus, but the more Royce got into it the stranger it became. Whereas the other old guys with beards tended to just sit up on their porcelain thrones and make with the thunderbolts, Odin had to work and sweat for his position. At least, that's the way Royce told it.

The gods, or the "Aesir" as Royce called them, seemed pretty much just regular folks. They had kids, held jobs, got feeble and eventually died. In between, though, came the magic swords and the flying chariots and the horses with eight legs. Other than that, old Asgard sounded like your average everyday trailer park, with silver shields everywhere instead of aluminum siding.

The head guy, the oldest of the gods, was Odin. In the beginning, it seems like he had the job purely on the basis of seniority. He'd been at the plant longer than anybody else, and the divine union appeared to take care of their own. That just wasn't enough for Odin, though, so he started looking for something else. Putting on some grungy clothes and a floppy hat, he went down to the mortal world and commenced to rambling. More than anything else, it seems, he wanted to be wise.

The first thing he did, the thing that had caught me in my tracks earlier in Royce's spiel, was trade his right eye for supernatural wisdom to some twisted old fart who lived under a big tree. Never mind why the twisted old fart didn't just use all that wisdom to make himself the head man; maybe he just wanted the eyes. Odin walked away a little worse for wear, never able to enjoy a 3D movie again, but he had the wisdom of the ages.

But it just wasn't enough to our boy Odin. He always needed more, like a junkie hooked on forbidden lore. By this point, normal folks walking around on the earth had started stringing each other up to the greater glory of Odin, in hopes that he would grant special knowledge to them. Odin, seeing this as a good enough plan, decided to take it one step further. He decided to sacrifice *himself* to Odin.

Royce seemed to ignore the practical problems of sacrificing yourself *to* yourself, so I decided to ignore it too. Either way, when he was done, there wasn't just a whole lot Odin didn't know.

Odin, though, being a generous sort of sky god,

didn't hold anything back. Once he had the mysteries of the ages in his sweaty little palm, he did the last thing you'd expect management to do. He just handed it over to mankind. All these little magic tablets he found, each with funky little letters on them... he just passed them out to people, and when they saw them they could learn everything Odin knew. How this was taken by the other Big Men In The Sky, Royce didn't mention, but I can well imagine.

In the end, which according to Royce hasn't happened yet, all the surviving gods in Asgard will get off their shiny butts and go stomp mudholes in the asses of the black hats, the Giants. Or the Giants will stomp mudholes into them; it's not clear. Either way, just about everybody ends up dying, except for one of Odin's sons and two regular folks, and the world starts over. There was all kinds of nonsense about giant snakes and swords of flame, but that was the general idea.

What this had to do with that yellowed piece of paper, or with a dead Greek writer, or with that guy chained to the mountain as an hors d'oeuvre for an eagle, I wasn't sure. What I was sure about was that it was one long story, and that Royce believed every word of it. But he was buying the beers, grateful for an audience, so I couldn't complain.

By the time Royce was all done, it was nearing on closing time, and the place had just about emptied out. I was started to feel a bit ragged, and so peeled myself off the stool and got ready to go.

I thanked Royce for his input, glancing over the pages of notes I'd got. He just beamed, throwing an arm around my shoulders, sure in his heart I'd taken my first step to full conversion. I hadn't, but I didn't have the heart to tell him.

On my way to the door, I snapped my fingers and spun around.

"I've got a package coming to me here," I called back to him, then across the bar stacking up chairs on the tables. "I couldn't give my own address, and figured I could swing by here to pick it up."

"Sure," Royce answered. "What is it?"

"Just a package," I said. "Won't take up any space."

"No sweat. I'll be here early tomorrow, since I'm leaving the next day. Have to get my stuff ready for the trip."

"Right." I gave a little wave, and then listed off towards the door.

Back home, only the second time in a month, I dragged the boxes out of the trunk and up the steps to the house. It was just a few minutes after 2 a.m., and I knew I was too awake to sleep any time soon. As tired as I was I wanted nothing more than to drop right there on the hardwood floor; but I'd spent hours staving off a drunk, and now all that nervous energy was just pouring out of my eyes.

Figuring I'd see what else dear old granddad had in his box of tricks, I fished around inside and came up with a stack of papers held together with a rusty paper clip. The type was smudged, but legible. Collapsing onto the couch and switching on a lamp, I started to read.

"An Encounter at Dusk"

(The following account is excerpted from Gallants All, *an early collection of rogues' tales by William Harrison Ainsworth, first published by Riley & Sons Ltd., 1833)*

In the surviving accounts of the activities of Reginald Taylor, the notorious highwayman known as La Main Noire to the French and the Black Hand in his native England, there is one episode which seems to stand apart from the work-a-day parry and thrust of his customary encounters. It was an occasion on which, one might hazard to say, La Main Noire met his match.

Late of Yorkshire, at that time living in France as a successful merchant, Reginald Taylor as his wont would take often to the open road in the hooded guise of the highwayman, thus to deprive wealthy aristos of their overburdened purses, and to convey these moneys into more deserving hands. Clad all in midnight sable, a pair of Dragoon pistols crossed in his belt, the gallant brigand continued in Louis the Well-Beloved's kingdom the work he had begun in George Augustus's. The king's infantry and musketeers pursued him in vain, and La Main Noire continued his activities unchecked.

One late summer afternoon, during that second year of the Austro-Prussian War, a well-appointed carriage was making its way along the wide road from Calais to the City of Lights. Its furnishings were of intricately worked brass, the curtains hanging in the well-fitted windows of a russet gold. The driver was a sturdy enough fellow, the dust of two decades in the seat still clinging to his hair. Of his passengers, he knew only that they numbered two men and one woman, dressed in the height of fashion and giving the distinct impression that they would not gladly answer any unnecessary questions.

Near dusk, the carriage was quick approaching the township of Amiens, where they would stop for the night. The driver, mindless of the road in front of him, thinking only of a soft bed, a warm mug of beer, and the company of an attractive jeune fillette, almost drove right over the man standing in the middle of the wide road, a pistol cocked and ready in each hand.

The driver pulled his team to a halt, and then gripped the reins tight, his gaze trained on the black clad man in the road.

"Throw down the reins, monsieur," boomed the voice of the brigand. "No harm will come to you."

The driver took little comfort at the man's words, still eyeing the cocked pistols. Relenting, he let slip the reins, and awkwardly raised his hands over his head.

"Good," the brigand commented. "Now, off the carriage." He gestured to the ground with one of the pistols, and stepped forward menacingly.

The driver nodded dumbly, and when his feet hit the dusty road he knew who the villain must be. It was none other than that scourge of the king's roads, La Main Noire.

"Now, open the door," instructed the highwayman. "And be quick about it."

The driver complied, stumbling around to the side of the carriage and, with a guilty look, opening wide the side door. Then he stepped quickly back, his eyes averted.

"You, in the coach," La Main Noire boomed. "Out into the open."

For a long moment, there was no movement, no sound, only the slowly dimming light from the setting sun, and the quiet rustling of the leaves. Then, with a quiet grace, a man stepped out, first to the running board, then to the ground. He was followed by the other man, and then the woman.

The first man, the taller of the two, was dressed all in gray, closely tailored, with a silk cravat at his neck and a shapely topper crowning his head. In his hand he carried a cane of ebony, capped in an intricate device of silver. On his lapel was a broach of silver, a stylized representation of a semicircular sun, caught either in the act of just setting, or just rising. He bore an almost bemused expression on his thin face, and his half-lidded gray eyes betrayed no fear.

Of the other passengers, the shorter man seemed almost a twin to the first, the gray of his suit a shade closer to white, his head bare, but in almost every other respect the mirror image of the other. He carried no cane, but on his lapel was another broach, the mate to the first. The woman, comporting herself with a haughty carriage, was dressed in a deep forest green, a bonnet tied around her elfin face, her auburn hair in a tight bun at her neck. Neither, like the first man, displayed the slightest fear or hesitation.

"Your valuables, gentles," the highwayman commanded. "Else you'll taste the spittle of these." Thereupon he indicated the pistols in his hands, with a grim nod of his head.

"We have little of value, as you would measure it," spoke the first man. "Take what you will and let us be on our way. We have pressing business in Paris, and I would not be late."

If the brigand was taken aback by the odd manner and forthright speech of his intended victim, he made no sign of it.

"I'll do my best not to delay you, monsieur," offered the highwayman, dipping his head in a mock bow. "But it would please me to know the names of such illustrious visitors." Here Taylor considered he might have netted bigger fish than originally he had suspected. Passing nobles might be good for an easy mark and a week of meals at a farmer's table, but someone of importance might prove more valuable indeed.

"Certainment," answered the tall man. "My name is Rahab, and my companions are called Salome and Samedi."

"Strange names for French highborns," Taylor commented.

"Indeed," replied Rahab, a slight smile playing about his thin lips.

"Tell me, Monsieur Rahab, of your 'pressing business' in the capital."

"Would that I could, sir, but I cannot," the tall man answered.

"Perhaps I have not made myself clear, monsieur," Taylor spoke carefully. "You consider my entreaty a polite question. It was not." Again, he made a meaningful glance at his pistols.

"I understood perfectly," Rahab replied. "It does not alter my response."

The highwayman's eyes narrowed.

"You seem confused, monsieur. Perhaps the weight of that heavy trinket," Taylor gestured to the half-sun broach with one cocked Dragoon, "has put you under some strain. If I might relieve you of it, perhaps your senses will return."

"Doubtful," spoke Rahab.

"What?"

"Doubtful that you might relieve me of my emblem, or that its lack would have any beneficial impact on my senses. My faculties, such as they are, are mine."

Taylor raised the pistol at his right, leveling it at Rahab's heart.

"I would have your 'emblem', monsieur, and I would have it now."

"Sir," Rahab answered calmly, "you may fire upon me, or either of my companions, at will, but you will not have anything from us."

"Noble sir," broke in the driver, panicked, "for the love of the holy mother give him what he wants!" The driver, though of stout enough heart, would not have any passenger of his shot down while in his charge. It might well have an adverse effect on his custom.

"I will not!" Rahab said firmly, only now allowing his voice to raise. "These emblems, though of little relative value, mark us as members of that holy fraternity, Les Enfants du Matin, and will not be handled by lesser hands!"

With that, Rahab took two long steps forward, and reached out his hand, wrapping it around the barrel of the pistol. Taylor, startled, flinched, and his twitching finger closed over the trigger. The pistol erupted with a flash and a sharp crack, and the shot was projected with unutterable force directly into the body of Rahab.

Taylor stared wide-eyed behind his mask, his mouth hanging open. In all this days and years working for the common good on the high roads, never before had he seen such a sight.

Standing before him, his hand still wrapped around the barrel of Taylor's pistol, was Rahab. The fabric of his gray jacket was torn and singed, marking the impact of the shot, but through the rent cloth Taylor could see no blood, no wound. Seeing his gaze, Rahab glanced down at his front, and then back up to Taylor's face, his expression grim.

"Had I the time," Rahab said, "I would take the cost of this suit from your own hide. As it is, that is a pleasure I must save for another day."

Rahab let his hand fall and, dusting off his front, turned to the driver.

"Driver, be so kind as to close your mouth, and then transfer to this man any of the baggage you think worth the trouble to this gentleman. Then to the seat with you, and let us be on our way."

With that Rahab motioned to his companions, and they climbed back into the carriage. Rahab made to follow them, and then turned back to the highwayman.

"In a rougher age I would have left you broken for this imposition, monsieur," said Rahab, "but I find that I have softened with the years. As it stands, I will leave you with this nugget of wisdom. You might do quite well terrorizing the small-minded and -hearted mayflies that buzz along your roads, cozened as they are by short, easy lives. But every man with even a small measure of vision must some day recognize that there are forces which walk the earth, older and stronger than his own. And before these, even the bravest of midges must inevitably fall."

With that, Rahab turned and climbed into the cab, closing the door behind him.

The driver, dazed, dumbly went about the business of handing the valuable cargo over to the highwayman and, without another word, climbed to the box and whipped the horses into motion. He drove on into the town, and the next morning on to Paris, were he discharged his passengers. Though he kept to the road until his death some fifteen years later at the hand of a drunken bravo, he never mentioned the events of that late afternoon, outside the town of Amiens.

As for Reginald Taylor's part, he soon returned to his native England, and shortly after emigrated to the New World, where he played some small part in the colonists' revolt. In later life he took to him a young planter's daughter as his wife, and settled in the wilds of Tennessee. By the time of his death at the age of seventy-two, long retired from the life of a highwayman, he had seldom mentioned his encounter with Monsieur Rahab. Often though, on late nights, watching mayflies swooping and darting around candle flames, singeing their wings and falling down to earth, he would reminisce to his children and grandchildren about the strange thin man and Les Enfants du Matin, and wonder after beings old and strong yet walking the Earth.

The FOURTH DAY

I was awoken early in the morning by the sound of the phone ringing. I'd been sleeping pretty restlessly, dreaming unsettling dreams about gangsters and cowboys and bulletproof Frenchmen, and so managed to skip the unfrozen caveman routine. Still, it took my vocal cords a few beats to catch up with my brain.

"Yeah," I croaked into the receiver.

"Spencer, did I wake you?"

"No, no," I lied, reflexively. "I'm up, I'm up." I dug the heel of my palm into my lazy eye, and then thought to wonder, "Who is this?"

"It's Amador, man," came the reply. "You said to call you when I found something."

"Lover?" I asked, blinking hard. "What? Found what?"

"Your boy Marconi," Amador answered. "I found him."

"What?" I said, immediately awake. "Where's he staying?"

"You should be able to catch up to him no problem. He's currently staying at the presidential suite at the Las Vegas County Morgue."

I dropped back onto the bed, my head slamming into the pillow.

"Shit."

Amador told me all about it: how Marconi had been found a couple of days before in a ditch just outside of Las Vegas filled with more holes than a wiffle ball. The local authorities had no suspect, no leads. It didn't matter much anyway. It didn't seem like the local cops were too sorry to see him go. The case was as good as closed.

I thanked Amador for the tip and asked him to keep me posted if anything new came up. He said he'd try, but managed to wheedle a pair of Rockets tickets out of me before he was through. I told him I'd do what I could.

Checking the clock, I could see it had only been a couple of hours since I'd come home. There not really being anything I could do, I decided to get a few more hours sleep before planning out my next step. It was a good idea. Sleeping usually is. It was too bad that I couldn't follow through on it.

I just laid there, staring up at my cracked ceiling, trying to figure out what I'd got myself into. One anonymous phone call and all of a sudden corpses are dropping left and right, and I still don't have a clue what's going on. All sorts of nonsense about mythological beings and ancient manuscripts, and all the while the lunacy my grandfather carried around with him all those years. It was getting to the point where I was having trouble keeping it all straight, trying to remember if the gangsters had anything to do with Odin, or whether that cowboy had stolen the book from Pierce.

Come to think of it, I pondered, there was a book in the cowboy story, wasn't there? And a guy named Pierce, too. I shook of the feeling of vertigo creeping over me. It was like the universe was conspiring to drive me crazy. I counted off the corpses: Stiles, Marconi... who was next? It occurred to me that I could just as well add my grandfather to that list when the phone rang again.

"Hello," I said, much quicker on the draw now that I was fully awake. "Amador?"

"You call me that again and I'll hang up," came the reply.

"Tan?" I asked. "What the hell are you doing up? It's got to be..."

"It's six in the morning here, slack ass," the old man growled. "It's when us grown-ups tend to get up."

I rolled over on my side and shut my eyes.

"What's up, you old crank?"

"I got a message late last night about our mutual friend." He answered.

"Who? Amador?"

"Say that name again and I swear to Christ I'm gonna hang up. Nah, your boy with the overdue book."

I shot upright, my eyes wide.

"Marconi?" I shouted into the phone. "Amador said he was dead."

"That's it," Tan hissed, and I heard the line go dead.

I waited all of two minutes, waiting for the phone to ring, and then punched in for call return. The line rang three times, and then I heard it click.

"I told you I'd do it," the old man said. "You didn't believe me, but I told you I would."

"Okay, okay. 'Someone' told me he was dead."

"Who?" he asked.

"Stop fucking with me, you senile shit; it's too goddamn early. Marconi, that's who."

"Oh, yeah," he sang through the line. "He's dead, you know."

I sighed deeply.

"What do you want, Tan?"

"If you're gonna speak to me like that I won't tell you." I stayed silent, and so did he. I knew this game. I knew how to win. "Alright, alright, I'll tell you. I made a few calls yesterday, people who knew Marconi, old gambling pals of mine, businessmen." He didn't specify what kind of "business," and I didn't press him on it.

"Anyway, I got this call late last night from this guy I knew from stir. He's a big dumb shit, good for nothing but hired muscle, but he tends to be around when important things are said and he keeps his ears open."

"Okay." I prompted. "Go on."

"Well, by some coincidence, right after Marconi turned up serrated in Vegas, there was an announcement about this charity auction gonna be held in Arizona."

"What kind of charity?" I asked.

"The best kind," he answered. "The 'Don't Ask Any Questions And You Won't Get The Wrong Answers' charity. See, the way it works is, say you're into a shark for a certain about of dough, right? And you can't pay up. So, like the walking clichés they are, they break your legs. Everybody knows this bit. But say after that you still don't pay. Sooner or later, your loan officer is gonna get impatient, and you end up in a ditch. Now, that makes the loan officer feel a whole lot better about everything, naturally, but it doesn't do a whole lot towards paying off your tab.

"So, they tend to take whatever you've got as kind of reverse collateral on the debt. If they like it, they keep it. If not, they sell it off. After this had gone on for long enough, somebody got the bright idea to organize things. You know, kill off a bit of bad debt, stack up the loot, and then invite your friends over to take it off your hands. Happens a few times a year these days. You can get some good shit, too. Better than a cop impound auction."

"What's all this got to do with Marconi?" I asked. "Did they take some of his stuff?"

"You bet they did. And they're auctioning it off with a bunch of other shit. Tomorrow night, as a matter of fact."

"Tomorrow, huh?"

"Yep, and you'll never guess what's on the docket."

"Not..." I began.

"You bet," Tan said. "A certain big book."

I stared up at the cracked ceiling and blew out a long sigh.

"Shit."

Five minutes later I was out of bed and wide awake, making plans to head to Arizona.

It seems that Tan's "friends" had figured that Marconi must have owed him something. Or at least, that Tan thought he did. Why else would he be asking after a worthless layabout like that? So in the interests of maintaining parity, they offered him a prized chair at the auction. Tan had no interest in sitting in it. I did.

The expense account provided to me by the publisher of Logion was coming in handy, no doubt about it, but I admit I was growing a bit anxious about the day the bills came due. With any luck, though, I'd have a story by then, and all would be forgiven. If not, I might find myself taking advantage of all those free drinks at Moon & Son a little more often.

Deciding there was no point in trying for any more sleep, I made a couple of calls to airlines and booked a flight to Vegas for early that afternoon. The auction was to be held a couple of hours outside of the City of Sin, south in Arizona, just after dark of the following day. If I got into Vegas early, I could poke around and ask questions about Marconi, get a good nights rest, and still have a chance to rent a car and get to the place with time to spare. I was getting in on the strength of Tan's good word, so I wasn't worried on that account. I only hoped I wouldn't do anything that would put the old man in Dutch with his old "friends."

At about nine o'clock, when I was fully ambulatory and trying to crib together something resembling breakfast from the odds and ends in the kitchen, there was a knock at the door. I decided it was to be expected. It was shaping up to be a day of surprise phone calls, unannounced visits, and unexpected travel plans. I dropped a dollop of honey onto bread so stale I didn't even need to toast it and made for the door.

There on the outside, his enormous girth almost entirely blocking the strained morning light, was Royce.

"Morning, Spencer," he boomed. "Am I in time for breakfast?"

My head rang with his every word, and without complaint I limply handed him the honeyed bread. He took it from me gratefully in one huge hand, and with the other held forth a small package.

"UPS came early," he announced, dropping the package in my hands. He smiled broadly and folded in the bread.

"Um...thanks," I managed, and then turned back inside. Absently waving Royce to follow, I padded on bare feet across the dusty wooden floors to the dining room and dropped down into a chair. Tearing the wrapping from the package in a long strip, I came up with a VHS cassette tape. "Oh yeah," I said, finally remembering what I was supposed to expect. With a groan and accompanying creaks, I pried myself off the chair and went looking for the VCR, left to gather dust in a closet after I'd bought the DVD player. Once I'd wired up the VCR and popped in the tape, it whirred unhappily and then sprang to life. Punching on the television, I fell back onto the chair.

Time codes scrawled across the screen, and then a header that announced the last Barbara Walters Interview Special, Tape 7832. Royce found a chair on the opposite side of the table and settled in, finishing off the bread. He fingered his cross and circle necklace while he chewed.

"You join some kind of tape club, Spencer?" he asked. "I thought everybody'd switched over to DVD."

"Nah," I answered, "just a bit of research."

"Oh."

That out of the way, we leaned back and watched the tape. It was the standard Barbara fare, nice shots of her and the interviewees walking slowly through English gardens, accompanied by faithful dogs, standing by water, skipping stones, all while her commentary rattled over the top like an aluminum roof in a hail storm. I recognized Pierce right away from the casual swagger of his walk and the insincere shit-eating grin that split his wrinkled face. Then the scene cut indoors to a quick tour of Pierce's Houston mansion while they talked. If you've seen one billionaire's private fortress, you've seen them all. Last came the actual interview, a two camera setup with Barbara and Pierce facing each other at an angle in matching Louis Quatorze, Pierce shifting uncomfortably back and forth in his chair. They were in his study.

Seeing the bookcases lining the walls, the rare prints, the sculptures, I felt for sure I'd seen that room before. It was to the first commercial break before I had it. It had that same crowded look as my grandfather's study, except you could tell that Pierce didn't *live* in his, and kept it mainly for show.

It was a few minutes after the commercial break that I noticed something over Pierce's shoulder and scrambled for the remote. I punched the rewind button and ran the tape back to the Pierce Mansion Tour.

"What?" Royce asked, leaning forward, still rubbing his necklace. "What did I miss?"

"I'm not sure yet," I answered. "Watch."

The tape had almost run back to skipping stones by the pond, so I hit play and let it resume normally. Again the cut to the interior of the Mansion, again the tour. Through the main hallway, the dining room, the den, and into the study. Once in the study, Pierce leads Barbara around the room, pointing out the masterpieces. An original Degas, a sword worn by Napoleon, an original edition of Gibbon's *Rise and Fall of the Roman Empire*. On and on. Then it happened. I hit the pause button.

"There!" I shouted, jabbing the remote at the screen. "See that?"

"See what?" Royce asked.

"Motherfucker has pointed out every knick-knack in the room that Barbara deigns to stop by, and look what he does here."

The two figures flickered on the screen, noise lines drifting like snow flurries all around them. Barbara stood to the left of the frame, her elbow at a glass case containing a large antique book propped up on a pedestal. Pierce stood to the right, his eyes darting briefly to the case. I hit the play button.

Barbara half opens her mouth, as though to speak, and begins moving her arm to point in the direction of the open book. Pierce's eyes widen, and his right hand shoots out and grabs Barbara above her elbow. He then points with his free hand to a portrait hanging above the mantle, and courteously drags her over to stand beneath it. The camera follows, and the book and the case disappear from view.

"That's the kazoo in the cracker jacks," I said, hitting the stop button. "That's the lucky prize."

Royce was thoroughly baffled, and looked like he was beginning to feel made fun of. I waved him off, telling him there was more honey in the kitchen. Without a word of complaint, he was out of the room and rummaging through the cabinets. I sat at the table, my chin resting in my hand, and watched the sequence through again, muted. It all seemed too easy to chart.

Pierce had this thing he didn't want anyone to see, or that someone didn't want him to show. He neglects to keep it out of sight when the camera people show, and panics when it catches the great Barbara's eye. He fakes her away from it, but knows it was in the shot. Then, through the interview, he keeps trying to position himself between the book and the camera, but by then it's too late. He knows he can't ask the crew not to shoot the book, can't ask them to edit it out, or they would immediately get suspicious. Two weeks later the show airs, the book in plain view, and someone, somewhere, notices. A few days later, it gets stolen.

I paused the tape a few dozen times and still couldn't get a better look at the book. But that someone, sitting somewhere, had gotten a good enough look. And then Marconi had gotten a call.

* * *

Royce had some more errands to run before heading into work, so he made his goodbyes, the last of the honey glistening on his chin. I turned off the television and stripped off my shirt, heading for the shower. At the last instant an unexpected panic washed over me, and I locked and double-bolted the front door before continuing to the bathroom.

I stood under the water for long minutes, just letting it wash over me. I had been running pretty much nonstop for the past few days on little food and even less rest, and the water felt as though it was pouring new life into me. I was waterlogged and pruned before I finally shut off the tap, but stepping out I felt revived, and a bit more ready to meet what the day would bring. Two phone calls and a bald monk with a videotape; whatever else came would have to be an anticlimax.

I briefly considered stopping in at the offices of Logion before leaving town, but thought better of it. I had very little to show for my time except vague notions and unanswered questions, and given the growing tab for my endeavors I thought it best to wait to make my big entrance. Shaking the wrinkles out of my suit, I dressed and then stomped into my boots. I dropped a fresh pack of cigarettes into a pocket and took the time to gas up my Zippo. Then I shoved a couple of clean shirts and a pair of sundries into a suitcase and stood in the middle of the living room, trying to remember what I was forgetting. My eyes fell on the cardboard box laying near the couch, half open, the contents just peeking out.

I hadn't expected to get any farther into my grandfather's stuff than that first magazine, but now my curiosity was beginning to mount. The never ending series of Taylors, the continuous mentions of one "Black Hand" or another… either it was all an elaborate hoax of the old man's, or else there was a long history of insanity here. In my own family? Or just some other crazy bastards who just happen to be named Taylor? Had my grandfather arranged to have the Black Hand Mysteries written in the forties just to add his name to this list of lunatics? Or was that what started him on the path in the first place, some unlikely and unlucky coincidence?

Whatever the answer, the question had worked its way into my overtaxed brain, and I realized I wouldn't be content until I had the answer. Fishing around in the kitchen drawers, I came up with a roll of packing tape. I sealed up the box, and then put it next to the door by the suitcase. I figured I would regret having to carry it around on the trip, but knew I couldn't help myself. The key to my grandfather's obsession with all that nonsense was in the box somewhere, and the sooner I found it the better.

The morning light was thin and feeble as I walked out the front door onto the porch, the suitcase under one arm, the cardboard box under the other. I locked the door awkwardly, the box balanced on my hip, and then stepped off onto the lawn. The grass was high and dry, the last colors of summer fading, and my boots disappeared from view with every step. I was reminded of my brother, and of the field near our grandfather's house, and I shivered like I always do.

After dumping the case and box into the trunk, I sat in the driver's seat, trying to figure out how to kill the next three hours. Royce was off at work, and even if he wasn't I think I'd had about enough of his good-natured company as I could stand for one week. Michelle was working on the translation, probably at that very moment, and wasn't much for conversation with a project before her. Amador was holed up in a dark basement somewhere in Houston, spinning his electronic webs through the ether, and my brother was off in parts unknown, doing whatever it was he does these days. Janet had left town months before, doing some kind of Korean walkabout, and everyone else either thought I owed them money or thought they owed me money, and either way it made things strained.

So I sat there in the car, in the dim light of an autumn Thursday morning, nowhere to go and nothing to do, with two mysteries circling like starving dogs in my thoughts. One old man's stolen property, another old man's senile obsessions. I lit a cigarette and started to drive.

I meandered for a while, then moseyed, and ended by just tooling around. The stop and go of the traffic, the electric mantra of red-green-yellow, the slight squeal of my brakes as I stepped on the pedal, all had a soothing effect. I concentrated on the simple task of driving and tried to close my mind off to unanswered question. When I finally pulled to a stop, I was in front of the airport. I still had two hours until boarding time.

Fuck it, I thought. I need a drink.

I was beginning to think I had a problem, then realized that the magazine was still picking up all my bills, so maybe it wasn't such a problem after all. I lugged the chains I forged in life into the airport and through security and, once in the bar glowing with tasteless neon and "local color", dropped them under the table at my feet. I ordered up a screwdriver, then another for good measure, and settled back to watch the television, the volume turned low, trying to pick out the whispered confessions of the people on the daytime talk shows.

By the time I got on the plane, all the questions were answered. The women who love too much and the men who wear their underwear had cleared it all up for me, and I hoped to enjoy the flight in peace.

On the plane I dreamt, and in the dream I was on a plane. I sat on a big, wide first class seat, the leather smooth under my hand. In the seat next to me sat a man dressed all in gray, with a silver-topped cane in his hands. On his lapel was a silver pin of a rising sun. The pin caught my eye, and I had the distracted notion that it was actually the setting sun. Then the man spoke, and I lost track.

"I wonder if I might borrow that?" the man spoke, pointing with the head of his cane towards my lap.

"What?" I said, my eyes never leaving his. They were cold, gray, like tiny cannonballs frozen in ice.

"Your magazine," he answered.

Then I broke from his gaze and looked at my lap. There, resting across my knees, was an enormous leather-bound book, locked with a heavy metal clasp. On the cover was a silver disk. As I looked at it the silver disk began to change, and I realized it was the necklace Royce wore. I wondered where I'd seen it before.

"Can I have that when you're through?" asked a woman's voice.

I looked up and sitting opposite us was a woman and another man, both dressed in the same shade of gray. Both had the sun pin on their clothes, though these two also wore nametags. "HELLO MY NAME IS SAMEDI" and "I'M SALOME".

"I… I'm not finished with it," I answered.

Then the flight attendant came up and took our drink orders. She leaned over the gray man sitting next to me and asked if I wanted a drink. Then I saw that she had a gun in her hand, pointed at my heart. I realized that she wasn't a flight attendant at all, but a robber, and wondered why I hadn't noticed the mask.

When I woke up, we were halfway over New Mexico. I felt fuzzy, wrapped in gauze, and the cardboard box in my lap was behaving entirely inappropriately. I managed to swallow twice and then blinked hard, trying to remember where I was. Involuntarily I glanced to my right, worried I would see the gray suit and the silver cane. Instead there was an unlikely looking man in a golf-shirt and sans-a-belt slacks, reading an in-flight magazine. I worked the box off my lap and onto the ground before I lost all respect for it, and then closed my eyes again. When the flight attendant came around to offer me a pillow, I checked twice to make sure she wasn't armed before shaking my head no.

It'd been a while since I had been in Vegas, and stepping off the plane I was reminded why. Each time I came back it was a little less the town I remembered, and a little more Disney. It was getting to the point where, aside from the neon and a couple of street names, it could have been a different city entirely. Kid friendly and family safe, but the kind of place where Dean Martin wouldn't have even stopped for gas.

Lugging my bag and the box through the airport concourse, maneuvering past the middle-aged housewives taking one last turn at the one-armed bandits before giving up and heading back to Kenosha, I found the rental car kiosks and arranged for transportation. I thought for a second that the girl behind the counter was interested, but then I joked about buying the insurance so I could run down children and old folks with impunity and that was over. She blanched, not getting the joke, and I decided to leave well enough alone.

Maybe it was too little sleep, or the weird dreams I'd been having the past couple of days, but I felt disconnected as I started up the car and turned out to the main strip. Like watching a pretty boring movie of my life, I was running on remote control.

I checked into a hotel on the other side of town, far away enough from the action to be cheaper and with less tourist traffic, but without question still Vegas. There were slot machines in the lobby, and the keys to my room came with a handful of complimentary chips. I dropped my stuff in my room, put a fresh shirt on under my suit coat, and then headed back downstairs. At the hotel's café, I had the waitress bring me the white pages and the special, and after wolfing down what passed in Nevada for chicken fried steak, ripped the page I needed from the phone book and tipped her all my chips. On my way out, the waitress started to kick about the mangled phone book, but saw her tip and decided to let it slide.

The doorman was happy to help out with directions, at least once I waved a couple of bucks at him, and so fifteen minutes later I was pulling into the parking lot of a rundown apartment building on the outskirts of town. Double checking the address, I locked up the car, and headed towards the rickety stairs to the second floor, trying to look as inconspicuous as possible. I probably shouldn't have bothered. In a neighborhood like that, being inconspicuous only makes you stand out all the more.

The lock on the door proved no problem, the work of a little over a minute. An antique 1.25" Mortise cylinder almost rusted through; I could have just shoved it open quicker, but professional pride demanded I do it the old-fashioned way. Tan would have been pleased. When I had finished, I pocketed the two slim picks and gently turned the knob. I wasn't prepared for what I found.

Either Marconi was a bigger slob than even Tan let on, or someone had really worked the place over. Particle board furniture was shattered into splinters and dust, and the ceiling fan overhead had been yanked out by the roots. The doors were ripped off the cabinets in the kitchenette, the drawers pulled out and tossed across the floor. In the small bedroom, things were even worse. A stained twin mattress had been gutted lengthwise, its ticking pulled out, the stuffing lying in a carnage of synthetic fibers all around. Someone had been looking for something, and they had been thorough. From the looks of the casual damage to the walls and ceiling, though, they hadn't found what they were looking for, and had taken out their frustration on everything else left standing.

I was poking around in the bedroom closet, trying to find anything still in one piece that might help me figure out who Marconi had been working for, when there came a knock at the door. It was followed by a gruff voice calling out, and then the sound of heavy footfalls in the living room. There are times when I regret my decision never to carry a gun. This was one of them.

I make it a rule never to go into a situation I don't know how to get out of, but overcome by the destruction of Marconi's apartment I'd allowed myself to get boxed in. There were no windows back in the bedroom, no convenient ceiling tiles to push out of the way and crawl through, no sideboard vents. I was stuck. Seeing no other option, I straightened up, dusted off my suit as best as possible, and walked into the main room.

The cartoon that stood there waiting for me screamed landlord. Sweat-stained undershirt, barefoot and Bermuda shorts, he was overweight, grizzled and balding. Smelling the stink of his cheap cigar, I wondered if guys like him were drawn into the property management field by genetics and cultural conditioning, or whether they got to looking like that only after taking the job.

"You a friend of Marconi's?" the sweat stain asked warily, eyeing me up and down.

I thought quickly for a clever story and, failing miserably, did the best I could. I was too tired for this.

"His cousin," I said in an East Coast accent. "Sal Marconi. In town for the funeral."

I stuck out my hand and he limply accepted, drawing his hand back as soon as was possible.

"Funeral, huh?" he said. "Didn't think enough people gave two shits about Marconi to pay for planting him."

"Well," I said serenely, every bit the grieving relation, "we may have had our differences, but Gian was still family, you know?"

"Sure, sure," he answered, apologetic. "No offense."

"None taken." I motioned at the destruction around us. "Did Gian always keep his place like this?"

"How the fuck should..." he began, then calmed himself and clamped down on the cigar. "Nah, he was a slob, but nothing like this. It was all tore up when the cops came by the other day to check things out, and they said it looked like there'd been a break in."

"You don't say."

"Yeah, but with his TV all busted up like that and nothing stolen, I figure it for a bunch of kids out for some fun. You know? Saw the place was empty, and decided to have a party." He paused, shifting his eyes. "I must have been away that night, 'cause I would have heard if something was going on."

"I'm sure you would have," I said, nodding. I was also sure that blanketed in the fog of vodka I smelled on his breath, he most likely was "away" most every night.

"Even so," he continued, "somebody's gotta pay for this mess. Marconi didn't keep any insurance, and the cops say that there's not enough left in his bank account even to cover his parking tickets, so I'm out a months rent right there, too."

"I'm sure that the family can work something out," I said, "cover any outstanding debts."

At that, he brightened up considerably, and probably would have shook my hand again if I'd let him.

"Alright, then," he said eagerly. "I figure with the clean up costs, and the rent, and the charges for repairs, minus his security deposit, it should come to..." He wrinkled up his forehead, trying to impress me with his mathematical prowess. I got ready for a big number. He didn't disappoint.

I promised him the family would cut him a check for the full amount as soon as the funeral services were done, and had him write down his mailing address on a sheet of shredded newspaper. I was all set to leave, figuring I'd overstayed my welcome and was only risking trouble, when he grabbed my arm and steered me out the door.

"Come to think of it," he said, suddenly my best friend, "I got a package here for Marconi the other day. After the cops were here. I was going to mention it but… well…" He stalled, waiting for me to finish up for him, to get him off the hook. I didn't.

"Anyway," he finally continued, squirming, "Marconi was always sending himself stuff when he was on the road, signature required, and those fucking delivery guys were pounding on my door all hours with shit for him. One week it was eight o'clock in the morning, on a Monday no less."

I shook my head in sympathy.

"Anyway, I always handed the shit over when he got back, and the bastard never once even thanked me." He looked at me guiltily, and added, "May he rest in peace."

"I'm sure he will," I answered.

The package turned out to be a Fed Ex mailer, stuffed full and mailed a week before. I thanked the sweat stain for his time, and promised to send him the check in a few days. He bobbed his head so much he looked like he belonged on a dashboard, and waved at me from the doorway as I made my way back to the car.

I waited until I was back at the hotel and safely in my room before I opened up the package, letting the contents spill out onto the bed. I was surprised to see a neat bundle of large denomination bills, a couple of matchbooks, and what looked to be pages torn from a ledger book.

I counted out the bills, coming to at least ten grand. It seemed that Marconi didn't like to travel with a lot of cash, though I was impressed by his faith in the good name of Federal Express. The matchbooks came from the seedier topless bars in the Houston area. The ledger page, scrawled in a shaky hand and smelling of spilt beer, was a list of numbers and names, added up with a tally at the bottom. If this was a record of Marconi's debt, it was no surprise he'd run into trouble. On the credit side, he had listed one number, a big one. It wasn't enough to cover all his expenses, but it made a good start. Out along side the big number, in block letters, was a name: LUCETECH.

I lit a cigarette with a match from one of the books, and stared long and hard at that name. I wasn't sure if I'd found a missing puzzle piece, or if things had just got a whole lot more complicated.

I managed to nap for a couple of hours that afternoon, waking in a cold sweat only once or twice, and by the time the sun set I was up again and ready to roam. I had nowhere to be for another twenty-four hours, so I had time on my hands, and thanks to the foresight of the dear departed Mr. Marconi, I now had money to burn.

Other people might have thought twice about spending a dead man's money, even a dead crook's. I might even have, at one time. But the way I looked at it, the money was doing Marconi no good as it was, and if I turned it in to the cops they'd have to impound it and wouldn't even get to enjoy it. I could have turned it over to the landlord, but I didn't expect for a minute that he'd have given the package to me if he'd thought there'd be cash involved. Any way I jumped, the money would just be causing someone trouble, so it was best I keep it with me, and see to it the cash found a good home.

I have little love for casinos, at least the latter day variety, but when in Rome… So I showered off the day's grime, dressed, and headed down to catch a cab to the strip. The doorman, unctuous, asked if I'd found my friend's address alright with his directions, and then hailed a taxi, his hand out bragging the whole time. I was feeling generous and Dean Martin, so I laid a hundred on him as I climbed into the cab. For one night, I was going to be an old time swinger, and leave worries about webs of intrigue and murder and lunatic relatives until the morning.

After the first couple of casinos, I was a star. The way I was dropping cash without blinking, and by my scruffy look, everyone eventually assumed I was Hollywood slumming, and hung at my elbow. I lost a month's salary at the craps table, won back half at blackjack, and drank whatever they put in front of me. It was Disneyland, with animatronics and out-of-work actors in goofy costumes, but if you squinted just right it was still Vegas.

I was at a roulette wheel in a casino whose name I'd missed, when someone put their hand on my shoulder and spun me around. I panicked, all swagger lost, remembering the trail of corpses that had led me this far. I was having trouble deciding on cowering in fear or coming up swinging when I looked into a face that was almost as familiar as my own.

"Amador?" I said.

"I've been looking all over for you," he answered, his face grim. "We've got to get you out of here."

I started to mouth a response, but was just too baffled – and maybe a little drunk – to even think straight. Amador got me to my feet, and taking my elbow led me away. The waitresses and pit bosses frowned at my back as we passed. The gravy train was leaving the station, and they'd have to make do with what I'd left behind.

When I finally sobered up, we were back in my hotel room, me lying sprawled on the bed and Amador trying to force a cup of coffee into my hands.

"Where did you come from?" I said, sipping the coffee and immediately regretting it. Wherever Amador had found the stuff, the people there must have been happy to get rid of it.

"You drink too much," Amador answered, loosening his tie and falling into a chair. "Always have."

"Tan's right," I said. "You *are* a prig."

Amador looked wounded for a moment, and then it passed.

"Maybe," he confessed, "but just think if it hadn't been me found you reeling at that table. Suppose it had been the guys who got Marconi. I could have slipped a knife in your ribs and been gone before anyone had noticed what happened."

"You were going to stab me?" I asked, still not up to full speed.

"No," he answered, "but I could begin to reconsider." With that, he finally broke a smile and was the Crooked Lover all over again.

He didn't look all that different than he had when we were kids. Still slim, with a dancer's figure and a bullfighter's build, with the right accent Amador could have gone far in Hollywood. As it was, he was probably the sharpest looking data processor the feds had on the payrolls.

"You lost the goatee," I observed.

"Nah, I still know where it is," he answered. "On the chins of half the guys working with computers these days. It's like a part of the uniform, and you know how I always felt about uniforms."

"Hey, you're the cop, not me."

"I'm not a cop," he shot back, sounding hurt, "it's just that when I decided to sell out, the FBI was the highest bidder."

"Lucky them."

I rubbed at my temples, and against my better judgment took another stab at the coffee. It was worse the second time round, but I was feeling more alert and starting to think straight.

"What the hell are you doing in Vegas?" I finally asked. "When we talked this morning, I thought you were still in Houston."

"I was," Amador replied, "but after we hung up I started to do more digging on this Marconi guy. He was mixed up in some bad business, Finch, more than your run of the mill job. Around noon, I was called to the office of the Regional Director. The big wheel, the head G-man, and he wanted to know what I was doing sniffing around the Marconi case."

"Marconi case?" I parroted. "He had a case?"

"So it seems. Turns out that the feds had been after him for a while, after he turned up in routine surveillance of some of the bureau's most popular people."

"Who? The mob?" I considered telling him about what I'd found on the ledger sheet, but decided to wait and hear what he had to say first.

"I don't think it's the mob, but they wouldn't tell me who it really was," Amador answered. "I'm not authorized for that information, insufficient security clearance they said. But they did tell me that these people were bad news, and from all indications it was them who had done Marconi in."

"'*Done Marconi in*'?" I mocked. "You've been watching too many movies."

"Maybe you haven't been watching enough," Amador said, bristling. "You've been spending too much time writing articles about movie stars and pop singers, and you've forgotten what these kinds of people are like. I tried to get you at home as soon as I left the Director's office, but you'd already left. I took some personal time off work and caught the next flight out. I've been hitting all the bars and casinos looking for you since I arrived."

"Why?"

"To warn you," he answered. "You've got to let this one go. You keep picking at it, something bad's going to happen. These kinds of people don't like to be picked."

"I'll take my chances," I said evenly, sitting up straight. "I always have." I was starting to get a little uncomfortable, and was glad I hadn't yet mentioned the money.

"Alright," Amador relented, spreading his hands wide, "it's your funeral. But remember this. If you get it in the neck this time, I won't be able to help you."

Amador got up from the chair, crossed the room, and opened the door. He paused in the doorway and, not looking back, repeated, "I won't be able to help you." Then he closed the door, and was gone.

I was jittery from the cheap coffee for the rest of the night, and I couldn't concentrate on the television. It was all true crime documentaries and mob movies, and I found I just wasn't in the mood. Fetching a bucket of ice from around the corner and coaxing a couple of cans of Pepsi from the machine, I set up at the table and stared at the walls. I was sobering up for the fourth time in as many days, and was beginning to think maybe Amador had been right about my drinking. I was usually only concerned with covering the tab, or getting some other sucker to pick up the check, but the sharp pain in my side told me that my kidneys were beginning to lobby for the minority position. Amador was gone, and I hadn't even told him what I'd learned.

After a while the wall started to get boring, and a quick scan of the television showed it just as bloody as ever, so I cut open my grandfather's box again, feeling like a junkie scrambling for a fix, and pulled out the next sheaf of papers from the stack. This one was typewritten, with scribbled notes in pencil in the margin, and seemed to be transcribed from a book. Filling a glass with ice and then pouring cola on top, I propped my feet up on the bed and started to read.

"An Evening at Rest"

(An excerpt from The Buccaneers of America: A true account of the most remarkable assaults committed of late years upon the coasts of the West Indies by the Buccaneers of Jamaica and Tortuga (both English and French), *by John Esquemeling, Dutch, 1705)*

Chapter 1

IN WHICH THE BLACK HAND RETURNS TO HIS HOME AT THE PALM, AND SHARES A DRINK WITH HIS DOUBLE

The Island of Mano, situated to the North and West of that famous island called Hispaniola, near the Continent thereof and in the latitude of twenty degrees and forty minutes, served as it had for some years prior as the secret retreat of the Black Hand and his crew. The Spaniards, who first set eyes on the island, named it La Isla del Mano, from the shape of its mass, which in some manner resembles an outstretched hand, or in the Spanish tongue *una mano*. The island is circumscribed by a number of inlets and coves, the protrusions and demi-peninsulas describing each having the look of fingers. The country is very mountainous, and full of rocks, and thus of the five principle points of access, only one is in any wise hospitable. This one is situated between the masses most closely resembling the thumb and forefinger of a man's hand, and as such the only welcome port and settlement on the island is to be found on the geologic analogue of that fleshy part of a human extremity.

At the outermost points of those two masses, called in a natural way the Thumb and the Finger, there are posted ever-vigilant guards, their gaze, and their two and twenty cannon and firearms, always trained at the sea beyond. The men, and in times of distress women, who occupy those porticoes are called by their mates Nails, in a hardly surprising happenstance.

Through this well-guarded entrance sailed the sturdy Rover, her crew well-ready to reach their Port of Call. At her helm stood the Buccaneer of note himself, the Black Hand, his steady grip steering the ship to harbor. The settlement thereto, in a manner which begins to betray the somewhat limited imagination of the inhabitants, was named the Palm. Though her more wistful denizens claimed the name derived from the cacao-nut trees which grew in profusion around the whole of the island, those with more sober judgment were quick to argue that there was no other reason than the main (or *La Main*, which they spoke in emphatic Gallic tones, so as to make clear their clever wits).

The Rover pulled to at the dock, and while tossing fastening lines back and forth, the crew on the deck of her and their mates already on shore hallooed their greetings, and hurled their jibes, back and forth. They seemed, for all the world, a collection of long-separated siblings, brought together at last for holiday feast. When the lines were made secure, and the ship finally brought to rest, the crew disembarked, making for their homes or taverns with a raucous glee, arm-in-arm with their bosom friends from the shore.

The Black Hand himself, the master and architect of the entire enterprise, was the last to leave the ship, and leapt with an easy grace from her side to the sturdy dock. Then, without a word to any of those in attendance, he made his way through the narrow streets to the high place whereupon sat his home.

A short time later, the Nails watched with careful eyes as another ship, another Rover, a mate to the first, also made its way through the Thumb and Finger to settle in at the harbor. If they thought it a matter of note to see the repeat of the previous circumstances, instant by instant, they made no sign of it. Again the ship was made fast at the dock, again the crew was greeted warmly by their comrades already ashore, and again disembarked with a merry glee. Again the Black Hand was the last to leave the ship, and again made his way through the narrow street, a mute shadow upon the darkened streets.

This second Black Hand, mirror image to the first, reached the high house in just the same fashion as the first, opening the sturdy door and stepping inside into the gloom. A dim figure, he made his way through the darkened house, up a narrow flight of stairs, to a closed door on the top landing. This door he heaved open, and slipped into the bright room beyond.

Inside was an air of warm conviviality, with heavy woven rugs upon the floor, a cheerful fire burning in a corner brassier, and a solemn-looking hound asleep against a far wall. In the middle of the room was set a wide table, with high-backed, wide-armed chairs on either side. On the center of the table was set a carafe, and a pair of glasses, both full of a wine the color of dark velvet. At one of the chairs sat a figure dressed all in black, his booted feet propped on the edge of the table, a merry grin splitting his face.

Welcome home, sibling, he offered. *Do join me in a drink.*

At that, the figure before him removed the hat from its head, and down came tumbling downy tresses of a golden hue. Off came the cloth mask covering the face from eyes to chin, and there stood before him a woman of striking beauty, a latter-day Aphrodite.

I see no reason why I should not, brother, she spoke in honey tones. *After all, I would say that I have earned it.*

Chapter 2

IN WHICH A TOAST IS DRUNK,
AND MUCH IS MADE CLEAR

The striking woman, now unmasked, seated herself across from the man she called brother, and watched as he poured her glass full from the carafe. Then, with graceful movements, he propelled the glass into her grasp, and then lifted up his own.

A toast, he announced.

To what, pray, dear Richard? the woman asked.

Why, dear Jane, he answered, *to that which is always toasted on the occasions of our reunion.* He moved the glass's rim to a fraction from his lip. *To our dear mother.*

To that fair lady, the sister seconded, bringing *her own glass to her full red lips. May her health long prevail.*

Both drew long draughts of the heavy wine, and then pulled the glasses from their lips.

Now, added the sister, *it is to me to offer the counter-toast.*

As is expected, the brother answered.

To the memory of our departed father, she toasted, raising her glass in salute to the portrait of the man that hung above the door-frame.

To that remembrance, the brother amended. *Ever may it be green.*

Again each drew a long draught, draining the glasses to the dregs. Then with a flourish each slammed the glass down onto the pitted table top, and regarded the other with a broad smile.

It has been too long, sister, the man observed. *Too long by half.*

Almost a full year, by my reckoning, the woman agreed, *since last we two met. Would that things were other than they are, and that we two could ship together. But that is not in our stars, brother, nor in the commission laid upon us by our departed father.*

What no one beyond the walls of that room knew, not even their own hand-picked crews, was that the two they knew individually as the Black Hand, and whom each served with a loyalty even unto death, were not the first to carry that name, and that each had in fact received the name and their solemn duties as their only inheritance from their lost father. Most inhabitants of the township of Palm, both those who stayed ashore and those who had berths on either of the twin Rovers, knew that more than one body carried as their own the aspect of the Black Hand.

What none guessed, however, was that one was a woman, and the other her brother.

The siblings' father, the late Arthur Taylor, originally of Liverpool, had taken on the name and guise of the Buccaneer Black Hand while they two were both in swaddling clothes, and had sallied forth for long years, carrying the torch of justice out onto the high seas. His targets, both kings' navies and freebooters alike, were relieved of their ill-gotten gain at a cutlass's point, and their cargoes of slaves or chained oarsmen were given their liberty, to live their lives as their maker had intended, free and without hindrance. When, in the fullness of time, Arthur Taylor was upon his deathbed, he lay on his two children, now most grown, the onus of taking up the torch of justice in their own hands, and carrying on the struggle he had begun. Each, he instructed, was to carry on as though he were the father embodied, and, from behind the mask which villains sailing the world's wide seas feared, fight against tyranny so long as their limbs had the strength. To the world at large the Black Hand would seem in fact a ghost, appearing one instant in the Carribe, the next at the Cliffs of Dover; and none would suspect that each was not the original, so complete would be the deception.

The task laid upon them was a demanding one, and there was little time for the comforts of home and hearth, but on the rare occasions that each was moored at the dock of Mano, they would share what little familial happiness was afforded them.

But enough of this, said the sister, reaching for the carafe to refill both their glasses. *We profit nothing recounting that which cannot be changed. I'm sure your adventures have numbered many in the long months since last we sat here at home, you and I, and I would hear of your exploits.*

The brother took the proffered glass, and studied the gently swirling liquid in the flickering fire's light. His brow furrowed, and he sat in contemplation for a long moment.

Very well, sister, he finally spoke, *though I fear there's little of adventure in the tale, I shall tell you what chanced this summer passed, when my Rover put to shore on an unknown island some thousand leagues from here.*

Chapter 3

In which Richard relates his Adventures of Late

We had been sailing some weeks without sight of land, the brother continued, *and our stores of food and water in desperate need of replenishing. There was some concern among the crew that our provisions might not hold out, and that we would be found adrift years hence, a ghost ship, haunted by the hungry souls of her crew. There was talk of an albatross sighted and killed the spring before, and of diverse other offenses given the gods of the sea over the course of our journey. But the bos'n, a pious fellow, would have no such blaspheming, and set to reading his holy book aloud daily, while perched atop the main deck, pronouncing that the Lord God had commanded us to have no other gods before Him. The bulk of the crew, though, as superstitious as their fellows the world 'round, were often heard to comment that they had no quarrel with gods before the Lord Almighty, but had qualms about offending any and all which might be coming after him.*

We sailed on thus for days, on glass-calm waters, the winds dying in our sails. The first mate was called upon to dispense rough justice in several cases of petty theft,; crewmen looting the rations of their mates for a crumb or swallow of water. Those which defied the law were given the lash, as their due, but this served as insufficient deterrent to the others, and still the unrest grew.

Finally, on a still, hot day, the sun hanging high in the sky, the fo'c'sle called out land ho, and we pulled the rigging to, pushing what little wind there was to drive us toward the sighted land. It was hours before we dropped anchor; the crew crowded in the bow like rats, anxious for solid ground.

The island was little more than a sand bar, a few score miles around, but it bore on its back trees and thick grasses, and birds could be heard over the sea air. There was water, then, and enough for us all.

Leaving the bos'n at the helm, the first mate and I, along with some dozen of our crew, put out in dinghies and made for the shore. The men rowed with vigor, eager to run aground and drink their fill of whatever water they might find.

Coming ashore, we beached the boats and made our way inland, cutting our way through the thick growth, reaching at last an inland lake. The first mate was the first to test the water, and through his broken teeth pronounced the water the finest he'd ever tasted. I let the men drink their full, and then instructed them to bring the casks from the dingy and to fill them to capacity. The mate and I then led a small party further inland to forage for food.

We had gone perhaps a dozen strides when one of the crewmen remarked on broken branches amongst the undergrowth. We at first thought this the work of a large boar, perhaps, or some other rough beast, but further on the mate caught sight of foot-prints which, though small in dimension, bore the unmistakable sign of human passage.

We proceeded more warily then, making our way inland with watchful eyes, every hand at the pommel of a cutlass. We heard indistinct sounds as we progressed, calls from the trees, but they were too faint and too far away to be identified. We reasoned that the inhabitants of the island had become aware of our presence, and were warning their kin of our approach.

After a slow hour's march through the trees, we came at last to a wide clearing, where a waterfall crashed gently down the side of a high rock. Gathered in the clearing, around the base of the rock, stood four and twenty children, of all sizes and ages, both male and female. They were clad in clean clothes, though some a bit ragged and torn, and from their complexions and attires seemed to represent each of the sea-faring races of the globe. The children were calm, almost serene, and looked upon our party with great interest.

The oldest of the children, a girl dressed in the manner of a young English lady, stepped forward from the mass and addressed our group.

Gentles, she said, have you come to take us home?

She spoke in the King's own English, did this strip of a girl, and looked upon us with eyes as open and honest as any I might ever have seen.

I answered her as best I could, saying that we had not come with those intentions, but that if she and her company needed transport to their homes my ship was at their disposal.

The girl nodded, as if she had expected no other answer, and then turned to look towards her fellows. Without a word between them, the children drew themselves into a single line, and then the English girl indicated that they were ready to follow.

Struck dumb, I signaled my men to turn and retreat for the shore, and then with the mate beside me stood and watched as my crew led the strange band of children out of the clearing and into the trees. As they passed, a number of the children turned to us and offered their thanks, and I was amazed to hear pass their lips every language with which I have become accustomed, and some many more besides. Only a fraction of those children spoke a word of English, it transpired, and on the main spoke no other language than their own. After careful count, the crew and I counted some dozen different languages, some good portion of which not one of my men could identify.

After replenishing our provisions, we raised anchor and set sail, this time for the coast of Spain. There is a nunnery there with which I have had some dealings, having aided them on one or two occasions when members of that order took to sea and met with misfortune. I knew they would take the children in and, should they be unable to find their own homes, at least find suitable accommodations for them.

In the course of our weeks in travel to the continent, I had occasion to question the older girl, and others with whom I could communicate, about their circumstance. From what I was able to gather, each of the children had, at different times, been the victim of some catastrophe at sea, either through shipwreck, or fire, or intercession of brigands. Somehow, miraculously, each of the children survived, and found their way onto the island upon which we had discovered them. From their accounts, the lost ships in question numbered at least a half-dozen, perhaps three times that many. Furthermore, in those infrequently travelled waters, it seems hardly likely that ships from so many ports of call would meet with calamity within swimming distance of a single speck of an island.

When I questioned the children about this, they could only say that they had been taken somewhere peaceful and safe, and then we had arrived to rescue them. There was the intimation that there was some agency at work here, as though someone had transported them to that island for safe keeping, or else to some other locale, and then to the island where we would find them. Where this other locale might be, in that empty and barren stretch of water, and whom the agents of their rescue might be, I could not say.

The bos'n, for his part, was sure it bore all the marks of the divine hand, and that angels themselves had rescued the children. Others of the crew spoke of Fiddler's Green, and other mythical places of seamen's repose. For myself, I have no such answer, no such certainty. As regards the lost children found ashore, I have only questions.

After reaching the waters of Spain, we sailed along the coast until we came to the nunnery. Then, putting to shore, we entrusted the children to the care of the sisters. Thereafter, our provisions stocked and our arms ready for action, we put again to sea, going north into the Channel, where we encountered an English ship heavy laden with goods, bound for Dover from the New World. She was at the end of a long journey, and we aided her in lightening her cargo. From there to Majorca, and then back to the high seas.

We must not have been far a'course, brother, the sister observed, *for in just that season I myself was steering my Rover through the Straits of Hercules, and into the wine-dark waters of the Middle Sea. My tale, too, involves members of a holy order, though in my case they were less charitable than the objects of charity themselves.*

Chapter 4

IN WHICH JANE RELATES HER ADVENTURES OF LATE

We had been sailing long weeks since last we had sighted another ship, the sister continued, *and my men grew hungry for some business to tend to. We came at last upon a galley ship, Spanish by her colours, lying heavy in the water, bound for the northern coast of Africa. There was a second ship close to, which had the look of a French vessel but flew no King's flag. The second ship was secured by grappling hooks to the first, and as we watched a boarding party swarmed from the second onto the decks of the first. They were, we had no doubt, freebooters, anxious for whatever booty they might take from the galley.*

Though we had no especial love for either the crew of the Spanish ship nor of the Freebooter, there is nonetheless something in the breast of man which stirs on seeing a crime in progress, the victim helpless, so we threw our lot in with the underdogs. Coming 'round the two ships, we sailed close to the Freebooter, and, grappling our own ship to her, made ready to send across boarders. The crew, ranged through the rigging, cutlass and pistols in hand, watched for my signal which, when the time was right, I issued.

Then, leaving only a skeletal crew aboard the Rover, we swarmed over the deck of the Freebooter, dispatching what little resistance we met, and then like garden frogs leaping from one stone to the next moved on to the Spanish galley. Using the freebooters' own rigging, we leapt to the deck of the galley, and with wild eyes met the scoundrels like a hurricane's gale. They, at first taken completely unawares, were slow to retaliate, but soon regrouped, and then tried to press their advantage, hacking their way through my crew, trying to drive us from the galley's deck. Their plan was an ill-considered one, however, for in trying to drive us from their prey they succeeded only in forcing a number of my crew back onto the Freebooter herself, where they were quite capable of repelling the scoundrels' attacks.

I myself, my Mate at my side, drove the attack onto the Main Deck, felling innumerous freebooters as we went, until at last the Pirate Captain and myself stood face to face, our gored blades in hand. He smiled a gap-toothed smile at me, and then offered some greeting or challenge in his mongrel tongue, which I could not fathom the meaning of, bowed his head, ever so slightly, and then came en garde. I lifted my cutlass before me, weaving its point in pirouettes in the air, and parried his every thrust, driving his own blade with a wrench away from its intended target. Long minutes we dueled thus, until at last he began to waver, and dropped his guard, and I made the killing thrust. He fell, his face a mask of surprise, and lay a blooded heap upon the deck.

The galley was taking on water now, the holes burst in its hull by the Freebooter's cannon below the waterline. Once the last of the Freebooter crew was dispatched, I urged my own men to go below, free what galley slaves they could, and tend to whatever booty might be salvaged from the ship. I myself made my way across the deck to the Captain's Cabin, my Mate still at my side.

The door to the Cabin had been burst open, and the Freebooters already inside, having only come back out into the open air when our Rovers' crew had come aboard. Inside, in the well-appointed cabin, I found a riot of corpses, littering the thick Persian rug. Each was lain in an aspect of distress, as though they had struggled against their death, and met a grisly demise for their trouble. One or two were women, high born from the looks of their clothing and the jewelry the scoundrels had yet to rip from their cut throats, and there were also three men dressed in the black robes of the followers of some Holy Order. They lay close by one another, each more gashed and mutilated than the last, and their cold faces bore expressions of such determination, the likes of which I have rarely seen. I could not place their Order, none carrying any of the distinguishing signs of the Benedictine or Dominican, though I did note that in the place of the expected Cruciform each wore a medallion showing a four-armed spiral, encircled with a band. These medallions, of silver, were hung on heavy cords about each's neck, and one of them had seemed to grasp the emblem at the moment of his death, so rigid still was his hold upon it.

The third of the mendicants, lying farthest from

the door, held clutched in his cold fingers a book, a thick tome bound in leather which, when we pulled it free of his grasp and inspected the contents, was comprised of pages of unimaginable age covered in dozens of different hands, in a dozen different tongues. Emblazoned on the cover was the same banded spiral, here engraved on a glittering silver shield. This Book, no doubt a text of holy writ, or else the history of their Order, I entrusted to the care of the Mate, and then turned to the business of inspecting the remainder of the Cabin.

When the surviving slaves had been transferred across the deck of the listing Freebooter, and were safely on the Rover, I gave the order to abandon ship, first the galley and then the Freebooter, and with the crew complete on the deck of the Rover, had them cut loose the grappling lines, and we were away. As we sailed on towards the north coast of Africa, there to discharge our passenger slaves, we watched as the two ships, locked in a deadly embrace, sank slowly beneath the calm waves, and disappear eventually entirely from sight.

The bounty of the ship, including the Holy Book, we carried in our hold, and have now been transferred to our island stores. What profit it will turn us, in days in years to come, who can say. As for myself, I have little time for reading and other civilized pursuits in this day, as I have other tasks to occupy my time.

Chapter 5

IN WHICH A FINAL TOAST IS DRUNK,
AND THE SIBLINGS BID THEIR FAREWELLS

A pretty trick, Sister Jane, spoke the brother, savoring the last of his glass, *turning on the brigands using their own tactics.*

They deserved no better, I suppose, answered the sister, *and we could do no worse. I wonder, though, at your tale. From whence do you suppose the children were brought to their island sanctuary? Another ship, perhaps, or from some surpassingly unknown land?*

To that, the brother replied, *I have scarcely an answer. It will remain, I would suppose, yet another of the questions which shall remain unanswered, like the floating island and the web-handed dwellers beneath the waves. The seas are deep, as you well know, and hold mysteries many and strange.*

The sister nodded her agreement, and then refilled their glasses, emptying the carafe of its dark wine.

A final toast, then, she recommended, *ere the night is done. To the mysteries of the ancient sea.* She then lifted her glass on high, its crystal catching the light from the brassier and sending it in rainbow shards against the far wall.

And to the pursuit of justice, seconded the brother, raising his glass in kind.

The two brought the glasses one final time to

their lips, and drained them each dry. Then the brother stood, and straightened himself.

To bed, then, I fear, dear sister.

Yes, she replied, standing herself. *We've much to do in the coming days, and scant time until we must take to the waves again.*

We must not wait so long a time again before re-uniting, the brother instructed. *I grow lonesome for familial company.*

As do I, my brother.

The two embraced, and then made for the hallway, where each retired to their personal chambers. Come the morning they attended to the business of readying their ships for another voyage, and within a fortnight each had again put to sea.

The Black Hand, in his diverse guise, spread its fingers of justice over the waves once more, and held injustice in its grip. Two years would pass until the siblings again would reunite, and then for the last time. For the present, though, each sailed with a lightened heart, knowing they were not alone in the world, even when faced with mysteries the depths of which no man might ever hope to fathom.

The FIFTH DAY

I managed to sleep almost to noon the next day, awoken only by the untimely entrance of the housekeeper, the sound of her jangling keys working its way unsettlingly into my dreams. She backed out, apologizing in broken English, but by then it was too late. Catching a glance at the bedside clock and seeing the time, I immediately panicked, realizing only after jumping to my feet that I had nowhere to be for a good seven hours.

I ordered up some room service, sticking to the old standards of pork products, breads and fruit. When it arrived, the fruit well past all concerns, the bread an insult to bakers everywhere, and the bacon and sausage menacingly discolored, I settled for a cup of coffee and flipped on the television. I'd learned years before that daytime TV was no place to spend any amount of time, and the disquieting children's programs and too-outrageous-to-be-true talk shows only served to deepen that conviction.

Giving up, I helped myself to another shower, made myself as presentable as possible and, packing up my gear, headed downstairs to check out.

On the way out the doorman solicitously offered to have my car brought around front, obviously hoping for one last easy tip. What cash was left was going to be needed that night if things played as expected, so I politely declined. He dropped the act and stopped just short of kicking me off the curb.

I had about a two-hour drive ahead of me, south across the border into Arizona, and had originally planned to spend the afternoon nosing around Marconi's haunts, seeing what I could find out. Amador's little performance the night before had gotten more of a reaction out of me than he expected, though, and I was a little gun-shy about making too many waves in the pool. It wasn't that I was particularly worried; I just didn't necessarily want to go looking for trouble. Best to let it find me at its own pace.

I decided I'd probably overstayed my welcome in Vegas, figuring that if I were to stick around any number of people might come out of the woodwork and stumble across me, not least of which would be Marconi's landlord itching for his fat check. That in mind, I gassed up the car, stocked up on cigarettes and snacks, and headed out of town to the south.

* * *

I'd begun to feel like my whole life was spent in cars, driving to and from hotels. I was having trouble remembering the last time I'd stayed in the same place three days running, or slept in my own bed for more than a couple of nights in a row. The life of the carefree reporter, so attractive just a few years before, was beginning to wear a little thin.

I had always laughed at people like my grandfather, tethered down and fenced in, like voluntary prisoners, rarely stirring even past their own front door. I knew that the old man had spent some time traveling when he was younger – the knickknacks and mementos that were crammed in the house to the rafters were proof enough of that – but from earliest memories he was just like another piece of furniture. I could remember seeing him out of the house only a handful of times, usually uncomfortable and suspicious. Now, a little more charitably, I could look back and see that in a sense the world had changed around him, and he seemed so ill at ease out in it because it was no longer the world he knew.

Normally, I wouldn't have given the old man so much credit, but I was in for a drive, and car trips tend to make me sentimental. Thinking about the old man, and the papers and books he'd obviously collected for years, I started to think of him in terms of the stories he'd kept. Like the Richmond Taylor of the pulp novel, all sophistication and class, perfectly in his element among the elite and the dregs of society alike. Remembering the odd friends who turned up from time to time, ancient men who arrived unannounced to share a quiet drink with my grandfather and then disappeared again, that seemed to make sense. I'd never really thought about it, but few of those guys I'd have picked out of a lineup as my grandfather's "type." Some were money, sure, like O'Connor and his ilk, but others seemed like they'd be more at home splitting a bottle with Tan than sitting up in Richmond Taylor's study sipping a glass of port. But still they came, seeming more to respect the old man more than like him, and sometimes with little gifts or a pat on the head for my brother and me. We hated them, of course, though we accepted their gifts without question.

One time, when the old man was feeling uncharacteristically familial, he had my brother and me sit on the floor snacking on cookies Maria had baked while he sat talking with another old guy. His name was Martin, or Martinson, or something like that, and he was a big, beefy bruiser of a guy. Bald headed, red as a beet, he had hands like hams and laughed loud and long whenever the chance permitted. He brought us little plastic police badges and cap-guns, and I liked him immediately.

The two of them were talking about old guy stuff, my brother and I not really paying attention, when the bald bruiser started in on the time my grandfather had spent out west. Suddenly my grandfather jumped out of his chair, told his friend to be quiet, and ordered my brother and me out of the room. The friend looked embarrassed, like he said something he knew he shouldn't have, and kept his head down while we kids shuffled out of the room, pocketing a couple more cookies as we went.

In retrospect, it's hard to imagine what my grandfather didn't want us to hear. It wasn't as if he cared about us hearing people talking about sex, or crime, or drugs. To be honest, he seemed hardly to care what we heard at all, so long as we kept ourselves clean and out of trouble. Later, he'd insist on intense study and physical exercise, which helped me make my eventual decision to leave, but when we were younger we were unwanted pets, to be tolerated underfoot on occasion, but best kept out of sight and out of mind.

I often wondered just what the old man hoped to accomplish with his work schedules and exercise regimen. After a few years of that, the toughest training Tan could think to put me through seemed like elementary school recess. But though I despised my grandfather for years for putting us through it, I never once really understood the point.

After studiously ignoring us from the age of five on, when we turned twelve suddenly we were the focus of every bit of the old man's attention. The day before we were to start the seventh grade, after

Maria had taken us shopping and helped pick out new school clothes and tried unsuccessfully to get us into coordinated outfits, my grandfather called us both down to the study and had us stand in front of his desk while he paced back and forth behind it.

He was quiet for a long while, aimlessly wandering along the wall and running his wrinkled hands over the stacked papers and books, brushing the display cases and framed prints. We were getting restless when, finally, he spoke.

He told us that we'd been wasting our time all the years we'd been with him, not once taking advantage of his obvious wisdom and years of experience. He had let it go on long enough, and had decided it was time for a change.

My brother and I risked a glance at one another, and I could tell he was thinking the same as me: the old man had finally lost it. Patrick, always braver in these situations than I, was about to speak when our grandfather came around the desk and put a heavy hand on my left shoulder, another on Patrick's right.

He kept talking, shaking us as he did, telling us about the dangers the world presented day in and day out. He said it was getting worse, that horrors unimaginable when he was our age had simply become routine, and that terrors undreamt of in those days were now being unleashed on the world.

For these reasons, he said, and for others he hoped one day to reveal, we had to improve ourselves, to be better equipped for the challenges of a changing world.

At this point I was starting to worry. This was sounding like something that might threaten to cut into my free time, already booked solid with MTV and superhero comics, and I could tell Patrick felt the same way. We had little choice, though, terrified of the old man as we were, and so we waited patiently while he spelled out his grand scheme. From what we could tell, it involved very little sleep, lots of study and even more exercise.

Up an hour before school for calisthenics, a cold shower, and then a ten block run to school. Then our normal classes, where we were naturally expected to excel, a midday meal of fruits and carbohydrates, then the ten block run home, an hour of martial arts exercises, and two hours of intense study in addition to our regular schoolwork. A few hours sleep, and up the next morning to do the whole thing again. Weekends varied only in that the ten-block run was a round trip, with a brief pause at the school playground for a drink of water, and the extra hours for study and exercise. Every day, seven days a week, every week of the year.

I managed to make it almost two years of that before finally throwing in the towel, packing a bag, and running away to New Orleans. But by that time it was too late. Though I could take on any grown man barehanded, and was better educated than most of my teachers, I carried away with me only two things: I hated my grandfather, and I never wanted to get up before dawn again.

I pulled into the town of Sizemore with time to spare and enough gas to get me the rest of the way, so I stopped at a fast food joint to fill up before continuing on. Sizemore was little more than an off-ramp and a blinking red light, with the requisite truck stops and fast food eateries. Identical to every other blip on the map, it didn't look like the town had been there more than ten years which, from what Tan had told me, sounded about right.

The auction, Tan had said, was to be held at one of the more secure locations in the American Southwest, which he figured would have proved a test to break into even in his best days. Built a decade before, an oasis in the middle of the Arizona desert, it had originally been intended as a health spa, to put it charitably, or a fat farm when you got right down to it. It did pretty well the first few years, made the investors real happy, and then the bottom fell out when their resident nutritionist was discredited by every medical journal in the country. Even the alternative types, having no problems with sticking yourself full of needles and setting them on fire, thought this guy was just a bit too far out. It could be said that the world simply wasn't ready for a diet composed entirely of reconstituted human waste, or the "Second Harvest" as the brochures discretely put it, but then again maybe it was just a horribly wrong idea.

In any case, when it was all said and done Second Harvest Enterprises was left with vast tracts of developed land in the ass end of nowhere, with the little gas-stop town of Sizemore the only thing to have profited from the whole farrago – understandably, as it was the only place within one hundred miles to offer non-feces-based foodstuffs to the starved and starving guests of the spa. Efforts to unload the property on the public market failed miserably, the entire affair having left in the mouths of investors a bad taste.

To the rescue of Second Harvest Enterprises came a consortium of business men and private citizens, who stated only that they wished to use the property for "company events." The sellers asked no questions, happily accepted an offer half the market value of the buildings alone, and quietly left with their money. The new owners didn't bother to change the name of the complex, though they did invest heavily in a state of the art security system and established a permanently staffed guard station on the premises. The good people of Sizemore, sorry to see the shit-eaters go, found any overtures to the new tenants quickly and decisively rebuffed, usually at gunpoint. They couldn't quite complain, however, when several times a year sharply dressed men and women poured off the highway from the private airstrip down the road, bought up everything in sight, and headed out to the former spa. The new guests were particularly fond of anything with local color, and the sale of curios, knickknacks, and "authentic Indian artifacts" skyrocketed. In the end, it was a pretty agreeable arrangement all around.

From where I sat in the window of the burger joint, thinking from the taste of the food that I'd accidentally thrown away the meal and was munching on the wrapping, I could see that the entrepreneurial spirit in Sizemore was in full swing. Indian blankets – manufactured no doubt in Taiwan – hung from racks set up in front of the gas station, and a collection of bleached cow skulls were artfully arranged under a tent in the parking lot of the truck stop next door. The burger joint, I noticed, had broken with franchise standards to offer the "Big Chief Whopper Meal" and "Buffalo-Sized Shakes." I'd settled for the white bread menu, cautiously, and was beginning to regret even that.

As I was finishing up the last bites of my flavored cardboard, a big black Cadillac sedan rolled to a stop in the parking lot and a collection of walking stereotypes climbed out. Watching them head inside, squinting in the bright sun even behind dark sunglasses, I wondered if they had any idea how much they advertised just what they were. They might just as well have been wearing nametags reading "HI, I'M WITH THE MOB." When one of the guys in the train caught my eye and I noticed the pistol-shaped bulge under his suit coat, I decided to keep all my clever observations and witticisms to myself.

Facing the window, my back to the entourage, I could hear them ordering in loud, east coast accents every themed item on the menu. The store manager, personally taking their orders and shouting them back to the guys staffing the grill, was obviously thrilled.

"So, you wanna eat it here, or head on up to the place?" I heard one of suits say to the others when confronted with the question of Here or To Go.

"I don't know," another answered. "Whatta you wanna do?"

"I wouldn't a asked ya if I knew, would I?"

"Oh, no we don't," came a third voice, a woman's this time, "we're not doing this again. Shit, it's like eating out with the Bowery Boys every time we stop. Jesus." I heard her sigh deeply and then add, "Let's just eat here, alright? We don't want to get there too early, anyhow. Makes us look desperate."

"Right," the first voice answered. "Just what I was thinking."

"I was going to say that," the second voice said eagerly. "Makes us look desperate."

"Jesus," the woman said. "How do you two get dressed in the morning?" I'd begun to wonder the same thing.

This being the middle of nowhere, and Arizona to boot, the tables all had little disposable ashtrays on them, those flimsy aluminum Frisbees that used to be stacked like communion wafers in every fast food joint worthy of the name. Never one to pass up a chance to smoke indoors, I pulled a cigarette from my pocket, lit it, and settled back to enjoy the show.

Their food ready to roll, the trio carried their trays to a table a few jumps away from mine and settled in to make do with their meals. I waited patiently, hoping to hear something useful from them before heading out. You never know what mobsters might let slip while enjoying a tasty burger, and I'm always primed for new material. Instead of conversation, though, I was greeted only with the sounds of chairs scuffing across the linoleum, and then contented chewing and gulping. I was glad I'd already finished.

"Hey," came a gruff voice at my elbow, and I almost started right out of my seat. I turned, trying for casual, and looked up into the wide face of one of the two men. "You done with that?" He jabbed a fat finger, heavy with gold, at the table in front of me.

"I-I…" I stammered, losing all cool. "I was just smoking…" I surprised myself; I'm usually good with gangsters.

"Nah, sparky," he said, his eyebrows knitted. "Your salt. You done with it?"

I looked from the bruiser to the salt shaker and back again. Then I nodded absently and felt the breeze as his arm shot past me to retrieve the shaker.

"Thanks," he called over his shoulder, heading back to his table. I heard him mutter something like "Spaz" under his breath, but couldn't be sure.

It wasn't until the woman spoke that I realized I was still staring at their group. The eating habits of the other guy were leaving me spellbound.

"You here for the auction?" the woman said a second time, more slowly this time and with emphasis. Suddenly I was the baffled foreigner, or the escaped mental patient.

"Yeah," I answered casually, treating her to a Louisiana accent. "Just got in a while back. In from N'Orleans, you know."

"New Orleans," she repeated, animated. "I love New Orleans."

"Really," I said, pushing my chair back and climbing to my feet, never breaking eye contact. "Which parts?" I had a real opportunity here, even after choking a second before, and didn't want to lose it.

"Oh," she said, apologetically, "I've never been. But I've heard a lot of nice things, and it always looks good in movies."

"James Bond," the monkey on the left said, dribbling sauce down his chin, "that was cool."

"Right, right," the other chimed in, "that crazy funeral thing."

The woman waved them quiet, and then turned back to me. From the obvious cost of her necklace and the way she ordered around the two mooks, I could see that she ranked in her organization. A chief's moll? Or daughter? Or, given the enlightened times, an exec herself?

"Who are you with, Mister...?" She left the sentence hanging in the air, waiting for me to finish for her.

"Cassidy," I answered. "David Cassidy. And I don't suppose I'm with much of anyone, aside from myself." I came up a few feet from her, and offered my hand. "I'm here representing certain interests who would prefer to remain... shall we say, nameless... at this juncture."

She took my hand and smiled.

"Charmed," she said, giving my hand a squeeze. "I'm–"

One of the mooks coughed, theatrically, and a bit of pickle went shooting from between his teeth to hit the other one in the neck. The other, ignoring the pickle for the moment, joined his companion in staring with narrowed eyes at the woman, giving her a none-too-subtle message.

"Relax," she told them both, "relax. He knows about the auction already, and he'll get the introductions soon enough." She turned to me. "These functions run best when there's a level of trust involved. Don't you agree, Mr. Cassidy?"

"I certainly do, ma'am," I answered.

"And besides," she answered, turning back to the pair, "if he should try anything, I know the two of you can handle him. Right? Otherwise, why did I even bring you along?"

The two exchanged a quick glance and then, shrugging, returned to their meals.

"Excuse them," the woman said to me, "but I don't pay them for their brains, if you get me."

"I get you," I said evenly.

She took my hand again, in both of hers this time, and smiled.

"I'm Angela Rosetti," she said, pumping my hand. "And that's Benny, and that's Nick." I nodded greetings all around, while the two guys studiously ignored me.

"And who're you with?" I said. "If you don't mind me asking, that is."

"Salvatore," she answered, like I knew who she meant. I did. "I normally just handle our interests on the west coast, SoCal mostly, but I'm the only one in the business with any kind of eye for art so I'm usually tapped to take the auctions."

I nodded. So she was an exec and not just window dressing. Though not the first time I'd met a mob boss in a fast food joint, this was still shaping up nicely. Besides, Louie the Neck had been nowhere near as nice to look at.

"Anything in particular you're after?" I asked. She sat back down, and motioned for me to pull up a chair.

"Officially, I'm supposed to be looking for Rockwell. It's a long shot, but the boss loves Americana, and you never know what these skells pick up in the way of payment or merchandise. Unofficially, I'm looking for late French expressionism. I'm building a new house in Anaheim, and I've got some wall space to fill." She took a sip of her soda, and then flashed her lashes at me. "And you?" she said. "What are you in the market for, Mr. Cassidy?"

The way she asked, the way she was looking at me, was making my knees quiver, and sent butterflies sumo-wrestling in my gut. I chanced a glance at the muscle, reminded myself why I was there, and plowed ahead.

"Nothing in particular," I answered casually, "though the interests I represent are always on the lookout for antique books." I paused, letting the last word hang in the air, looking for some reaction. None came. "Something of a bibliophile, I suppose you could say," I added, relaxing.

"Hmm," Angela hummed, giving nothing away.

"When we finish up here," she finally said, "we're heading on over. You want to follow us in?"

"Sure," I answered. "I've never been here before, and the directions I got from my principle were a little sketchy."

"Great," she said, clapping her hands. "Maybe then I'll have someone to talk to." She leaned in close, and I got two nostrils' full of her perfume.

"There's a certain old world charm to these things, but the conversation is usually for shit. I mean, I can only listen so many times to the story about how Rocky Stompanato took out that whole group of Triads single-handed, or to the one about what Mack Diamond did to that spic he caught in bed with his wife, before it starts to get old. You know what I mean?"

I nodded, trying to smile. I was getting in deep now. Movie stars and pop singers seemed a whole world away.

I followed the limo up the narrow road from Sizemore to the compound in my little rented Ford. Angela had offered to let me ride up with them, but I wanted my ride handy, so politely declined. For a second it looked like she might want to ride with me, but the two mooks stepped in front of that one and ushered her into the waiting limo. They eyed me as I walked back to my Escort, one of them thoughtfully patting the bulge under his arm.

The road dead-ended at the gate which still read "Second Harvest Ranch." There was an electrified gate on rollers in place across the entrance, made of reinforced chain-link and topped with razor-wire. From either side stretched a steel-banded fence some ten feet tall, crowned with electrified nettle and razor-wire, with a sentry tower visible a hundred or so yards off to the left and right. I could hear the sounds of guard dogs barking within, and a couple of uniformed thugs with assault rifles made a slow circuit into view as we pulled up, circling the other perimeter of the fence.

The limo driver pulled up to a TV monitor and two-way radio set on a pedestal a yard from the gate, and after a few seconds the gate rattled open to let him in. As soon as his rear wheels had passed inside, a row of barbed spikes popped back out of the pavement, pointing at me like accusatory fingers. I took off the parking brake, and rolled forward, the gate sliding back into place as I came.

The TV monitor flickered on, and a security guard's bored-looking face filled the screen.

"State your name," his voice crackled over the intercom.

"I'm here as proxy for Tan Perrin," I said, leaning out of the window. I felt like I should order fries next.

The voice on the other end of the intercom sighed, and the security guard looked directly into the camera.

"State your name," he repeated automatically.

"Um, Cassidy," I answered, "David Cassidy. But I don't think I'm on your list. Like I said, I'm here as proxy for..."

"I heard you the first time, sir," the guard answered in beleaguered tones. "But I still need your name for my records."

"Okay, you've got it." I didn't want to push too hard, but neither did I want to seem like a pushover. Either way would have sent up red flags, and I didn't know if Tan's name carried enough clout with these people to weather that.

"Yes, I've got it," the guard said, writing on something out of my line of sight. "And who are you representing?"

"Tan Perrin," I answered, allowing a bit of annoyance to creep into my voice. I was remembering every heavy I'd ever run into and trying to imagine how they might react. "You want I should call him up, see if we can get this worked out?"

The implied threat worked.

"No, no," the guard replied hastily, "that won't be necessary. Mr. Perrin's right here on our list. Looks like he called ahead about you coming, but doesn't look like he gave your name."

"He wasn't sure who'd be available," I answered, sounding pissed, "but if that's a problem for your little dog and pony show here, I'll turn right back around and let him know you don't want his business." I blew a cloud of smoke at the camera lens and added, "It's not like I don't have better things to do with my time, better places to spend my money."

The gate in front of me shuddered and then started to roll open. I saw the barbed spiked just beyond fold back into the ground, and turned back to the monitor.

"Come on in, sir." The guard smiled. "Sorry about the inconvenience."

"I bet you are," I blustered, and then drove on through the gate. I found a place to park amidst the ocean of limousines and luxury sedans, and turned the engine off. My hands were shaking, my palms sweating. I was out of practice in this business, but it was starting to come back to me.

Angela found me again just after I entered the main building. I was standing in line in what I thought was a registration desk or a coat check, but on getting to the head of the queue found I didn't have what they were after.

"Are you carrying, sir?" the primly professional woman on the other side of the desk asked.

"What?" I said.

"You should have been provided a list of controlled items with your invitation," the woman recited, a robot in a nice business suit. "We must look after the interests of *all* our guests, you must understand."

"No, I don't–" I began.

"She means, 'Are you packing?'" came a voice behind me. I turned to find Angela standing a few feet back, her arms folded across her chest, smiling at me. "Well," she went on, "are you, Mr. Cassidy?"

"Um, no," I answered. At that point, my whole inventory included only a pack of smokes, my lighter, my wallet containing the last few thousand left over from the night before, and the CDr I'd burned after talking to Tan about the auction. I unconsciously reached into my pocket, feeling the sharp corners of the jewel case; I hoped it would be enough.

Angela and the woman behind the desk must have thought I was doing a final check for any firearms, because when I came up empty handed they both smiled at one another and nodded. The woman behind the desk make a couple of quick marks in the big ledger in front of her and handed me a fan with the number "23" printed on it in big, block characters.

"The auction will be in the main conference center," she recited, pointing to the rear of the building automatically like a flight attendant miming exit signs, "and is scheduled to begin–"

"That's alright," Angela broke in, threading her arm through mine. "I'll show him the ropes."

As she led me away into the foyer, I straightened my tie and tried to shake the wrinkles out of my slacks with alternating steps.

"You look fine," Angela whispered in my ear, sensing my concern. "Most of these jokers couldn't get dressed in the morning without two other guys helping them."

"Thanks," I said, walking a little taller and casually scanning the room for familiar faces. It wouldn't do to be recognized, not yet at least. "If you don't mind me asking," I said to her, placing my hand over hers on my arm, "and I don't want you to take this the wrong way, but why are you even talking to me? You outclass me by four to one, and I'm sure there's lots of guys more important than me around."

"Sure," she answered, "almost all of them. But they can also be the most boring sons of bitches you'll ever have the misfortune of meeting. Like I told you, if I hear their fucking stories one more time I swear to god I'll shoot 'em all myself, and to hell with the business's image."

"You think I'm so much more interesting?" I asked.

"I don't know, but you haven't started to bore me yet." She tightened her grip on my arm and gave me a sharp look. "Besides, I can always shoot you later if it comes to it."

I tried for a good-natured response, but managed only nervous laughter. Either Angela didn't care either way, or couldn't tell the difference, because she joined right in and steered me over to the bar.

I ordered up a screwdriver and a scotch and soda for the lady, and then we stood talking quietly in the corner, sipping our drinks. Angela pointed out the capos and dons as they crowded into the room, commenting on this one's changes in fashion style since taking on a new mistress, and on that one's obvious color blindness. I started to relax, feeling like I was at someone else's prom, and joked with Angela about the heavy hitter with the lisp who spat on everyone in proximity as he talked, but who carried so much weight that no one dared say anything. Angela wondered if he knew he was doing it, but given the spattered eyeglasses and hastily covered drinks of those standing around him, I found it hard to believe he couldn't.

"These guys," Angela explained, "are here mostly just for the company. There's so few places these days where people in our line of work can get together and just relax, ever since big business moved in and took over Vegas. So every time there's one of these shows out here at the ranch, they come flocking in to catch up on old times. Those that aren't out to kill each other, that is, but even some of those."

I confessed to Angela that this was my first time at the ranch, playing it off like I always had obligations elsewhere when invitations had arrived before.

"Oh, it's pretty sweet," Angela said. "Security's tight, which is nice. The chick at the welcome desk over there – the one who asked if you were packing – is a fifth-level black belt, and has a stun gun in the desk drawer in case she can't get in too close. That's one of the only rules of the ranch: No Guns. The guards here can carry, but they can't come into the main house. That archway we came under is really a metal detector, and if you tried to get in here with a piece the guards'd be on you with Tasers and mace before you could make a move."

I nodded absently, hoping the x-rays hadn't somehow scrambled the disc.

"There's guns enough outside, though," Angela went on. "I left Benny and Nick with their buddies on detail outside, and they probably still haven't finished stroking each other's rifles." She caught my confused look, and laughed. "They've got a range set up just outside the front gate. Helps the muscle get their aggressions out while they're stuck hanging out here. You let those guys go too long between killing something, they start to get jumpy." She paused, glancing at the windows to the bright light beyond. "I wouldn't want to be a rabbit around here when one of these shows goes off. Those boys don't know when to stop."

I wasn't really feeling any better about my decision to come after hearing all this, but I was saved any further good news when the lights overhead flashed on and then off.

"Come on," Angela said, grabbing my elbow and dragging me towards the conference room. "I want to get a good seat before the big wigs show up."

Considering who we'd already seen milling around, I wondered just what Angela's idea of "big wig" entailed. I was about to find out.

The conference center, the rows of aluminum frame chairs with upholstered seats and backs arranged to face the raised podium at the front, with aisles down the middle and either side, could have been nestled anonymously in any midscale hotel from California to New York. If you didn't notice the mob bosses and contract killers taking their seats, that is, which I couldn't help but do.

"Now, that's interesting," Angela said in a stage whisper as we found our place.

"What's that?" I asked guardedly, scanning the crowd.

She gestured, nonchalantly, with her chin towards the front of the room.

"You usually only get business types at these things," she answered, "but now and again civilians with underworld connections make an appearance. When they do, they're typically escorted by somebody in the business, you know?"

I forced a chuckle and answered nervously, "Well, art appreciation knows no borders, right?"

Angela smiled slightly.

"I couldn't agree more," she said in silky tones, "but still and all. Check out those folks at the front there, those three on the left and those geezers on the right."

I followed her line of sight and finally noticed who she meant. To the left of the podium, looking calm but deadly serious, were two men and a woman, all of them groomed to perfection like they'd just stepped out of the pages of a fashion magazine, wearing tailored business professional attire in shades of gray.

Opposite them, across the aisle on the right side of the room, sat an odd assortment of gray and bald heads, shifting uncomfortably, darting glances around the room. They were all dressed in non-descript suits and ties, but I was able to recognize at least a few of the faces, and knew they were more used to wearing uniforms or judges robes. I didn't mention it to Angela, but unless I was mistaken, at least one of the Joint Chiefs of Staff and a couple of Supreme Court judges were in that group, and one face I recognized from the business pages of the New York Times but couldn't place.

"Not the regular crowd?" I asked casually, behind my hand.

"Not hardly," Angela said, suspicious. "They don't seem the types to be serious art collectors. Still, they must know which strings to pull or they wouldn't be in here."

I thought for a minute, and then lobbed another question at her.

"Don't people worry about being caught out?" I asked. "I mean, these civilians you're talking about. Don't they have any problems getting seen at one of these things?"

Angela shook her head.

"No," she answered, "the type of people who normally come to these things, both in the business and out of it, usually aren't in a position to worry about anything like that. They're powerful enough that they don't give a shit who sees them where, because they don't have to. It's the nickel and dime players who have to worry about aliases and being incognito. The most powerful move with impunity through anything, any situation, because they're practically invisible by nature."

I nodded, my eyes shifting between the two groups at the front of the room, when a couple of cartoon mobsters took to the podium at the front of the room and started the show.

"That's Dominick Carerra," Angela whispered in my ear, indicating the thick-fingered don taking the microphone. He was in his late fifties, with slicked-back white hair and an expensively tailored suit. As he flexed his grip on the microphone, a pinky ring caught the light. If you looked up "mobster" in a pop culture dictionary, this is the guy who would be staring back at you. "He always plays auctioneer at these things. If you ask me, he's a frustrated comedian, and being head of the Chicago syndicate doesn't get you many chances for public speaking, if you get me. So he volunteered to head this operation up when the families bought the ranch a few years back, and he's been up there with Mr. Microphone every chance he can get since."

I blew out a breath between my teeth, hoping Angela didn't notice my slumping shoulders. Tan's tip had been right on about Carerra running the show. Now I just had to hope that the disc would do its job.

"Alright, alright," barked Carerra dramatically into the microphone, waving the murmuring crowd of mobsters quiet. "It's time to get this party started, right?"

A wave of reluctant nods and grunted agreement moved through the room, as the boys left off their bloody reminisces and settled into their chairs.

"Okay, I'd like to welcome all of you to this little fund raiser, and I want you to know it's great to be here with you again. There's a lot of familiar faces in the crowd tonight, a lot of old friends, so it's nice to see that not *all* of us bought the farm this past year. Ha ha."

Polite laughter rippled through the room, punctuated by some hearty guffaws. Carerra, satisfied with the response, continued.

"There's some new faces with us here tonight, as well, so maybe this would be a good time to cover some ground rules, yes?" Carerra took a breath, and his tone got a bit more severe. "The past few days, the ranch has been the site of some, shall we say, unpleasantness. On three separate occasions, for those of you who don't know, someone has tried to force their way onto the property. Small groups, well equipped, and armed. Now, I'm not mentioning any names, because we don't have any, but this kind of thing just isn't right. Our security systems out here are nothing to sneeze at, you know, and our guys are some of the best, but if not for some unseasonal thunderstorms and lightning flashes, at least one of these little commando raids might have been successful."

There was some noise from the crowd at that, and some unhappy faces.

"Now, I'm not pointing any fingers, and I'm not about to start a witch hunt, but I just want to remind everyone that we're all businessmen here, so let's act professional. Storm-trooper raids aren't professional. Most of you here ponied up a bit of the scratch we needed to buy this place, and your contributions help us keep it up, but it looks like someone has forgotten one of the first rules of business. You don't shit where you eat."

Carerra leaned forward, tightening his grip on the microphone.

"You all with me?" he said forcefully, scanning the crowd. He got a chorus of nods in response. "Alright, then, let's start the bidding."

It was over an hour before they got to the lot I was after, so I took the chance to scope out how things were supposed to work. The image of the mob boss playing auctioneer was a difficult one to swallow for a while, especially considering the lame jokes he tossed in between lots, or the jabs he tossed off at the winners and losers at each round of bidding. It was like a livestock show, celebrity benefit, and roast all rolled into one, disconcerting mess. I kept reminding myself to take Dom the Joke Man seriously, though, remembering what Tan had told me about him.

There were some pretty choice items put up for bid, all things considered, and if I had any amount of money to play with, I might have shot for one or two. As it was, Angela walked away with a Degas thought lost by the art world decades before, and even a prized Rockwell. The most heated bidding came over a few vintage cars and antique firearms, and for a minute I thought the thing was going to come to blows, two heavyweights trying to outbid each other, neither willing to back down for fear of losing face. In the end, the monkey on the right ended up winning a couple of guns, while the monkey on the left ended up with the cars. Carerra did his best to keep everyone happy and in their seats, but I for one didn't want to be around outside after the dust had settled. Not that I wanted to hang around outside anyway, not after what I planned to pull.

Finally, one of the lackeys brought up the next item for bid, and it was the book. The same I'd seen on Barbara's special, the same one that Marconi had pinched and ended up getting greased over. It was sealed in a Lucite box, the cover about the dimensions of a letter size sheet of paper, but practically as thick as it was wide. It seemed in pretty good shape, considering its probable age, but then again it was missing at least one page. Through the Lucite, I could make out the well-worn leather covers, the metal clasps, and the silver disk on the cover, though not well enough to see any detail on it.

"Okay," Carerra began, checking out the card attached by a red thread to the corner of the Lucite case, "item number forty-nine: Antique Book, Some Wear, With Metal Highlights. The bidding starts at five hundred. Am I bid five hundred? Any bookworms in the house?"

I clenched my fists, waiting to see what would happen next.

What happened next was a pair of fans jumping up and down so much it could have air-conditioned the whole room, number 17 over with the mystery trio in gray on the left of the room, and number 45 across the room in the hands of the incognito Supreme Court Justice. Within a few minutes, the high bid had jumped from $500 to just over fifty thousand, and didn't seem about to slow down any time soon. As nondescript as the two groups of "civilians" might have wanted to be from the outset, they were certainly attracting more than their fair share of attention now, as the mobsters and hitmen settled back to see which group would snap first. A few of the onlookers had begun to consider seriously bidding for themselves, figuring that anything someone else wanted that badly must be worth something.

"O-kay," Carerra sighed wearily, looking from the Lucite box and back out to the crowd. "I am bid fifty thousand, do I hear sixty? Can anyone beat sixty?"

I swallowed hard, steeling my nerves, and climbed to my feet.

"I will," I said, as forcefully as I could manage.

Angela tugged at my sleeve, and snatched up my fan from the floor.

"You just wave the fan, Cassidy," she said, chuckling. "You don't have to pop up like a jack-in-the-box."

I waved her off, my palms sweating, my eyes never leaving Carerra. In their respective corners, the holders of fans 17 and 45 were looking at me hard, with those if-looks-could-kill looks.

"You're an eager one, aren't you, kid?" Carerra said. "So, what do you bid?"

I shoved a hand into my suit pocket, and felt the hard edges of the jewel case.

"Information," I answered, proud that my voice hardly cracked at all.

Carerra's thick eyebrows knitted together, and he looked at me quizzically.

"What?" he asked.

"Information," I repeated, straightening up a bit taller, trying to come off the dangerous guy.

"Alright, kid," Carerra finally said, "I'll bite. What the hell are you talking about?"

"I've got information to sell," I answered, pulling the jewel case from my pocket and holding it up for him to see. This was a bit of stagecraft on my part, the disc inside little more than a prop, but I figured I needed it for the kind of play I was trying for. "On this disk are a few choice files I've pulled from my collection, about the murders of Sonny Bianca and his family, about what really happened to Mayor

Kelly's daughter, about what's buried in the foundation of the First Federal Bank of Chicago, about..."

"Okay, okay," Carerra said angrily, banging the microphone against the podium like a gavel, sending a shriek of distortion and feedback through the P.A. system. "So you got a little dirt," he said, trying to play it cool. "So what?"

I knew so what as well as he did. For all their tendency to boast and brag when around family, there are still some messes even the loudest mob boss doesn't want to get mixed up in, things he's done personally that he should have passed off to a subordinate, or even secret transgressions against other mobsters. Bad business, all around, and that was precisely what I was talking about. Enough dirt to bury Carerra, thanks to my contacts over the years and a few dashes of spice from Tan. As soon as Tan had told me who was hosting the auction, and always did, I remembered the half dozen stories about him I'd heard but could never use, for fear that he'd manage to get me killed before someone else got to him first. But desperate times and desperate measure, so here I was with my ass hanging out and a disc of pure dynamite waiting to go off in my hand, hoping Carerra would jump the way I'd guessed he would.

"So what," I answered, as evenly as possible, "is that I'm not part of any family, and worse still, I'm a reporter." I paused for a second, letting that one sink in, and heard chairs scraping against the floor as the heavies around me started to their feet. "And," I added louder, "if I don't make a call at a certain hour tonight, everything on this disc will be automatically emailed to every newspaper and FBI office in the country, along with a few other choice morsels I've collected over the years."

Carerra fumed, but kept his place. So far no one had clubbed me from behind or stuck a knife between my ribs, so I was ahead of the game. I just hoped I could make it to the end of the play without collapsing on my shaking knees, or wetting myself, or both. I'm not nearly so tough as I'd like to make out.

"Okay, okay, everybody stay cool," Carerra finally said, waving to the room. "Alright, Mr. I'm-Really-A-Reporter-And-I'm-So-Fucking-Clever, what do you want? Huh? What's going to keep your yap shut?"

I nodded towards the Lucite box on the podium next to him.

"That book, and a clear path out of here," I answered.

The combatants in the bidding war didn't like that one bit, and jumped to their feet. The Justice, acting like he thought he was back at the bench, actually shouted "Objection!" while the guy in the gray suit with the 17 fan across the room just shouted "The Book is mine" in a screwball accent.

"Somebody shut them up," Carerra said out of the side of his mouth, and while he rubbed his chin a few lackeys made their way to the front rows and convincingly argued that everyone should keep to their seats. Not happy about it, but not seeing any options, everyone sat back down and kept quiet, their eyes never leaving me.

"Let me ask you something, Reporter," Carerra said, his head cocked to one side. "What's to keep me from just having my boys break your neck, burn the disc, and let the chips fall where they might? Hmm? Are you that convinced you've got the goods on me, or that I even give a shit about my reputation?"

"No," I answered calmly, "but I know one thing for sure. You don't shit where you eat. It's not good business."

Carerra looked at me for a long minute, tapping the microphone lightly against the palm of his hand, and then nodded.

"Okay," he finally answered, "you've got a deal. Give me the disc, take the book, and get the hell out of here. And if I ever see you or hear your voice again, I will personally rip off your head and shit down your neck, you get me?"

"I got you," I started to say, taking a step forward, but the outbursts from the party on the left and the party on the right drowned out my words. I couldn't make out what they were saying, but I got the distinct impression that they weren't happy.

Carerra snapped his fingers, and more lackeys and bruisers appeared from the wings to join those already waiting at hand.

"Keep those mugs quiet," he ordered, indicating the two parties in front, "and if they give you any trouble, kill them."

The lackeys nodded mutely, and within seconds had the situation well in hand. The former bidders weren't happy, but they seemed content now to bide their time.

I made it to the podium without incident, and handed over the disc as with his other hand Carerra passed me the Lucite-encased book. With it firmly in hand, I decided not to waste any time with idle chat, and hurried towards the door. The mobsters and killers looked on as I passed, vaguely bemused, as though I had provided a bit of dinner theater and they were thankful for the distraction. A few seemed sorry to see me go, not eager to get back to the business of the auction.

At the door, Angela caught my elbow, smirking.

"I was right about you, *Cassidy*," she said in a low voice, her mouth near enough to my ear to give me the shakes. "You certainly weren't boring."

I smiled back, wishing for better circumstances, and beat feet the hell out of there. I still wasn't sure if I'd make it to the car alive; getting out onto the road was another thing entirely.

As it was, I made it out without incident, the car untouched and the Lucite case on my lap. Once back on the main road, the electric gate swinging shut behind me, I hauled ass through the gathering dark, passed up Sizemore without a backwards glance, and made it Flagstaff in record time. I ditched the rental car in a parking garage. Lugging my suitcase, the cardboard box of my grandfather's things and the Lucite encased book awkwardly across the street, I bought a ticket at the Greyhound station for the first red-eye heading east. In just over an hour after leaving the ranch, I was nestled in a cramped bus, the suitcase wedged under my seat, the cardboard box at my feet, and the Lucite case in my lap.

I was too wired to sleep and was looking at another five or six hours in that seat, so I figured I'd take a peek at this book that was worth so much of my time and trouble and so many other people's lives. I couldn't figure the case, though, and didn't want to risk damaging the book in the dim light trying to get it out. The passing scenery was ghostly gray in the darkness, and not much to look at in the light, so I didn't have a choice but to pull another piece of madness out of my grandfather's box to give me something to focus on, and hopefully calm me down a bit. I pulled out a sheaf of Xeroxed papers, with a rusty staple in the corner holding them together, and started to read.

The Blake Hande

Dated sometime after 1430, this ballad represents one of the earliest surviving of its type. It is preserved in one fragmentary manuscript copy in Cambridge University Library, MS Ff.7.97, folios 94v-109v. It is presented here as re-edited by Professor E. Mettler (Cambridge University) from the original MS. This text, along with the critical apparatus, was first presented in *Scoundrels and Rogues: Forgotten Ballads of the Medieval Period*, 1898, eds. E. Mettler & J. Boanerges.

Introductory Notes

Despite parallels with early Robin Hood legends, notably *The Gest of Robyn Hode* and *Robin Hood and the Monk* (both anon.), the ballad of the Blake Hande seems to predate either of them, and may well have served as a precursor, if not inspiration, for both.

The setting for the story is the close of the Eleventh Century, during the 3rd Crusade. The principal figure, who by the end comes to be known by the nom du guerre of "Blake Hande" or *Black Hand*, is Edward, the son of a tailor. Desiring to win the respect and admiration of his countrymen, Edward allows himself to be impressed into service as a foot-soldier. It is his earnest hope to win his spurs through his valor, and thus ennoble both himself and his family.

(Throughout the body of the text, the editors have included glosses and commentary drawn substantially from later versions of the tale, which, it is hoped, will help fill the gaps left by those portions lost over the years.)

The Blake Hande

Lythe and listin, gentilmen,
That worke upon the lande;
I shall the tel of a gode yeman,
Hoos name was the Blake Hande.

Eduard was hys name at birthe,
In a humbl family borne
Hys mother a humble taylors wif
Hys faders handes wel worn.

He grewe to lern to cut an sewe
A taylors life he mede
But dremed dyd he of other fates
And wher the roads might leade.

When Richard of the Lioun Heart
Agains the Saracin did war
Eduard saw a chaynce to teke
An thoght to winne his spurs.

Edward the Tailor's Son joins a massing of soldiers and knights, nobles and commoners alike, led by Richard the Lion-Hearted. They cross the Channel and make their way through Europe, coming at last to the Holy Land. They meet and fight against the forces of Saracen repeatedly, sometimes knowing victory, sometimes defeat. Finally, in a melee near the Muslim-held Jaffa, Edward himself is separated from the bulk of the English contingent and finds himself lost, cut off in the wilderness.

Away from the eyes of hys fellowes
A wanderynge alone was he,
Until in the mydden of a grene wode
Spyed a Moor beneth a tre.

Al arrayed for battle,
Hys sworde helde in hys hande
Mede Eduard redy for the charge,
To dye in that foregn lande.

The Moor aspyed hys comin,
An made no move to fyght,
An proved for all hys fearsom mene

He was a peacefel wight.

Than Eduard was a tyred and sick
Of swordes and bowes a bende
Sew made he peace with that dark moor
An made of he a frende.

Edward and the Moor spend several days travelling together. The Moor speaks English well enough to communicate, and entertains Richard with tales of his home, and of the great mysteries and legends thereof. The Moor finally tells him of the fabled, half-legendary Order of the Black Hand, which has acted as a force against mindless aggression and slaughter in the Moorish lands for countless ages.

Now of thys solem Order
Of the handes of Blake,
The Moor he did long recovnt
They work theyr fellowes seke.

"Agains the Kynges an Prelates al,"
The Moor he clearley sayed,
"Each Brothere of the hande of Blake,
Does lifte up prode his hede."

"Each mann they saye, and evry childe,
Must hys own choyces meke,
An sew they strugle al lif longe,

Each with handes of blake."

Edward and the Moor become friends as they travel, recognizing each other as brothers beneath the skin, and each resolves to see the other treated kindly, with humanity, should they be found by his own countrymen. Unfortunately for the Moor, they stumble across an encampment of English soldiers first, who toy with the Moor brutally for long hours before finally killing him.

Eduard than entreats the peeres
To putte awey ther swordes,
Let the Moor go wit them than
A prisonner at hi worde.

The peeres thoght hi wordes a gest
An bede him meerey speke
An geve the Moor unsemely dethe
An cut Eduard on his cheke.

It is at this point that Edward abandons forever his dream, his hope, of becoming a knight. He now has something grander, more noble, towards which to strive. He leaves the English camp that night, the blood hardly dried upon his face, and makes his way home, alone, to England. Arriving at his father's home, he finds the old tailor three winters dead, his mother nowhere to be found.

Came Eudward to the taylor's home
Wher lyved hys parens bothe
An founde he ther no livynge sole
Nor sygne they lyved for sothe.

Away a fro the home he fonde
Depe in the grate grene wode
The plece his fader restes hi hede
Beneth a crude woden rode.

Hi mother he could fynd no synge
Nor any grave she laye
Butte kne he than she too had mete
Her oun tru dyeing daye.

Kne he than that bothe had fel
Benethe som cutthrotes sworde
The work of som vile bishoppes hande
Or els some crule landelorde.

Edward, born the son of a simple tailor, trained as a soldier by the Kingdom's finest, dedicates his life and all his efforts to the opposition of tyranny and injustice, both at home at abroad. Having seen too many sons of peasant families fall under the Saracen's spear in a war few of them could even hope to understand, Edward sees the leaders of his own country as a greater threat to liberty than a foreign king in far-off lands could ever be. Inspired by the Moor's tales of his country's legendary order, he ceases to be Edward Tailor, and ever after is known only as the Black Hand.

Sew Eduard than he left that plece
Cladde in livrey al of blake,
An toke him to the grene wode,
To fyghte for al mens seke.

An from that daye onne,
In evry cornere of the lande,
The people loved an nobles feyred
The name of the Blake Hande.

The SIXTH DAY

I woke folded double in the cramped seat as the bus pulled into the station in El Paso. I'd slept a little, fitfully, dreaming in Middle English, but didn't feel at all rested. Coaxing my aching muscles and groaning joints into motion, I managed to climb out of the seat, get the bag, book, and box arranged in an awkward hold, and stumbled from the bus and out into the stale morning air. It was just past dawn, and already I was remembering why I didn't like El Paso.

Not bothering with a cab or rental car, I hoofed it the few blocks from the bus station to the nearest flea bag motel. I checked in under the name of Richmond Taylor, and lugged my things up rickety metal stairs to my shoebox room. The bed looked like it had been used as a prop in one too many professional wrestling bouts, and the sink in the bathroom wouldn't stop dripping, but the air conditioner seemed to work and the door locked solid.

Dropping my things unceremoniously on the floor and stripping to the waist, I struggled hard against the urge to a) shower, b) shower and then sleep, or c) screw the shower and go right back to bed. I didn't feel like I'd really rested in days, which I hadn't, but my nagging conscience told me I had important things to do before I even thought about rest.

First, I had to call Tan and give him a heads up that he might be expecting trouble. He'd known it was coming, naturally, having passed me the invite to the auction and given me the skinny on Carerra. Still, it was only good form to let him know that I was out of it, and that there was a chance there might be some ill will directed his way after vouching for me. Ill will, to say the least.

The phone rang at Tan's place a good six times before anyone answered, which was unusual enough in and of itself. More unusual still is that it wasn't Tan who answered, a first.

"Hello, who is this?" came a frantic voice on the other end of the line, a woman's and in no mood for niceties.

"Who is this?" I echoed, and then added. "Cachelle, is that you?"

"Spencer, baby, I'm so glad you called," she answered in a rush. "I've just been worried sick, sick I tell you, and I didn't know what to do. The doctors are no good, and the police are even worse. I oughta throw a hex on the whole lot of them, watch me if I don't."

I settled back on the bed, cradling the phone against my shoulder, and pulled off my boots.

"Slow down, Cachelle," I said. "Take it slow, from the top. Where's Tan?"

Cachelle let out a heavy, rattling sigh and continued.

"Tan's in the hospital, sugar, and he's in a bad way. Somebody broke into his place late last night and made a mess of him and his rooms. I heard the crashing around and called the cops, but by the time they showed up whoever it was had already gone. That ambulance took its own goddamned sweet time to get here, pardon my French, and I'm surprised Tan didn't just up and die on us before we got him to the hospital."

Two questions were jockeying for first position in my head, waiting to jump.

"How is he?" won the race by a nose, with "Who did it?" following close behind.

"Well," Cachelle answered, breathy, "Tan is... well, he could be better, sugar. They've got him all hooked up to monitors and computers and wires and tubes, and they're breathing for him and pushing his blood around and listening to his insides, but he hasn't woke up yet. They don't know for sure yet if he will, or if he does whether he'll still be... still..." Her voice broke, and I didn't have the heart to make her go on for a second. I just sat on the edge of that crappy bed, one boot off and the other on, naked to the waste and unable to feel a goddamn thing. I was numb, empty, and I could hardly hear her talking for the noise all the screaming thoughts in my head were making.

I steadied myself and tried for a follow-up.

"Okay, Cachelle, I know." I was trying to stay calm, trying not to blow up and set her over the edge. "Do the police know who did it? Did they get them?"

"No, no, no, they don't know who did it, they don't have any damned idea," she wailed. "Somebody just busts into somebody's house and messes them up like that, and the police don't even know where to start. They were asking *me* if I knew who did it!" She snuffled loudly into the phone. "Then there was that note this morning, and they didn't even know *what* to do with that."

"Note?" I repeated. "What note?"

"I found this note this morning on his bed stand, right next to his hospital bed, and it hadn't been there fifteen minutes before because I'd looked. I'd been up in that room with Tan all night, and I know *I* didn't put it there."

"What did the note say? Do you have it with you?"

"No, the police took it, ignorant know nothings, but I can see it still like it was right in front of me, I don't think I'd ever forget."

I pulled a ballpoint and a spiral out of the side of my suitcase, and propped the spiral open on my knee.

"What did the note say, Cachelle?" I repeated.

"It said, '*They were able to break your bones, but we can hurt you worse.*' And it had a phone number across the bottom. The police tried calling it or tracing it down, but nobody answered, and they can't even figure out who has that number."

I took a deep breath, and held it.

"Is there any chance you remember the number?"

"It's burned in my eyes, Spencer; I couldn't forget it if I tried." Then she rattled off the numbers, a toll-free 888 prefix and the full seven digits.

I gave Cachelle the number of the hotel and asked her to call me as soon as she knew more. If she couldn't get me at the hotel, she should call my home number and leave a message, and I'd get back with her as soon as I could. Cachelle insisted we pray together before hanging up. I couldn't argue, and once we'd done our Amens she was off to try to clean what was left of Tan's place. It was the only thing she could think to do, and to be honest I was kind of wishing I was there with her to help. The only thing I could think to do was to call that 888 number, and I would have taken cleaning up over that in a heartbeat.

It took half an hour of planning and replanning, but in the end I figured out what had to be done. Still on the edge of the bed, still with one boot and no shirt on, I punched in the first of two numbers I needed to call and crossed my fingers. I just hoped he was back in town, and that it was still early enough that he hadn't left for work yet.

"Yeah," came the groggy voice on the other end of the line.

"Amador," I sighed. "Great. Stay right there, I'm going to call you back."

"What? Do you know what time it is?"

"Early," I answered. "Now don't go anywhere."

"I've got to talk to–" I heard him say, but I clicked off the line before he could finish.

Next up came the hard part. I pulled a cigarette from my suit coat, lighting it with my Zippo, hoping to soothe my nerves, or least give my hands something to do. Cradling the receiver against my ear, I punched in the 888 number and held my breath. My hands were shaking, so much so that the smoke rising up from the cigarette jetted into tight spirals that almost circled back on themselves above me. It occurred to me that I was putting myself in a considerable amount of risk for a single story, but realized at this point it wasn't even *about* J. Nathan Pierce anymore, or shady land deals, or any of it. I just wanted *answers*.

The line rang once and then clicked on. I heard silence on the other end.

"H-hello," I said, putting my bravest face forward.

"Mr. Finch," came the answer, a man's voice like nails on a chalkboard.

"That's me," I answered, trying for glib, "who are you?"

"That's not important, Mr. Finch. I assume you received our... message?"

I tightened my grip on the receiver, white-knuckled and sweaty palmed.

"Don't touch my friends again," I barked, "or I will find you and kill you myself."

The voice on the other end laughed mirthlessly.

"Charming, Mr. Finch," he said, "but hardly germane. You have something we want, and to be quite honest we'll do whatever we like to you or your friends until we get it."

I forced myself calm, aiming for collected and reaching just short of "not panicked," which would have to do.

"What's in it for me?" I blustered. "I've been through a lot of trouble to get this thing."

"You'll go through quite a lot more if we don't get it, Mr. Finch. What's in it for you is the continued well being of yourself and your friends. Need I point to a certain Mr. Marconi as a rather unpleasant object lesson?"

That clinched it. I just hoped my plan would work.

"Alright, what do you want me to do?" I answered. I was trying to put a hint of desperation into my tone, and found I was hardly faking at all.

"We would like to meet, Mr. Finch, to arrange a transfer of the item from your care to ours. Where are you now?"

"California," I lied. "Los Angeles."

Again the mirthless chuckle, and chills ran down my spine.

"A nice try, I suppose," he continued, "but I'm afraid the Caller ID on your phone places you squarely at a hotel near the center of El Paso, does it not?"

Now I was panicking for real, all thoughts of acting gone. I snapped back open my Zippo and held it up to the phone.

"Hear that?!" I shouted, rolling the wheel and setting up a flickering banner of flames. "That's my trusty all-weather lighter, and if anyone fucks with me here I'll introduce it to your little book club member and see how well they get along. Do you get me? I'll fucking burn it if you come near me!"

"Calm yourself, Mr. Finch," he answered. "No one would dream of intruding on your privacy. Shall we arrange a more neutral location to meet, then? At some later time?"

I breathed deep, relieved. So far it was going fine.

"Tomorrow night, six o'clock," I answered firmly. "San Antonio. In front of the Alamo. It's then and there, or nowhere, and I burn the damned thing right now."

The voice on the other end of the line sighed dramatically.

"Very well, Mr. Finch," he answered reluctantly. "Tomorrow night at six o'clock in San Antonio. We shall speak further then."

"Don't forget," I shot back, leaning forward, trying to regain a bit of my lost self-respect. "The Alamo."

"I shall remember," he answered, but I got the impression he hadn't caught the joke.

I paused only to relieve my overburdened bladder, which had threatened to give way at least twice in the course of the conversation, before calling back Amador at home. The way he answered, you would have thought it had been years.

"Shit, Finch, what the hell is going on...?" Amador began, practically shouting before I cut him off.

"Hang on, Lover, I've got to run something down for you quick, and then you can say whatever you like. This thing that started with Marconi has gotten really messy, really quick, and I've ended up with something that these fuckers want. I've arranged to meet them tomorrow night in front of the Alamo to hand this shit over, and I'm pretty sure once they lay hands on it I'm going down like a shot. They've already put Tan in the hospital, beat half to death, not to mention Marconi, and I don't really think they'll have that much problem with adding me to the list. I need you to pull whatever strings you can, get the Feds there in force, and pick these fuckers up before they pick me off. The Bureau'll be able to solve a string of murders and beatings, and I'll get to go on breathing. What do you say, man, can you do that for me?"

Amador let out a long sigh on the other end before answering.

"Sure, Finch," he finally said, "of course, I'll make the call right now and get the shit lined up. But I told you something like this was going to happen, didn't I?"

"Don't pull that nagging shit on me right now, okay, Amador, I am just not in the mood for it."

"Alright, alright," he answered, "but I think this thing is already messier than you know."

"What are you talking about, man?"

"It was just on the news," Amador answered. "J. Nathan Pierce was found murdered this morning; shot to death in his own home."

There was no hope for sleep after that. I finished up with Amador, giving him the details on the time and place of the meeting, and numbly hung up the phone. Half undressed, I paced back and forth in the motel room for a while, one foot bare and the other booted, before finally stripping down and going through the motions of a listless shower. The water-flow was tepid and weak, but I hardly noticed.

Back out, I didn't even bother to get dried off before I got dressed again, and grabbed up the Lucite case. I cracked it open, and dropped the heavy book out onto the bed. The silver disk on the cover caught the light, and shifted like mother of pearl when the book was moved. It was set into the leather of the cover, the curved edges overlapped by the material around it. I was able to pry the metal clasps loose, and flipped the book open to the first pages.

Where was Michelle when I needed her? I couldn't make the writing out at all. It was all little swirls and lines, maybe Greek, but it could have been Klingon shorthand for all I knew. I flipped a few pages ahead, carefully, the delicate pages rustling like dried leaves as I moved them. The handwriting seemed to change every few pages, the types of letters or alphabets changing every few more. The writing was so small and tightly packed that my vision swam just looking at it, and I felt a headache coming on. I flipped to the end of the book and found the last sections written in an alphabet I recognized, at least, though I couldn't make out the words, followed by a bunch of blank pages. This was getting me nowhere. I needed motion, needed to get my feet moving, or I'd burn myself out from all the pent up frustrations.

Dropping the book back into the Lucite case, I took it into the bathroom and hid it above the ceiling tiles over the toilet, sliding them carefully back into place so that everything looked kosher. I didn't really think anyone was going to track me down just yet; the threats I'd made about burning the thing seeming to have the desired effect, but still it made sense not to take any chances. I stomped into my boots, grabbed up cigarettes, lighter and room key, and was out the door.

Three old men haunted my steps, two dead and the other just barely alive. Two that shaped my childhood, made me the man I was, and one who had played Roadrunner to my Coyote for months, my very own white whale. All that was over now, I realized, any story long gone. Whatever land swindles or dirty deals Pierce had been mixed up in had somehow paled in comparison to the growing pile of corpses around that damned Lucite-encased book. The publishers of Logion wouldn't be too happy about that, I figured, but I decided I didn't much care. All of this had stopped being about the story a long time ago, for me at least, and now I just wanted the answers. What was this book, and why was it so important to these people? What did this Lucetech outfit have to do with it, and if they were one of the groups at the auction, who were the other people? Who was the voice on the other end of the phone, the ones who had put my mentor in the hospital? And who had been the one to call me in the first place, to put me onto the book's trail?

I didn't have any of the answers to the questions I'd started with the week before, and now had a few dozen more piled on top. My head was swimming in riddles and mysteries, but one thing kept forcing its way back to the forefront. Tan laying in that hospital bed, barely alive, Pierce full of holes in his spacious and well-appointed home, and my grandfather dead and buried.

How had my grandfather died? I hadn't asked, and no one had mentioned. I'd assumed it was just old age, just his worn out body finally giving up the race and moving on to greener pastures (or under them). He'd looked so old, one foot in the grave already the last time I'd seen him, that it was a shock he'd made it as long as he did. And when had been the last time I'd seen him? Had it really been over ten years?

It had not been, in retrospect, my most shining hour. To be honest, I'd acted like a spoiled brat, but it was years before I realized it, and by then it was much too late.

After the first summer I'd spent in New Orleans with Tan, when I'd just turned fourteen, I was forced to return home to San Antonio to finish out high school. Tan, who seemed to have no ethical problem training me in the art of cat burglary, balked at harboring a runaway. So it was back to the house on Crescent Row, back to breakfasts in the kitchen with Patrick and Maria, and the stony silences and occasional outbursts from my grandfather.

Still, things had changed at my grandfather's house after that summer. I'd left off the training regimen the old man had drilled us with all those years, and the old man left off forcing me to follow it. I still worked out, running and doing free weights, but only because they were the sorts of skills Tan had insisted were vital to a burglar's success. I did well enough in school, too, I suppose, again following Tan's advice. Tan had taken a more holistic approach to the art of crime than most, I guess you could say, and considered the uncultured thief little better than a cutpurse. A true thief, he always said, had to be an artist as well as a craftsman, and that demanded literacy and an appreciation for the finer things. I swallowed it all, naturally, considering how impressionable I was and how impressive Tan had seemed.

My grandfather only mentioned my summer away once, a short while after my return. I'd just shown up a few days before school was to begin that semester, looking no worse for wear, and went back up to my room. Maria, for her part, couldn't stop fawning over me and scolding me mercilessly, by turns, while Patrick was a little jealous of my little adventure, which he'd been afraid to come along on, and more than a little worried about how the old man might react. At the dinner table that night, my grandfather hadn't said a word about it, just demanded I pass him the green beans and that was that. I was home.

It was a week into the school year when, on my way up to my bedroom after school, the old man called me into his study. He was sitting behind his big desk, the piles of papers and books that only grew larger and taller with every passing year almost hiding him from view, while I stood waiting, my backpack in hand, shuffling my feet. I was scowling, I'm sure, offended at this interruption in my daily routine.

"There are roads," the old man finally said, his hands folded on the desktop in front of him, "paths a man must choose to walk down. The road we walk is what defines who we are, how we see the world, and how the world sees us. Every man should be free to choose his own path, free to choose the person he will be. That is, unfortunately, not always the way of things. There are forces in this world which conspire to restrict our choices, or unduly influence us one way or other. These forces are the very face of evil. In my experience, all that is good and true is a natural extension of individual liberty, and anything impinging on that liberty is an aspect of evil. There comes a time for some of us when the struggle against these forces, the attempt to eliminate these figurative 'road blocks,' not for ourselves alone but for others, becomes the highest calling. To insure the liberty of others – their freedom of choice – becomes the path that we walk, and defines who we will be."

I must have pulled some face, or else rolled my eyes at the length of his oration, because the old man shot out of his chair, slamming his bony hands against the desktop.

"Understand," he barked, "that everything I have done is for your own good. I chose the path I walk long before you were born, long before your mother was born, and I will walk it until the day I die, though slower now and with less strength. It is anathema to my very existence to force a way of life on you or your brother, to choose for you the life you will lead. I have only presented you with options and equipped you with the skills I think you will need, so that when the time comes you will be able to choose wisely, with open eyes and an open mind. For me that choice came early in life, and for others it comes much later. For you..."

He paused, rubbing his spotted hands over his wide forehead, sighing.

"I don't know what you will someday face," the old man continued, "but I know that most likely I will not be there with you. The choice you will make, the choice your brother will make, those belong to you. Your choices, in the end, are the only things that are truly yours. When you decide, try to remember the things I have taught you. Maybe then I will still be with you, at least in part."

He stopped and stood staring at me, his expression surprisingly tender. When he hadn't spoken for a while, I shifted uncomfortably, slinging my backpack over my shoulder.

"Am I dismissed?" I snarled. I sounded nastier than I'd intended, and regretted it almost immediately. I tensed, expecting reprisal.

"Yes," the old man said wearily, slumping back into his chair. He waved a hand towards the open door. "Go on, get out." He propped an elbow on the armrest of the chair, his face shielded behind his hand.

I left, quickly, and stomped up to my room. It would be the last time the old man spoke more than a few sentences to me in a row, though he tried that one last time.

It was the night of graduation, years later, and I was ready to go. I'd written back and forth to Tan, since that summer, planning out when I would come back and what I would do once I got there. Tan had been giving me little exercises to do, summer study before the first day of school, a list of books and articles as long as my arm to study up on. I'd passed my senior finals, perhaps not with flying colors but passed nonetheless, and I was done with high school. The things I felt I couldn't live without I'd packed in one suitcase and two small backpacks; everything else I just considered dead weight. I had a bus ticket in my pocket for a six o'clock Greyhound for New Orleans. By the next day, I'd be back at Tan's, on my way to a life of cat burglary.

I made one more pass around my room, making sure I hadn't forgotten anything, slung the backpacks one over each shoulder, and hefted up the suitcase. Turning out the lights one last time, I was out in the hall and down the stairs, ready to roll.

Patrick was at the kitchen table with Maria, eating a quick bite before heading over to the high school for the ceremony. One look at me and they both knew what I had planned, though I hadn't breathed a word of it yet.

Patrick was spit and polish in his crisp new white shirt and silk tie, his hair trimmed and styled. We maybe hadn't been as close the previous few years as we'd been as kids, but we still got along fine, and I couldn't help but think I'd miss seeing him around every now and again. From the pained look on his face that he was trying hard to hide, I got the impression he felt the same way too.

Maria, for her part, wouldn't make eye contact with me, but chased peas around her china plate with a spoon and muttered to herself under her breath. I think she'd been expecting something like this every day since I got back that summer, years before, and now that the moment had arrived she'd lost faith in all of her rehearsed responses.

We made with some painfully small talk, each of us taking for granted that this would be the last time we'd see each other for some time to come, but none of us brave enough to say anything of substance. Patrick made some offhand remark about a party planned for the post-graduation festivities and Maria scolded him a bit, reminding him that he wasn't to stay out too late, not to drink and drive, and all of the expected remonstrations due an eighteen year-old boy on graduation night. Patrick didn't bother giving me too many details about the plans, and Maria didn't waste a breath trying to scold me. I was leaving the house, and leaving along with it the right to take part in those sorts of discussions.

Finally, I said something along the lines of "Well, gotta go," and made the circuit of the table, if a bit reluctantly. Kissing Maria on the cheek, her fingers digging into the flesh of my arms as though she might still keep me from leaving if she could somehow keep me immobile. Shaking hands with Patrick, awkwardly, thinking that it was the adult thing to do, but uncomfortable and not knowing when to stop, feeling that there were things I should have been saying but wasn't.

I was all set to go, and then grandfather appeared in the doorway. He had a package under one arm, about a foot square, wrapped in black paper with a silver ribbon, and a long thin box wrapped in the same style in his other hand.

"Where...?" the old man began awkwardly, looking me over, taking in my luggage and then the expressions on the faces of Maria and Patrick. "I had thought..." He broke off and straightened up, composing himself. "I have hired a car, as I thought we would take in a meal on the town after the ceremony this evening."

"I have some stuff to do," Patrick answered weakly, "but I can put it off a little while."

"Good," my grandfather answered, not taking his eyes off me. "These are for you," he indicated the packages with a nod of his head, "but I had hoped to present them to you on our return from dinner." He paused, a pregnant silence hanging in the air as he waited for me to answer, and finally added in a voice that sounded almost wounded, "I've had them wrapped."

I was having trouble meeting the old man's gaze, but he wouldn't stop looking, and wouldn't stop waiting for me to answer. Finally, I couldn't take it any longer.

"I don't need your stupid shit!" I shouted. "I don't need it, and I don't need you! I've had to put up with it all this time, and now I'm leaving, and there's not a fucking thing you can do about it."

Patrick blanched; Maria's mouth hung open; but my grandfather just kept looking at me, his face set.

"I always hoped..." he said softly. "That is... I–"

"I don't care!" I spat back, my voice shrieking. "I'm leaving."

I hitched up my suitcase and stomped past the old man towards the door. Without a second glance, my face burning and my eyes watering, I shoved the door open and was out on the street. I was eighteen, and so far as I was concerned I was never coming home again.

It would be years later before I realized how petulant and small I'd been that night, how little like the adult I'd thought that I was, but I'd learned by then there are some doors that once opened can never be closed, and some bridges you can only cross once. I'd made my choice, and I had to live with it.

I must have walked for the better part of the day through the streets of El Paso, thinking things over, trying to fit the puzzle pieces together. As the light began to dim and my last cigarette burned down to the filter, I figured I'd had enough of walking for one day and decided to head back to the motel to try to get some sleep. I'd start early the next day, rent another car, and make the drive to San Antonio in time to get my plans in motion.

My stomach rumbled loudly all the way back to the motel, not having gotten much attention since the burger joint in Sizemore the day before. At the convenience store, along with a few packs of smokes and the requisite Pepsi, I bought a handful of what the owners were optimistically calling "burritos," odd little fried lumps of something brown that dripped orange grease through their wax wrappers and rustled with an unsettling sloshing noise when dumped into a large paper bag. I fished out enough bills to cover the damage and continued on to the motel.

I should have picked up a roll of antacid along with the burritos, I decided, after the second one had disappeared down my craw, but by that point it was too late. The first two were sitting like bricks in my gut, but I was still hungry, so I sent numbers three and four down to join them, swigging as much of the Pepsi as I could with every bit to mask the taste, and being quick to light up a cigarette when it was all said and done to try to clear the air.

Managing to get both boots off this time around, I sat on the edge of the bed, just staring at the powered-off television set, trying not to think. On impulse, I called down to the front desk to see if I had any messages, but as near as I could make out from the mumbled squash of syllables they spit back I didn't have any waiting. I was about to hang up when it occurred to me that the desk clerk at a flea bag like this might not be the most reliable avenue of information in the world, and if Cachelle had tried to get a hold of me they might just as well have hung up on her as taken a message. I clicked off the line and then punched in my home number, thinking there might be voice mail waiting on my answering machine there.

There was a message alright, but not from Cachelle. It was from Michelle Orlin in Austin, out of breath and frantic with excitement, going on and on about something or other. She left her cell phone number on the message and insisted I call her as soon as I got it, day or night, whatever the hour.

I was tempted to wait, to call sometime after all of this craziness had a chance to go away. I had already had about all the news I could stand, all of it bad, and didn't want to run the risk of getting that last proverbial straw. My camel's back, humped and pained, could never have taken it.

Michelle had seemed so enthusiastic, so damned happy, that I just couldn't bring myself to wait. With any luck, she'd have some kind of good news, anything to lighten the load.

"Hello, this is Michelle." Through the light static, she sounded sort of drunk.

"Hello, This-is-Michelle, this is Spencer." I was wishing I was drunk, too, now that I had the chance to think of it.

"Spence! Ohmigod, I'm so glad you called!" She was running at 45 rpm here, all of her words run together, a long speedy string of syllables; I was still at 33-and-a-third, but I did my best to keep up.

"What's going on, Michelle? I'm kind of in the middle of some shit right now–"

"I was right," she cut in, as though she hadn't heard me. "I was right about it, I can't fucking believe it, this is the biggest thing that's happened to me in my entire fucking life!"

"What is...?" I started, and then get an idea. "Is this about that paper?" I asked. "The one you're looking at for me?"

"Of course," came the answer, "what else would I be talking about? It's all real, Spence, it's all fucking real! It's the whole play, well, more or less – the whole goddamned thing."

"It checked out?" I asked. "It's that guy, that… um…?"

"Aeschylus," she answered, scolding. "Yes, it's got all kinds of other stuff, too, but it looks to be the full text of Aeschylus's *Prometheus Unbound* right in the middle of it all, if you can believe it."

I rubbed my chin. This was nowhere near as exciting news to me as it seemed to be to her.

"Sure," I said offhanded, "I can believe damn near anything at this point."

"Oh, me too, Spence, me too!" Michelle gushed. "But I've been doing some checking about a weird reference in the play, something about the 'stain-handed followers of Prometheus.' It sounded familiar, so I copied out some stuff that might tie into it. I've got a whole package of shit for you, man. I finished the translation this morning and I couldn't think straight about anything else, so I've been running around like a crazy person all day putting this stuff together."

She paused for a breath, and I took one of my own on credit.

"Are you at home?" she continued. "I'll run it by right now. I can't wait for you to see it."

"No, I'm still out of town," I answered. "Or out of town again. In El Paso, actually."

"Erh," she snarled. "I'm sorry." She felt as favorably about El Paso as I did. "Well, is there a fax number there? I really want you to see this stuff; you're not going to believe it."

"Hang on," I told her, "I'll check."

I dropped her on hold and picked up another line to call down to the desk. It took a while to get across to the desk clerk what I was after, but after some coaxing I came up with a fax number.

"Got it, Michelle," I said, clicking back on the line. I gave her the digits and told her to go ahead and send everything on. I wasn't sure how much I was going to get out of it, but there was always a chance it might give me some idea what the book was about, and maybe even why these jokers wanted it so badly.

I finished things up with Michelle, promising to call her as soon as I'd had a chance to look the thing over, and then made my way downstairs to the front desk. There was some trouble with the fax machine, I was told on my arrival, which seemed to be cleared up quickly enough when I produced a twenty and asked if it might be of assistance. The pages came through, a whole ream of them, and shuffling them into some kind of order I climbed the stairs back up to my room.

The burritos gone, the Pepsi following close behind and the cigarettes and ash tray my only friends, I propped my feet up on the bed, spread the fax pages out on top of the sheets, and started to read.

Prometheus Unbound
by Aeschylus

What follows is a fragmentary, abridged version of Aeschylus's lost play, *Prometheus Unbound.* It has been compiled from extant fragments, notably the Arabic manuscript (Codex 1785a-9) discovered by Michelle Orlin, then of the University of Texas-Austin. Though the Orlin Fragment is still under some dispute, the bulk of popular opinion holds it to be genuine, and is presented here as under the verifiable (if not verified) authorship of Aeschylus.

Characters

HERACLES
PROMETHEUS
CHIRON the Centaur
CHORUS of the Followers of Prometheus
PHOSPHORUS, a son of Eos
HESPERUS, a son of Eos

A rocky mountain-top, within sight of the sea. PROMETHEUS is manacled to a rock, his head bowed.

PROMETHEUS

Here am I, and here have I been. Long suffering the cruel torments of the merciless lord of the gods.

Chained here countless years with shackles of iron to this cold spire of unforgiving stone.

Of all that live on the earth, and under the seas, and in the skies, only I, Wise-Before-the-Fact, know when my torments shall cease.

When the man born of that cruel lord will come to free me, and his bitter victim to take on my sorrows.

Long suffering, for my love of man, for being too good a friend to the creatures of the day. Punished here for my sin, for saving the race of man from sure destruction.

I gave them knowledge of their own state, and placed into their hands the thing which would save them.

But wait, what do I hear? Some footsteps approach. Some new audience for my torments, or the agents of my release come at last?

Enter HERACLES and the Centaur CHIRON.

HERACLES

[To Chiron.] Here we have reached this wilderness, this unmarked desolation, home to one alone.

That god of old, who in daring to slip the bridle-rope of Zeus was chained here with manacles of iron,

To be food for that o'er flying eagle by day, and to shiver in his chains by night.

Prometheus, forethought, who gave to man that prize of the gods, all-fashioning fire.

CHIRON

Now the race of man is close on the heels of the gods, pursuing them to the foothills of Olympus itself.

No longer are men content to be the play-pieces in the games of gods, but have themselves grabbed control of play.

HERACLES

Still the hard heart of merciless Zeus softens with the course of time.

Like a stone in a fast running stream, the sharp edges of his ire are now rounded smooth,

And he finds after long ages forgiveness in his heart for the traitor god, his cousin.

The Father sends me, upon my labors, to loose Prometheus from his bonds, and to set another in his place.

CHIRON

Thus come I, who sore-pained seek for death, though still immortal, pricked by a poisoned arrow from your strong bow.

I, Chiron, whose suffering is but a shadow of Prometheus's, have come to take up his pains as my own.

Down into Hades cast, to the River Lethe, I will find forgetfulness there, and lose my pains among the shades.

HERACLES

Follow close by, then, Wise One, as I go about my work.

PROMETHEUS

Come they closer now, the prophesied agents of my release, the noble archer and the wounded centaur.

Look now, how Heracles raises his horn bow, and pulls back the string which no man but him can draw.

He notches to the bow one of his faultless arrows, fletched with the quills of the Stymphalian birds.

He sights along the arrow, and lets fly into the blue sky, and down comes the loathsome eagle, chief agent of my torments.

HERACLES

The deed is done, the still proud traitor's tormentor fallen.

Now, Chiron, will I lead you into Tartarus, to offer yourself up for Prometheus' sin.

The Sons of Dawn will be along presently, with the rising of the sun, to relieve Prometheus of his bondage.

Exeunt HERACLES and CHIRON.

PROMETHEUS

Kinder gods than ours bless you, noble Heracles, and you, pitiable Chiron.

To you, each of you, will be given a home among the stars, that future races of men may look upon you with reverence.

Now I wait, for those Sons of Dawn, who will release me from my torment.

Enter the CHORUS up the mountain, bearing a torch.

CHORUS

Hail to you, our proud patron, true father of us all.

As you sculpted the first man and the first woman from dumb clay,

So too did you bring to us all-fashioning fire, and all bring us up out of savagery.

We follow you and wait on your pleasure, we the Stained-Handed followers of Prometheus.

PROMETHEUS

It lightens my heart to hear it, that I have not suffered here only to be forgotten

CHORUS

Never forgotten, Wise-Before-the-Fact. This pith of fennel *[indicates torch]* we carry always before us, to keep us ever mindful.

PROMETHEUS

And to shed light into the dark corners.

CHORUS

And thus keep ignorance at bay.

PROMETHEUS

So you carry on my work among the race of men, you creatures of a day, carrying the light to your brothers?

CHORUS

Just as you instructed our fathers before us.

PROMETHEUS

Then never will cruel Zeus, or any new-found lord after him, hold sway over the lives of men.

CHORUS

Our lives are our own.

PROMETHEUS

Then could I be shackled here another thousand years and bear the torment, for I know my sacrifice not in vain.

But listen, others approach.

Enter Phosphorus and Hesperus.

PHOSPHORUS

Come we now, the awaited sons of the Dawn, to relieve you of your burden.

HESPERUS

We, the Children of the Dawn, will lead you from this place, and out into a prouder world.

PROMETHEUS

Long have I waited and known you would one day come. I welcome you, then, as a father his sons.

PHOSPHORUS

Now, Hesperus! I will free his shackled hands, and you see to his bound feet.

HESPERUS

There, the bounds broken, the ring pulled loose from stone.

PHOSPHORUS

The manacles shattered, the chains are tossed aside.

CHORUS

Rise now, father of us all.

HESPERUS

Rise and come with us, and we will lead you from your place of torment.

PHOSPHORUS and HESPERUS help PROMETHEUS to his feet, and lead him from the mountain.

CHORUS

We will stay on after, Prometheus Fire-Bringer, and hold the torch high for all to see,

Every man and beast, every god on the earth, or under the seas, or in the skies, and every passing wind.

We shall hold it forth, with our own stained hands.

Each member of the CHORUS produces a torch, which they light from the first fennel. Then they disperse, leaving the stage from all directions, their torches held before them.

THE SEVENTH DAY

I had trouble sleeping, and when dawn came, the first light of day spearing into the room through the slits and tears in the ancient curtains, I finally gave up trying. It had been one of those nights when every bump was a killer at the door, every rattle in the vents some nefarious something out to get me. The air had been hot and close, no matter how high I'd turned up the air conditioner, and the sheets clung to my clammy flesh as I moved. My head ached, my eyes burned, and my thoughts were racing. All in all, I wasn't in very good shape.

Peeling myself from the bed sheets, I showered as best I could again in the tepid trickle, did a sniff test on my shirts and sundries to pick out the most clean (or least dirty), and got suited up. I considered calling Amador to check the plans for the meet, but realized there was a good chance that whoever the Black Hats were they might have succeeded in tapping the motel phone lines once they learned where I was. For all I knew, I was being watched right then. I hoped not, as it might sour my plans, but in the end there wasn't much I could do about it one way or another. Packing up my gear, and ditching the Lucite case in favor of a large Sears department store sack I'd found in the bathroom trash as a less conspicuous means of transporting the book, I hefted my load and headed out into the world. It was a little after seven o'clock, and the butterflies in my stomach reminded me of first date jitters, or the trip to the doctor to get the results of my blood work.

From the front desk of the motel, I had to rouse the desk clerk from a peaceful slumber on an army cot hidden behind the counter. What the hell, I figured. If I couldn't sleep, no one should be able to. I paid my tab with most of the cash I had left over, leaving me with a few tens and twenties huddled together for company in my wallet. I phoned a cab and rode to the airport. The cabbie dropped me off in front of the rows of car rental outlets, taking the meager tip I could manage with a kind of stoic silence. He didn't offer to help me with my bags and box, and I didn't ask.

I hurried past the first rental outfit guiltily, somehow thinking they might recognize me as the guy who ditched one of their cars out in Arizona a couple of days before. Realistically, it was unlikely the car had been reported in yet as abandoned, sitting in the parking lot of the

Greyhound station along with the cars of all the other bus travelers. Still, I was in a paranoid mood, hardly to be blamed, and my paranoia was only going to get worse.

The second rental outfit I came to was out of anything suitable, but the third one had a mid-sized sedan with a functioning air conditioner and an AM/FM radio, and they'd take a credit card for the rental and insurance. That worked for me; I was hardly in a mood or position to be picky.

A half-hour later I was on the road, heading east into the flat, barren wastes of West Texas, hurrying to an appointment in my own personal Samara.

A couple of hours into the trip, my bladder about to burst and the grumbling in my gut telling me I had better eat something soon, I pulled into a roadside truck stop to look for a restroom and food, in that order. I managed to meet both of my requirements, though just barely; the restroom a far cry from what I'd call restful, and the sandwiches I ate only food in the broadest sense of the word. Still, I choked it down as quickly as I could, dropped another twenty on cigarettes and sodas for the road, and headed back out to the car. There was a payphone next to the door, and I figured that if I was going to try to assuage my fears with a call to Amador, this was the time to do it. I knew he would come through for me, but at this point every bit of reassurance would help.

My collect call to his house went unanswered, and at his office I just got voicemail. I decided against leaving a message, figuring it might cause problems. You never knew who might be listening in. At this point, I was half convinced that every phone line in the state was tapped, even those to the FBI offices where Amador was.

Back in the car and on the road I switched on the radio, hoping a bit of music might keep my mind off of things. After an hour of Puro Tejano, the lie was put to that little theory. For the most part. I was still expecting the worst, but now I was expecting it to come accompanied by the maddening sounds of a non-stop accordion.

The fax I'd got from Michelle the night before hadn't cleared up much for me, and I was hardly surprised. If anything, I was even more at sea than I had been before. As I drove, I ran through what I knew over and over, and was more confused every time I did.

There was the book, which contained on at least one page of writing about some secret cult, with ties to the mythological figure of Prometheus. The notes Michelle had scribbled in the margins of her translation indicated that Aeschylus, the writer of the play, had been censured at least, and possibly even killed, because he had exposed secrets of this Cult of the Light Bringer in the action and dialogue of his play. There was some mention made of the stained hands of the cult members, which set off in Michelle a cascade of associations, leading to the article clippings and Xeroxes of encyclopedia articles she'd sent along. A whole laundry list of "light bringer" deities throughout world mythology, and references to secret organizations reported to be known by the symbol of the stained hand. Or by black hands.

This is where my train of thought started to derail, and everything stopped making sense all together. A number of the articles Michelle had sent along concerned secret organizations from various nations whose names, when translated into English, meant more or less "The Black Hands." Thinking about the odd history my grandfather and his family had with that term, and all of the crazy legends and stories boxed up in my inheritance, I found it pretty hard to swallow that this was all some giant coincidence. Still, I was completely unable to come up with anything resembling a rational explanation, or any sort of causal relationship between them. What were the chances that the weird shit my grandfather had collected during his declining years of senility had anything to do with the story I was working on and the mysteries I found myself drowning in, much less that I would stumble across them all at around the same time? Slim and fucking none. Still, the fact remained that I had found the term in places and situations so far apart that they couldn't possibly be connected, so coincidence seemed the only possible answer.

In the interests of saving what little sanity I had left, I decided that the only acceptable answer was that my grandfather's family had a generations-long lunatic obsession with dressing up and playing masked hero, which may or may not have included my grandfather himself, and that it was just a weird bit of synchronicity that they chose a name sometimes associated with this Greek cult. A nagging voice at the back of my mind kept asking about that "Cult of the Black Hand" mentioned in that Middle English ballad, but I hadn't made it this far in life not being able to ignore the voices in my head, so that voice went unanswered. The simplest answer was best, and that was all there was to it.

I arrived in San Antonio ahead of schedule, hours before the scheduled meet. Parking in a pay lot a half-dozen blocks from the Alamo, I collected my things, putting a pack of cigarettes into each pocket, and hefted the Sears shopping bag with the book. I suppose I could have passed for a tourist in a pinch. Seedy tourist, with a fear-of-God look on his face, but tourist nonetheless.

I made my way to the Alamo in a hurry, not that I had any reason to rush. I had hours to wait, and it was only force of habit that led me to arrange a meeting in an open place where I could while the hours ahead of time scouting the area, watching for possible traps and potential backdoor exits. I knew a spot at the edge of the Alamo Plaza where I could squirrel myself away on a bench in a corner, keep an eye on the whole scene, and not be spotted. It didn't hurt that the spot was a coffee shop that served the best pastries I'd had outside of Paris and San Francisco, and where their coffee was served black and bottomless. I was jittery and nervous enough as it was; the coffee was bound to be no help at all.

An hour and a half-dozen cups of coffee later, I was proved right. My paranoia had kicked into overdrive and my thoughts just couldn't stay still. I was having no problem keeping to my seat, though; I'd poured enough coffee into me that if I stood up, I'd be having to empty my bladder every fifteen minutes. At least sitting down I could keep my mind off of it.

Paranoia was getting the better of me. I had to fight to resist the temptation to try Amador on the phone again, to call Cachelle to see how Tan was doing, or to run screaming for fear of what might happen for that matter. My thoughts ran in tight circles around the mysteries I couldn't seem to solve, the questions which bred like rabbits, one after the other.

I also couldn't stop checking on the book, leaving it first on the ground against my left foot, then holding it on the ground between my feet, and finally ending up with it on my lap. Every few minutes I gripped the edges of the book through the paper of the Sears shopping bag, as though it might have disappeared. I tried to do it unobtrusively so as not to draw attention to myself, or to it. But I couldn't help myself.

Finally, I took to opening the bag and peeking inside. The disk on the front of the thing intrigued me. It looked like silver, mirror bright, but seemed to shift as the light hit it. There seemed to be a spiral motif engraved on it, or it might have been the grain of the metal. Either way, as I moved my head from side to side slightly it looked something like a spinning pinwheel of metal, or silvery water running down a drain.

I wondered what sort of metal it was, to be untarnished after so many years. The clasps that held the book closed were of iron, it seemed, and looked every century of however many hundreds or thousands of years old the thing was. The metal disk, though, looked newly minted, like a silver dollar fresh off the presses. It couldn't be any newer than the rest of the book, though, because it looked as though the leather of the cover was cut around it, like it had been built up around the thing.

I started to wonder if I could even smudge or mar the thing if I wanted to. If I touched it, would it leave a print, or would it impervious even to that? And just what did the symbol mean – if it was a symbol – the curving spiral vortex? And why was it on the book in the first place?

My head buzzing with questions, I reached into the bag, my palm grazing the silver disk. As I watched, the illusion of movement increased, and it looked as though the disk was a living, moving whirlpool of metal.

And the world opened up, and the spiral swallowed me whole.

And the world opened up…

And the spiral swallowed me whole…

And the world opened…

And the spiral swallowed…

And the world…

And the spiral…

And…

I was standing on a featureless white plain, unable to distinguish any features, unable to see horizon or sky, walls or ceiling. San Antonio, the Alamo, the coffee and the pastries, the whole world… all of it was gone. Silence roared in my ears, and to my surprise the fear in my gut was gone, my hands firm and still. I looked down at myself, the only thing visible on which I could focus, and saw that my clothes were neat and clean, my boots shiny and new. I was polished and immaculate, free of sickness or fear.

I tried to take a step forward, but even though I could see my feet move below me, I didn't experience any sensation of motion. No feeling of kinesis. Without any landmarks, only featureless white in every direction, I had no point of reference. I crouched down and tried to touch the ground, but felt nothing. Patting my legs and chest and slapping my hands together, I could still feel the fabric of my pants and jacket, could feel the stinging of the slap, but the ground of whatever it was couldn't be felt any more than it could be seen. It was a blank to all of my senses.

"Well," I said aloud, my voice sounding small and distant in my ears, "this is either the afterlife, an experiment in sensory deprivation, or the last stages of madness. I'm not sure which I'd prefer."

I tried to take a few more steps forward, jumped to the side, and hopped up and down in place; anything to feel some sort of difference. Nothing.

"Okay," I said as loud as I could, "I'll bite. What the hell is going on here?"

A voice answered, loud enough to rattle my teeth, coming from everywhere and nowhere.

"A QUESTION," it said.

This was the voice that scared the crap out of Chuck Heston in *The Ten Commandments*, this was the voice that every super alien in *Star Trek* shared. This was loud, deep, and resonant, and sounded like the bells of final judgment. This was the voice of thunder.

"Right," I said, more than a little uneasy, looking up as though it would do any good. I wondered if this was how all the other lunatics felt, when the voices in their heads finally started answering back. "So where's my answer?"

The voice didn't speak, but suddenly directly in front of me hovered an enormous disk, liquid silver and churning in a rotating spiral. Without any frame of reference, it was impossible to tell how big; it could either have been ten feet tall and ten feet away, or a hundred yards tall a hundred yards away. Either way, it looked big. Stretching my arms tentatively forward, I couldn't reach it. Like a giant pool of mercury running down a drain, though I couldn't remember which way it went in which hemisphere. This one ran counterclockwise, whichever hemisphere that meant. And it was familiar.

"I get it," I said. "It's the same as the thing on the book, the one in the Sears bag. Is that what this is about? Did the disk do something to me when I touched it?" I ran through the possibilities in my head: coated with fast-acting hallucinogens, maybe, or possibly some weirdo superscientific virtual reality trigger. Nothing made sense, but then nothing about where I was standing was making much sense, so that was par for the course.

"A QUESTION," the voice said again, my teeth on edge.

"Two, actually," I started, and then got quiet as the spirally disk in front of me changed again. It seemed to shrink, or recede, one of the two, and then the image of the book's cover appeared, the disk set right on the cover. It looked so close I could reach out and take it, but when I tried I caught only air. I took a few quick steps forward, and the perspective on the book didn't change, coming no nearer, growing no larger. The things I was seeing must just be images, then, or else real objects hovering always just out of reach.

"Right," I said again, "I got that. The disk on the book. Sure. But what is it? And who are you? What the hell is this all about?"

I felt strangely calm. My emotional state was a like the environment, really. Flat and featureless. Maybe it was part of the process, part of whatever drug or technology or mumbo-jumbo was making me see and experience all of this in the first place. I realized, for the first time, that I really should be a lot more freaked out that I was.

"A QUESTION," the voice boomed again, and I was beginning to wonder if he knew any other words. Then he proved me wrong, adding, "BEHOLD, AND LET YOUR EYES BE OPENED."

I shrugged. This was having the same emotional impact as a late night TV infomercial, so I was sure somebody was monkeying with my reactions somewhere.

I didn't have time to worry about it much longer. The image of the disk on the book grew bigger again, or closer, or closer and bigger at the same time, the book dropping away and disappearing and the mercury spiral coming so near and so large that it blocked out my view of everything else. I got a horrible feeling of déjà vu, and then the spiral opened up, and swallowed me whole.

And the spiral opened up...

And swallowed me whole...

And the spiral...

And...

I was elsewhere, now, somewhere on another order of magnitude, and I seemed to have left my body behind. I was in a new environment, but though I could see and hear and feel and taste, if I tried to find my hands, or legs, or touch or see any part of my body, I came up empty. I was a disembodied set of sensations, floating in mid air, like the POV of a movie camera in some Hollywood blockbuster. That was weird enough; what came next put it to shame.

I was looking at a mammoth city of crystal towers and spires, floating on a glittering sea of stars, with an arching sky of blinding light overhead shaded from one end of the spectrum to another, a rolling, vivid rainbow of burning color. I knew, beyond a shadow of doubt, that I was looking at the Crystal City. I knew the names of the towers and spires, knew who lived in each room, knew the names of each of the vivid points of light in the sea of stars, knew the patterns and movements of all the colors overhead.

I was working on dream logic. I had only to look at a thing, and I knew everything there was to know about it. Impossible knowledge appeared in my thoughts as though just remembered, like I'd always known it but had forgotten until just that moment.

Was this what the disk did? It was like moving into a vivid, three-dimensional hypertext, where I selected object by sight and was privy immediately to everything there was to know about it. Where had the disk come from? I thought again. Who had made it?

As though in response to my voiceless question, my perspective changed. My point of view rushed towards the city, in over the sea of stars, through the glistening towers, to a spire that stood taller than almost all others in the city. I looked at it and knew it to be home to the Messenger of Mysteries. It was home to Raziel.

Blink, and I was inside the spire, in a room made of crystal, walls and floor glowing with living flames, and the ceiling open to the burning sky of colors above. The room was empty of furniture or decoration, without doors or windows. Only the open sky above, the walls of burning crystal, and the figure standing at the center of the room, head bowed.

I looked at it. Even though I could only see the figure's back, I immediately recognized Raziel. The messengers, I knew at that moment, did not have names, not as we think of them at any rate. The messengers had functions. Raphael, the Messenger of Healing. Uriel, the Messenger of Fire. Gabriel, the Messenger of Strength.

Raziel, the figure in the crystal room, back to me, was the Messenger given dominion over Mysteries, over Secrets. Only Raziel, of all the Host in the Crystal City, was privy to the secret plans of the Name, only Raziel the Almighty's one true confidant. Raziel knew what the Name had in store for each of its subjects, great and small, and it was at times almost too great a burden to carry.

I wondered what this messenger looked like, who I now knew as closely as myself. I blinked, and my point of view shifted again. Looking at Raziel before me, I saw the most perfect creature I had ever seen. Flawless and pristine, the face I saw was the untouched ideal for every sculptor and every painter who had ever tried to capture beauty, and I knew now that they all had failed. This was a vision of utter untouched perfection, and I ached to see it.

I knew, though, that had I looked upon the face of Uriel, or Raphael, or Sidquel, or Hasdiel or any other of the countless legions of messengers in the Crystal City, I would have been looking at the same face. The faces of messengers were mirrors, I suddenly knew, that reflected the light of the Name. One was the same as another, so long as they all stood in the Presence. Only by turning from the Name would they lose their pristine beauty.

But wasn't Raziel turned from the Name now? Face turned towards the floor?

No, I realized. The Name was not in one place in the Crystal City, sitting on a throne in some tower or other. The city was the Name, and all who dwelt in it bathed in its presence, breathed it in with every breath. You could not look anywhere in the Crystal City and look anywhere but on the face of the Name.

But Raziel was trying to look away, or thinking of doing so. The latest of the Mysteries to be revealed, the latest plans the Name had made, troubled Raziel.

The Name had turned its attention to the World.

The World, with beginning and end, was completely unlike the eternal perfection of the Crystal City. In the World, creatures were born, grew and died, without ever knowing firsthand the radiant splendor of the Presence. They had only hints and glimpses, if they were lucky, of the glory of the Name. Impossible to conceive for a messenger like Raziel, who had never once felt the absence of the Name's love. Worse yet, though, it was the Name's intention the inhabitants of the World would be forced to *choose* whether to accept the love of the Name or not. They would be able to turn forever away from the Presence and never feel it again.

What would the alternative be? What would someone choose over the warming radiance and the eternal grace of the Name?

That was the Mystery revealed to Raziel, the Secret that burned deep in the messenger's thoughts.

There was to be a revolt, a war in the Crystal City.

The Name had already decided.

Blink.

Blink again, and Raziel was leaving the spire, floating up over the city. I followed.

Though it had no wings, Raziel flew over the whole of the Crystal City, and I followed. Passing the messengers in their places, passing messengers flying on their way, I knew as Raziel knew which were destined by the Name to turn against It in the coming revolt, which where destined to lose their way and fall. Azazel, Sariel, Barakel, and all the others.

Finally, Raziel came to the tower of Sammael, the Messenger of Death. Sammael, who loved the Name as much as any messenger in the hosts, and was more loved by the Name than most. Sammael, who would lead the revolt and take the role of Adversary in the World. Sammael, who would become the tempter.

"Welcome, O Messenger of the Mysteries," said Sammael, as Raziel alighted on the tower.

"Greetings, Beloved Messenger of Death," replied Raziel, head inclined in respect.

"What brings the great keeper of the secrets to my humble tower?"

"It is of a secret I would speak to you," answered Raziel, "though my heart trembles at the thought."

Sammael, I could see, was taken aback by this. The two messengers looked enough alike to be twins, but there seemed something more open and loving in the face of Sammael. Raziel's face showed only worry, and the strain of secrets he couldn't bear to keep.

"Why?" Sammael was confused. "My dominion is over life and its end. I've nothing to do with secrets."

"This secret, though, has something to do with you."

Blink.

Blink again, and I knew that Raziel had told Sammael of the secret, that the divine plan had been revealed, and the role of the Messenger of Death in the coming war made known.

I looked at Sammael and saw a great change.

"I would not revolt!" cried the Messenger of Death. "What have I done to displease our Lord, that It would choose me for such a role? To spend an eternity turned from the Presence, tempting these pathetic creatures away from Its grace?"

"It is the Name's plan," answered the Messenger of Mysteries, "and it is ineffable."

Sammael paced the crystal floor of the tower room, hands clenched.

"I won't do it," Sammael announced firmly, head shaking from side to side. "I won't revolt. I will refuse to take part, and stay here in the Presence, never to turn away."

Raziel nodded. It was as hoped. Without Sammael to lead the revolt, there would be no war in heaven, and the creatures of the World would exist without temptation, each able to follow their own path unhindered. Without the interference of the legion of the fallen, as Raziel had seen in the divine plan, the creatures of the World would have true freedom of choice and would be able to come to the grace of the Name unencumbered by the treacheries of the Adversary. The divine plan would be disrupted, but in the end the divine purpose would be served, generations of the World's creatures choosing to worship the Name of their own free will.

The expression on Sammael's face soured as Raziel and I watched, and the Messenger of Death continued.

"But will It not punish me," Sammael went on, "for refusing my place in the divine plan? Will It not then cast me down, merely for choosing to worship It instead of rebelling against It? And am I not now rebelling, in my own way, for rejecting Its will?"

The Messenger of Death, one hand striking the other, prowled the room, reminding me of a caged panther testing the borders of his prison.

"This is not fair!" shouted Sammael. "To have spent an eternity in loyal service and be cast aside for the sake of some lunatic scheme."

"Have a care," Raziel replied. "It is still our Lord, and we dwell in Its mercy."

"Its mercy can go hang," Sammael answered. "It is lunatic, which you must see to have revealed these plans to me. You must agree, O Messenger of Mysteries, to have broken your covenant with the Name!"

Raziel fell back a step, expression confused.

"But..." the Messenger of Mysteries began, "I had no wish to offend our Lord. I had only wished better to serve It. There was a flaw in Its divine plan, it seemed to me, which I could resolve to Its better uses."

"A flaw?" sneered Sammael. "Then you admit that the Name is capable of error, to have produced something imperfect. Perhaps it has always been imperfect and flawed itself, only we have been blinded too much by Its power and our overmuch devotion to see it for ourselves. Perhaps It has bred that blindness into us! What proof have we that the Name created the World in the first place? The Name created the Crystal City and those who dwell within it, and we are Its creatures, but who is to say that It did not simply come upon the World already hanging like a jewel in the void? We messengers were created to turn our faces always towards the Name, and all that we know about what lies without the Crystal City is what *It* wills that we know."

"Sammael, please..." Raziel tried to interrupt.

"The Name is the Almighty Lord of the Crystal City," Sammael continued, undeterred, but perhaps the time has come for a new Almighty. Perhaps the time has come for a change."

Raziel opened its mouth to speak, but the Messenger of Death did not notice.

"I will speak to the others of this," Sammael answered. "There are some who will see what we have seen, and join with me to correct these errors. We shall finds the flaws and imperfections all, and root them out."

Sammael extended a hand towards Raziel.

"Will you join me?" the Messenger of Death answered.

"No!" shouted Raziel, confused. "I cannot. You cannot. This is not right. This is what I sought to avoid..."

Sammael cut Raziel off, angrily.

"Fine," Sammael barked, "it is always your choice. But remember this, O Messenger of Mysteries. Any who do not stand with me in my purpose stand against me. Sibling or not, I will not abide any who stand against me."

Sammael turned from Raziel and sped from the tower, off to seek others to join in the revolt.

Blink.

I blinked again, and Raziel was back in the crystal spire with the burning walls, eyes turned again to the floor.

I knew in that instant that Raziel had discovered the role the Messenger of Mysteries was to play in the coming revolt, the one divine secret previously unrevealed. It was Raziel who was to incite the Messenger of Death to rebel, Raziel who was to set in motion the first volley in the war that would rage through the Crystal City. In going to Sammael, and trying to prevent the war from beginning, Raziel had only been playing the role set down in the divine plan, working the Name's will. The war would come, and soon, and in some small way it would be Raziel's fault.

"No more," Raziel said, eyes turning towards the roil of color overhead. "This is unfair, even if it *is* the Name's own will. I will have no part in it."

"Nor should you," I heard a voice from the other side of the crystal room call.

Raziel turned, and my point of view followed along behind.

On the far side of the room, standing against the burning wall, was another messenger. At first I thought it was Sammael, come again to tempt Raziel to the revolt, but then I realized that this was another, kinder messenger. This was Thelesis, who had dominion over Free Will.

"What would you of me, O Messenger of Free Will?" asked Raziel, crossing the room to where the other stood.

"You have made a decision, and it is my purview to oversee it," answered Thelesis.

"Am I to be punished?" asked Raziel. "Are you to report my misdeed to the hosts, and witness to the Almighty of my transgression? For choosing a course counter to the will of our Lord?"

"Hardly, Beloved Messenger of Mysteries," answered Thelesis. "I have come to join you." A slight smile played on the messenger's face, the most beautiful and perfect expression I had ever seen.

Looking on the two together, I understood why Thelesis had come, and what need Raziel would have for the Messenger of Free Will. If any who dwelt in the Crystal City would agree with Raziel's view of the divine plan, I realized, it would be Thelesis. Free will, in Raziel's view, would become in the World a lie, a sham, a pretense for the celestial chess game that would play itself out between the armies of the Name and the armies of the Adversary. The two powers would vie for the attention and loyalties of the creatures of the World, and in doing so would deny them the true freedom to choose their fate. Coerced one way or another, through plans they would never glimpse or guess at, the creatures of the World would be little more than pawns in the game of forces beyond their reach. In Raziel's eyes, the risk that they would never know the love of the Almighty was too great. The rules of the game would have to be changed. And for that, Raziel would need the help of just one other messenger. Raziel would need the help of Free Will.

Raziel smiled in return and took Thelesis's hand in a firm grip.

"Then let us leave," said Raziel, stepping forward. "Let us leave the hosts and the city and the coming war behind and find our way somewhere beyond the schemes of the Name."

"Let us leave," agreed Thelesis.

The messengers drew closer together, rising slightly in the air. They turned slightly, hand in hand, and vanished from sight without a sound.

Blink.

Blink again, and the messengers were floating in a formless void, hands still clasped together.

The void was Kaos.

Kaos, the primordial absence of life, of heat, of light, against which the city of crystal hung like a diamond against black velvet. It was empty and vast, and it was the new home of Raziel and Thelesis.

The two messengers, hanging motionless in the void, waited for the war to begin. From their vantage point they could look upon the home of the messengers, where even now I could see flashes of light spearing out into the darkness. The revolt had begun, Sammael leading the revolutionary faction in its charge. The Name's forces, led by the Messenger of the Name, Michael, would be repelling the attack, taking heavy casualties, but in the end driving Sammael and the others from the Crystal City.

From far across the void, Raziel and Thelesis saw their sibling messengers falling, pouring like a cascade of burning stars from the city of crystal out into the darkness. Forever they seemed to fall, through the timeless void, until they reached at last the place appointed for them, the dark mirror of the Crystal City: the Grave.

The Two, Raziel and Thelesis, watched all of this without comment, neither wanting to be the first to speak. In silence they watched the revolt, the progress of the war, the losers' fall and their inevitable end. Not until it was done, and the city of crystal returned to normal, the dark valleys of the Grave finding their final shape, did Raziel speak.

"The war is through," the Messenger of Secrets said. "Now the game has begun."

The two messengers turned their faces away from the Name, and for the first time cast their gazes upon the World, hovering in the Void.

From their vantage point, the whole of the World could be seen at once, both physically and temporally – the full reach of the universe, galaxies without number and distances stretching out so far they bent back upon themselves. And not just Space, but Time, a function of the World which Raziel and Thelesis had never before experienced, was also laid out for them. The two messengers could see all of the ever-branching paths, from the white-hot beginnings with the first cries of the World's birth to the final frigid echoes of its death rattle.

Taken as a whole, it looked like nothing so much as a brilliant glass globe in which swirled figures of light and shadow that danced faster than the eye could imagine. The patterns changed as I watched, again and again, but one theme was constant throughout. The images spiraled, always spiraling, like planets in their orbits, turning in their course as worlds were born and died, as whole epochs of civilization waxed and waned.

Seeing this, and all that would happen, Raziel knew it had done right. In the Crystal City, the messengers, their faces turned always to their creator, even when away doing Its work, were denied Its vision, and so to them the plan remained ineffable. To the Messengers of Mysteries and of Free Will, though, it was all very plain; they saw the scheme, and what they had to do.

Better to understand the World, and to be accustomed to the pitch and yaw of Space and Time, to Gravity and the other Laws, the Two created for themselves another world, set off in the void, as identical to the real world as they could make it. It was the same as the World, in more ways that not, but it was empty of life; of the trackless, almost infinite expanses of their boundless reality; only that part in which Raziel or Thelesis moved knew life.

And I watched as they introduced into their notional realm, this Otherworld, the same Laws that govern the World, or rather that the World itself lays down. There, in their Otherworld, feeling gravity's pull and the seconds swirling past, the Two waited and watched the World.

Denied the panoramic view of the far void, they saw history now as it happened. The Earth cooled, its waters collected into seas and oceans, the hot belly belching up mountains. They watched the first life emerge, tentatively, testing the World as a child tests the water in a spring lake with a toe. They watched life develop and grow, taking on the many guises they had glimpsed from the void.

They were, of course, still much as the messengers in the Crystal City, since even the ravages of time and space can do little to the Children of the Name. They were without distinguishing features and without sex, each looking enough like the other that they could have been a mirror's image. As life progressed, they watched.

Wanting to grow closer to life, to gain understanding through imitation, they mimicked the habits of the living creatures. Swimming in nutrient soups in their world's oceans, drawing in sustenance through their extremities; gliding along by waving the cilia they grew, groping for light and warmth.

As life developed, their interest grew, and so more closely did they imitate. Using teeth to chew and hands to grasp and feet for walking rather than just perching. When the pongoids first appeared, the hairy apes so close in appearance to the messengers themselves and yet still rougher, harsher, they decided to take a final step. Seeing how life continued, and recreated itself, they chose sex for themselves. After that thought, there stood on that empty world not two identical messengers, but a man and a woman, as similar as brother and sister.

Raziel turned to Thelesis and took her hand in his. He led her through the forests of their Otherworld, to the valley they had chosen to be their home.

They discovered passion then, the hot, involved intimacy that two sexed creatures can know, and they learned something else. Love.

In the Crystal City the messengers love each other as a matter of course, but only through their love for the Name, seeing in each other an aspect and reflection of their creator. But the two messengers on their little world learned a different love, less perfect, more mutable, the love for another in and of themselves. In that moment, if not before, they became truly flawed, no longer perfect, as much living creatures as immortal celestials. In time their love bore fruit and, with the tender aid of Raziel, Thelesis brought forth the first of their children. A daughter, whom they named Anael, after their love.

The hairy apes of the World grew, becoming more like the messengers with each passing generation, until at last the Name took one among them and placed him in a secret place. In that garden paradise, the Name taught him to speak and to reason, named him man, and put the garden into his care.

In time, the man Adam grew lonely. A wife was given to him, and together the man and the woman lived in harmony in the garden.

From the Otherworld, Raziel and Thelesis watched, as their daughter grew tall and strong beside them.

Blink.

The images flying past slowed, and I came again to my self. It took me some time to remember myself, so lost in the pageant had I become. It was the voice of Free Will who woke me to myself again, sounding from the Otherworld.

"It ends soon," Thelesis said to her husband Raziel. Their daughter was nearby, engrossed in the epic struggles of an ant colony fighting to extend their empire nearby. Anael could understand the speech of the ants, barking orders back and forth between them; she could understand the speech of all the living creatures Raziel had brought from the World to their home for her to study.

"Yes," answered Raziel at last, turning to his wife. He had been lost in watching his daughter at play, as much engrossed in his study of her as she had been in hers of the ants. The messengers had not known children in the Crystal City, each of them born fully formed and prefect at the merest thought from the Name. A child was a mystery, even to him.

"Then it will be time for you to act?" Thelesis asked, lowering her eyes slightly at her husband.

"As we have planned," Raziel answered, his tone betraying his fears. "They will be tested, first one and then the other, with the trials of Free Will. If they act as the Name expects, they will find themselves driven from their home, and driven from the sheltering arms of their god."

"And made prey for the temptations of the Adversary," Thelesis added.

"Just so," agreed Raziel.

Thelesis stood and walked to her husband's side.

"Is your own little act of creation complete?" she asked, her tone gentle. "Have you completed the gift?"

Raziel lowered his eyes. "Yes, though it threatened to drain the life from me. It is done, and ready for its purpose, should the need arise. Should the man and the woman be driven from the garden and out into the world."

"They will," answered Thelesis confidently, a slight smile on her lips. "It is a question of Free Will, after all."

I blinked, and time passed again.

Raziel and Thelesis stood together now, looking upon the World. Anael was a short distance off, in a heated discussion with a lion. A lamb stood nervously a short distance away, keeping its eyes on the lion and Anael both. The daughter of the Two looked older now, more like her mother than before, but with something of her father's severity around her eyes. She was not alone now, either, it seemed, as I could see three infants of close ages, all boys, crawling around and between their parents' feet.

"Now," said Raziel, his expression grave, "it comes."

"I told you so," replied Thelesis, threading her arm under his.

From the Otherworld, the Two could see the man and the woman, finally tested by free will, ejected from the garden. They had made their choice, and the consequences were theirs to live with from that day onwards.

The garden was closed to them as they exited, the entrance guarded by the flaming sword of a messenger from Crystal City until it could be sealed off to the outside world forever.

"They are Sammael's now," Raziel said. "They are the Adversary's."

"Or the Name's," reminded Thelesis, "should they be coerced to It."

"Either way," answered Raziel, "they will not be free. Not truly, until they can make their choices of their own volition, temptation or divine intervention aside."

"Agreed," said Thelesis. "So you will be going, then? To bring your gift to them?"

Raziel nodded, silent, and held his wife closer to him.

I watched as Raziel moved away, stopping to rest a hand on the shoulder of his daughter, who paused briefly in her discussion with the lion. He continued on to a pillar of carved stone. From a cavity cut in one side, he drew out a small wrapped object the size of his open palm, holding it delicately.

Raziel whispered a word I couldn't make out, and a glittering sphere appeared in the air in front of him. It stood taller than Raziel himself, though not by much, and looked like a shining globe filled with stars. Turning to look one last time at his wife and children, and clutching the wrapped object to his chest, he stepped into the sphere and was gone.

I wanted to know where Raziel had gone. My perspective followed.

Raziel sat on an outcropping of rock on the side of a large mountain, the sky a brilliant blue overhead, the sun warming his skin. He sat casually on the rock, back against the rising mountain, looking out over the plains below. The wrapped object rested on one outstretched hand, held before him, as though offering it to someone.

I wondered who. And then I knew.

This mountain, which later generations would name Horeb, stood on the World, the original of which the Otherworld was the duplicate. Raziel had come here from his home across the void to bring a gift to the living creatures, to deliver them from the games of Celestial Chessmen.

A man appeared on the mountainside before Raziel, scuffed and bruised from his climb. Not a man, I realized looking upon him, but The man.

"You called me," the man said, and I could understand every word. He found his footing on the sliding gravel of the mountain, and stood proudly facing messenger.

"I did," Raziel answered, smiling. "I come to offer you a choice, O Man."

The man shifted warily, casting a glance back down the mountain to the plains below, where his wife was busy looking after their two infant sons. He knew all about choices, and about their consequences. They were far, far away from the garden now.

"I have come to make a gift of knowledge," Raziel added, and Adam stiffened still.

"There is work to be done," the man replied, beginning to turn. "I have had enough of knowledge, enough to last a long life."

"Wait a moment," Raziel answered, beginning to unwrap the object. "This knowledge is a tool, not a test, and can be used or discarded at your whim."

The man narrowed his eyes.

"Who are you?" he asked. "An agent of our Lord? Or another aspect of the Tempter in the garden? Which direction do you drive me with your intrigues, to Heaven or to Hell?"

"Neither," Raziel answered, smiling, and held forth his gift.

It was a silver disk, mirror-bright, bearing on it an image of the World as seen from the void beyond, spiraling like a living thing beneath the metallic sheen. I found I could not direct my attention away from it.

"This is a key to hidden mysteries," Raziel explained, turning the disk in his hands, "opening doors to secrets undreamt. Into this emblem have I put a portion of myself, a fragment of my being and wisdom containing the sum of all that I have seen and learned. In it, you will find the answers to every question you could ever conceive of asking, the history of your world from beginning to end, from first light of dawn till the final crack of doom. If you take it from my hands and use it all the days of your life, you will be a free creature, able to ferret out deception and coercion and face the world with eyes open. Never again will you and yours be pawns in the games and tests of the Name or the Tempter, driven towards either the Crystal City or the Grave. You will have the heavier burden of choosing your own road, and living with the consequences."

The man walked slowly forward, his eyes locked on the silver disk in the messenger's hands.

"This is a trick," the man said, but he didn't believe it.

"It is not a trick," Raziel answered. "It is a choice."

The man looked from the silver disk, to the messenger Raziel, to the disk and back again.

"To live free," the man said, "would be a good thing." He smiled, a little sadly, and took the disk from the messenger's hands.

Raziel smiled, but as I watched the image of the messenger and the first man on the mountain side wavered, slightly at first and then spinning and rippling with greater and greater speed. I felt dizzy and lost as the world in front of me became a roiling spiral of motion and light.

And the world opened up, and the spiral swallowed me whole.

And the spiral swallowed me…

And the spiral…

And…

I was back on the featureless white plain, and when I reached up to rub my eyes cartoonishly was surprised to find I had hands again. Hands to rub with, and eyes to rub. I patted myself down and was satisfied everything seemed to be in order.

It also seemed like my emotions were back in working order again. All through the show, I'd been a pretty passive observer, like my reactions were being tamped down, but now I was starting to feel like myself again.

"Alright," I said out loud, "let me see if I have this straight. There's something out there that might be the Judeo-Christian God, or might just be some extradimensional all-powerful whatchamacallit, and either way it's got a city full of angelic messengers created to do its bidding. And a couple of these angel-types turned anarchist and took off on their own, made a magic silver disk, and gave it to man. And now it's on the front of the book."

I was skeptic enough not to accept at face value that one of the world's set of mythologies had an inside line on being true. For all I knew the villain of the piece had it right, and what had passed itself off as "God" to a bunch of Semitic nomads thousands of years ago was just an interloper from hyperspace and not the "creator" at all. It was academic at this point, though, because clearly *something* had been around and messed with humanity.

Whatever it was, the booming voice wasn't talking. Or maybe it was just waiting for me to ask it something.

"So who are you, mystery voice? Are you the angel? The disk? What?"

"YES," boomed the voice from everywhere and nowhere.

"Great," I answered under my breath. "So how did this little magic dingus that knows all end up on the cover of a moth-eaten old book? And who wrote in the book in the first place?"

"A QUESTION," the voice boomed, "BEHOLD, AND–"

This was starting to sound familiar.

"Wait, wait," I shouted, waving my arms. "Don't do the whole super-Imax total immersion show again! I think one ride on that coaster is enough for one lifetime." I rubbed my hands together. "Is there anyway you could, I don't know, just answer my questions?"

There was silence for a moment, and I fancied the voice was off somewhere thinking things over.

"I think I can answer your questions," said a more human sounding voice from behind me. "If you prefer a more mundane approach."

I wheeled, startled, and standing there before me was the messenger from the story, the one who split heaven and tried to change the rules.

"Are you..." I started, nervously. "That is, you aren't a... you know..."

"A messenger?" said the figure before me, smiling openly. "No," he added with a shake of his head. "I am the emblem itself, the disk of which you speak. Or an aspect of it, at any rate."

I looked him from head to toe. He was a bit taller than me, as perfect an image of human beauty as the messengers had seemed in the Crystal City, dressed simply in a blinding white suit.

"Wait," I said, "you mean you're the guy with the booming voice." I waved my arm overhead. "The sound of thunder with the limited syntax?"

The figure in front of me smiled again.

"In part, yes," he answered, "and in part, no. There are many aspects to the Sefer Raziel, all parts of the whole."

"The Sefer Raziel?" I asked.

"The book of secrets," he answered. "The Book of Raziel. That was what the sons of the first man came to call Raziel's gift. The name was remembered ever after, though in time most had forgotten its true meaning."

I started to pace back and forth, the figure before me finally providing a point of reference. It was nice to be able to move again, in my own body at last.

"Okay, so answer my questions already, if you can," I said. "What happened to the disk after the 'first man' got it? How did it end up on the book?"

The image of Raziel seemed to think for a moment, and then answered.

"This book of secrets," he began, "this Sefer Raziel, made free creatures of the first man and his family. Their sons grew tall and strong, schooled by their father in the mysteries of the Sefer Raziel, free from the influences of the divine or demonic. When one of the first man's sons chose to slay the other, he did it of his own free will. He made his choice, and was driven from the presence of his family in consequence. He would live as an outcast, the Lord's mark upon him, but not as a pawn in the games of kings."

This was going to be story time, I could tell already. I decided to keep quiet and hear what the thing had to say.

"Anael, first born of the Two, had grown fond of the outcast son, watching the long years from the Otherworld. When he was driven out to live alone in the wilds, she found herself sleepless with worry over him and ached to see his loneliness and pain.

In the end, Anael left her parents and family on the Otherworld and traveled to the World to take as her husband the outcast son of the first man. Anael would be the first child of the Two to travel to the world of men, but she would not be the last.

"The sons and daughters of the Two, calling themselves the Children of Dawn, grew more numerous as the generations passed. Though long-lived and strong, they were with each passing generation less divine beings than their parents were. They peopled the Otherworld of their parents, learning the ways of the World, and making of their home a paradise. But they grew bored with the tedium of perfection and longed for the challenges of the flawed.

"Meanwhile, the sons of Adam kept close hold on the Sefer Raziel, and as the generations passed hid its wisdom and secrets from their brother men. Some of the Children of Dawn counseled their father Raziel to take back his gift, or else make plain a show of his power, to remind the men of the World of their place. But Raziel would not. Having broken with the divine plan and intervened in the destiny of men, he was now content to wait, and watch, seeing the World unfold before him. He would act when the time was right. Raziel was a lenient parent, though, placing no prohibitions on his children, or on their interaction with humanity. In time, more of the Children of Dawn left their homes on the Otherworld, traveling to the World to seek excitement and adventure in imperfection. The short-sighted sons of man, encountering the wandering Children of Dawn over the generations, came at last to view them as gods themselves, gods of sky and water, fire and war. Many of the Children of Dawn accepted the praise and prayers of the sons of man, setting themselves up as absolute rulers of the earth.

"The keepers of the Sefer Raziel, though, knew the truth. The silver disk, mirror-bright, showed them the truth of the world and taught them the story of Raziel, the messenger who sacrificed himself for the sake of man, who turned his back on the Crystal City and the undying love of the Name that men might live free. The light of freedom, bought at so high a price, was guarded jealously by the sons of Adam through whose hands the Sefer passed. Enoch, Noah, Solomon.

"In time, the keepers of the Sefer revealed portions of their secret knowledge to their brother men, shadows of truth to set them on the path to liberty. They encoded the secrets in the form of parables and stories, the unvarnished fact becoming veiled fiction, the thing itself becoming symbol. The Sefer Raziel became the torch of light, stolen from the heavens, the messenger Raziel the Lightbringer fallen from the skies.

"Through cultures and centuries the keepers of the Sefer moved, passing the disk from the desert-bounded sons of Israel to the water-bordered sons of Greece. Among the Greeks, the Cult of the Lightbringer was founded, the parables and symbols codified for the good of all men. To those beyond the inner circle, the Lightbringer was Prometheus, fallen Titan bound to a mountainside for his overmuch love of man; to those inducted into the secret rites of the Lightbringer, he was known as Lucetius.

"In time, along with science, mythology, and politics, the Greeks gave to the Roman conquerors the Cult of Lucetius. The Sefer Raziel itself, the cherished centerpiece of all wisdom, was kept in secret in Rome, kept close by the secret history of the work of the Cult through the centuries. The Cult of Lucetius, though, had extended its arms east into India, and further into China, and north into the lands of the Norsemen. The brothers of the cult identified each other by use of a secret symbol, a four-armed spiral set in a circle, the symbolic representation of the Sefer Raziel itself.

"Strengthening and renewing the purpose of the brothers of Lucetius, at the culmination of their secret rites and meetings the followers of the Cult would reenact symbolically the story of the Lightbringer, and of his gift to humanity. Lighting torches and repeating their sacred laws, the followers of Lucetius would go out into the world to work towards the improvement of their brother men's lot. In time, legends would arise over the boundless good will and sacrifices of this secret order of men, who fought for justice and freedom with hands stained black.

"With the rise of the Cult of Lucetius, its followers working everywhere for the liberation of their fellow men from the oppression of outside forces, the Children of Dawn found their worshippers dwindling in number, their influence on the wane. No longer able to play the great god on the hill, many were forced down into the cities and towns of men, forced to pass as brother men. They gathered power to themselves by force or coercion, having developed the taste for control. So involved became the long-lived Children of Dawn in their mundane pleasures that when they first discovered the roads to the Otherworld had been closed, they hardly seemed to care. But in time the sons and daughters of the Children of Dawn would grow weary of the World and long to return to the Otherworld. It was whispered among them that the Sefer Raziel of their first father might contain the keys to regaining the Otherworld, but over generations and continents the Children of Dawn could not locate the Sefer, so well was it hidden.

"Over the centuries, the Cult of Lucetius, now called by some the Order of the Black Hand, seemed to forget its original purpose. The Sefer, bound to the ongoing history of the Order, was cloistered away from view, seen by few, touched by almost none. The symbols and parables of the shadow teachings, devised to hide knowledge of the Sefer Raziel while sharing its wisdom, in the end eclipsed the true teachings of the Order. As the years passed, the followers of the Lightbringer were less and less in the world working their fellow man's good, and more and more hoarding power and prestige to themselves. Stories of the black-handed men who had in golden ages appeared out of shadows to fight oppression receded into legend, and then were nearly forgotten all together. The Order, splintered and secretive, grew in different lands and cultures into varied forms, with different aims, but always identified by the sign of the four-armed spiral, the torch, or the stained hand. When the book was lost at sea between the old world and a newly discovered land rich with opportunity, the Order lost its secret beating heart, and the gifts of the Lightbringer, the hope for true freedom for all living creatures, were seemingly lost forever. The Order would survive, but would resemble its first birth no more than the Grave resembled the Crystal City, becoming a dark mirror image of itself."

I stood looking at the image of the messenger for a long while before I realized he had stopped talking. It seemed that, my question answered, he had nothing more to say.

"What?" I finally asked. "Is that it? There's nothing more?"

The image of the messenger smiled slightly and nodded his head.

"Those are the answers you sought," the image replied, "when first you touched the disk. Control of the Sefer Raziel is a difficult matter, but you have done well. I hope you do as well in times to come." He paused, and then added, "For your sake."

Then the image wavered in the air like a mirage, and I braced myself. This was where I came in. The man before me was replaced by a man-sized swirl of light and color, a spiral which grew and grew until it engulfed me entirely.

And…

The first thing I noticed was the cramp in my leg, then the pain in my back, then the man in the gray suit pointing the gun in my face. I was back on the bench in the Alamo Plaza in the same position I'd been in when I reached in the bag to touch the disk. The Sears bag was still in my lap. I hadn't gone anywhere, it seemed; everything I'd seen and done taking place only someplace behind my eyes and between my ears, but I had no idea how long it had been.

"You were late meeting us, Mr. Finch," the guy with the gun said, and I recognized his voice from the phone the day before. The one who had left the note by Tan's bedside and threatened my friends.

I knew who he was, now, looking at him face to face. I'd seen him once before, with the other two gray suits at the auction in Arizona. He hadn't been pleased when I walked out with the book, but he seemed happier now.

"I hope you are well," he finally added, when it looked I had fallen mute.

"Peachy," I managed, my eyes on the barrel of his gun.

"Delightful," he answered. "Allow me to introduce myself. I am Rahab, and my companions," he gestured to the man and woman behind him, the same pair from the auction, "are Mr. Sunday and Ms. Veil."

"Charmed," I muttered.

I did my best to stay composed, but I was started to get really worried. God only knew how long I'd been lost in the Electric Kool Aid Acid Test, but Amador should have shown up long before. There should be FBI agents and cops all over the place, ready to pounce on whomever showed up to meet me. Instead, there was just this charming guy with his charming gun and companions, ready to introduce me to a bullet.

"I trust you have the item with you?" Rahab said, but I wasn't really listening. I was thinking back over what I'd seen in the disk and the things I'd been reading the past few days.

"Wait," I said, pointing at Rahab, "I know who you are. I should have remembered the name. You guys," I indicated him and his companions, "you're the Children of Dawn, right? Jesus, that's nuts. You guys really exist."

Rahab sneered.

"Flatterer," he deadpanned. "Guilty, as charged. Now please tell us where the item is, Mr. Finch. My companions and I have some traveling to do, and we'd like to get started as soon as possible."

No longer leveled out by the calming effects of the disk, this was getting to be too much to take.

"Wow," I said, sounding like a high school cheerleader. "You guys are trying to get back to that other planet, or dimension, or whatever, right? The one the two angels made. Am I right?"

Rahab took a step forward, leveling the gun.

"Our quest to reclaim our ancestral homeland is none of your concern, mayfly." He snarled, and jabbed the pistol barrel at my face. "Give me the book now, or I will simply peel it from your cold, dead hands."

"Wait a minute," I scolded. "Play the good Bond villain and answer my questions before you kill me. You tried to steal it from J. Nathan Pierce, but me you just kill outright? What, do I not rate?"

"No," came a voice to one side, "I'm afraid that was us, Mr. Finch."

Both Rahab and I turned, and I'm not sure which of us was the more surprised. My first thought was one of relief, but that didn't last long.

"Thank God," I said, seeing Amador standing just a few yards away, but my gratitude slipped pretty fast when I saw who was standing with him. The Supreme Court justices, the member of the Joint

Chiefs of Staff, and the other bigwigs from the auction. All armed with matching pistols, all smiling like the cat that just ate the canary and had the goldfish for dessert.

I knew at once what had happened. Amador was in their pocket. They'd bought him off at some point, either after the auction, or before, or even years ago for all I knew. Whoever they were, he was their man, and I was screwed.

"I'm sorry," Amador said sheepishly, looking from me to the collection of bigwigs and back again. "But I told you I wouldn't be able to help you. Why didn't you listen?"

That helped place his betrayal before the auction and my call for help, at least. Small consolation.

"Don't apologize," said one of the Supreme Court justices. "Everyone has their price. Even Finch has to agree with that."

"Sure," I said wearily. "Whatever."

I was just trying to figure out who was going to get to kill me, whiling the time watching the trio of demigods in gray point their guns at the high rollers and big wheels pointing their guns right back at them.

"So let me get this straight," I said, doing my best Columbo, trying to enjoy my last moments. "You guys," I pointed to the Supreme Court justice and friends, "hired Marconi to cop the book from Pierce, right? So why didn't you just buy it off of Pierce, if you were willing to pay?"

"We did," snarled one of the captains of industry.

"We beat them to it," answered Rahab in a lyrical voice. "After seeing the book of secrets revealed after so many long centuries on that infantile television program, my associates and I contacted him immediately to make an offer. We negotiated what all involved felt was a fair price and arranged a meeting. By the time we arrived to retrieve the item it had already been stolen, its whereabouts unknown."

"Which was you guys," I said, pointing to the bigwigs. One of them, absurdly, nodded proudly like it was all a grade school show and tell.

"So who are you guys, anyway?" I asked. "Since I'm probably about to get killed and all."

The bigwigs remained silent, Amador averting his eyes in shame.

"What?" I shouted. "Don't any of you guys go to the movies? You're supposed to explain all of this stuff before you kill the hero!"

A man in a blue pinstripe suit stepped forward from the back of the group, one of the ones who'd been at the auction. He was the one I recognized from the business pages, and now I remembered who he was. Billionaire entrepreneur and industrialist, second only to Gates and Jobs as one of the most influential figures in the world of computers. What was the name of the company he ran, again?

"We are the secret lords of the earth," he started, in the voice I remembered from the television spots. The company name started with an L. "We are the keepers of the hidden ways, who rule the rest of mankind from the shadows. We are the trunk from which branched the Freemasons, the Golden Dawn, the masters of Thule who became the Nazis, and every other society of secret mankind has known. We are the bearers of the torch, and the followers of the Lightbringer, the sacred cult of..."

"Lucetech!" I said out loud, snapping my fingers, the name finally coming to me.

The guy in the blue pinstripe suit stumbled for a moment, losing his place in his speech.

"Um, yes," he finally answered. "I was about to say the Cult of Lucetius, but Lucetech is one of our legitimate faces of business."

"Not so legitimate that it doesn't stoop to paying three-time losers like Marconi in cash and then killing him when he loses the goods, though, eh?" I jibed.

"This is pointless," Rahab shouted, gesturing with his pistol. "The secrets of the silver disk are ours by birthright, and no one but us will have them."

"The book itself is the lost history of our order," shouted back the blue pinstripe suit, "and the Sefer Raziel our key to absolute power. We have searched for it too many centuries to give it up now!"

Tensions were rising, and there was a symphony of hammers being pulled back and clips being slammed into place. This was not turning out quite as I'd hoped.

"No, I think not," said a familiar voice behind me, and everyone froze like a statue. I turned in my seat, and saw a tall man in a trench coat, with a wide black hat shading his face. I followed him with my gaze as he walked around the bench and in the midst of the firing range, and realized that no one else had budged an inch. They were literally frozen in place.

"You are all disappointments to me, to be honest," the man said, turning from the bigwigs of Lucetius to the jihad-happy Children of Dawn. "None of you are what I had hoped. To think of the potential wasted, the good you might have done."

The man raised his hand and snapped his fingers, and the pistols and guns disappeared in a flash. He snapped them again, and the two groups, now disarmed, were again free to move. None of them, though, seemed able to speak.

He turned to me, taking his hat from his head, and smiled.

"You'll forgive me these little dramatic flourishes, Mr. Finch," he said, "but I find that I have become rather melodramatic in my old age."

I knew him at once. I'd just spent countless centuries with him in the vision of the disk and talked to his image for some time after that. He was the original, the Messenger of Secrets. He was Raziel.

The Children of Dawn were getting nervous, but acting outraged to hide it. The Lucetius folks on the other side were just baffled, but doing a pretty good impression of furious all on their own. Me, I was just bewildered.

"The usefulness of the key to secrets has passed, I'm afraid," he said, addressing me. "In the dawn of man's history it served its purpose, but at this stage of development man cannot help but find ways to pervert any tool that comes into his hands, turning it to selfish ends. Men no longer need crutches, I would think, their free will inborn now as a result of the good works of those well meaning past generations. We could put it to a test, though. Yes, a test would suit perfectly."

He been talking so casually, calmly pacing back and forth, that I had almost forgotten the serious mess I'd very nearly found myself buried under. The silently mouthed protests of the groups to the left and right told me they weren't too happy with the way things were shaping up, but their inability to do anything about it meant I wasn't too worried.

It had been quiet for sometime when I realized that Raziel, the angel in the trench coat, was standing patiently in front of me, as though waiting for me to speak.

"Um, okay?" I said weakly.

"Excellent," the angel answered, gripping his hat with both hands. "Then the test is this: To whom,

Spencer Finch, will you give the book? Or will you keep it for yourself?"

I looked at him blankly for a long while, then looked first to the group of businessmen and politicians to my left, then to the group of near immortal beings to my right, and finally to the Sears bag sitting heavily on my lap.

I thought about it for a long while and couldn't come up with an answer.

"You know," I finally said, my hands resting on the shopping bag, "this thing seemed to be more trouble than its worth. These jokers…" I waved an arm at the two groups, "are just looking out for themselves, and there's every chance that whoever doesn't get it is going to come gunning for me. Hell, whoever gets it is probably going to come gunning for me, just for the sake of form. And if I keep it… well, I've taken that E-ticket ride once, thank you very much, and that was enough for me. Any other secrets or mysteries in my life can stay mysterious for all I care."

I stood up, the shopping bag gripped tight.

"If it's all the same to you, Mr. Raziel Angel Guy, I'd rather give it back to you. It is kinda yours after all, isn't it?"

The Lucetius folks and the Children of Dawn were none too pleased to hear that. A couple of them, tired of playing the silent majority, decided to make their point physically, and rushed towards me, bloody murder in their eyes. The angel just snapped his fingers again, shrugging at me apologetically for the excess, and everyone was frozen again in their spots.

"You would give it to me?" Raziel asked, looking at me and ignoring the silent screams of the groups to either side. "And sacrifice the possibility for untold knowledge, or for undreamt power or wealth? I'm sure if you were to keep it, there are many who would pay well to touch that disk just once, just for an instant."

"Yeah," I said, "but I guess that's a risk I'll have to take. Hell, it's only money."

Raziel nodded slowly, and walking forward carefully took the shopping bag from my hands. He opened it up and, reaching in, pulled out the book for everyone to see.

"This," he said, "is mine." He waved a hand over the silver disk, which popped out of the leather cover and into his hand without ever crossing through the intervening space. The cover was left smooth and unmarred, as though it had always looked that way.

Like a stage magician, Raziel waved the hand holding the silver disk once, and when the hand came to rest the disk was gone. Sent back, I guessed, to the Otherworld, or to the Void, or wherever.

"This," Raziel continued, holding up the book itself, "is yours, I should think." He handed it back to me.

"What?" I said. "Why?"

"Because only your family has continued the work begun by the sons of the first man, generations ago. Only your family, your forebears and their forebears before them have continued to struggle against oppression in all its forms, and to work towards the free and untainted existence of their fellow man."

"The Black Hand," I whispered.

"Yes," Raziel answered, nodding. "Unlike these sad dregs," he waved a hand at those to either side, "your family, with no hope of personal gain, not even knowing the true heritage of their calling, has struggled century after century for their brothers. Even you, in your way, continued the struggle."

"Um, wow," I said, back in high school cheerleader mode, unable to form a complete sentence.

"Keep the book," Raziel continued, "and these will not harm you." He waved his arm, and the two groups disappeared, like their pistols had just a few moments ago. "They are back in their appointed places and will not trouble you again. Keep the book, and honor the memory of your forebears."

I nodded mutely, taking the book from him and clutching it to my chest.

Raziel put the hat back on his head and turned to walk away.

"Someday," he said, as an afterthought, "you will have to come and see my home, come and see the

Otherworld. I've brought others of your kind there over the generations, children in distress, lost souls with nowhere else to turn. Most choose eventually to return here, to your world, but some have stayed on and made their homes there. In your search for a better world, I think you would be strengthened to see that one does exist, at least somewhere."

"Um, okay," I answered, giving a foolish little wave. I felt as though I'd just been invited over for dinner by Elvis Presley, or maybe Gandhi, and wasn't quite sure how to respond.

"I'll leave you now," Raziel finished, "as I can see you're much in need of rest. But as I told you last week, I am most sorry to hear of your loss. My condolences."

With that he turned, took three steps away, and disappeared.

I was left standing in the Alamo Plaza, the sun beginning to set, the secret history of humanity clutched to my chest and an idiotic expression on my face.

Dazed as I was, I managed to make it back to the rental car, something so mundane that after the events of the past few hours it seemed extraordinarily normal in comparison. I carefully placed the book into the cardboard box of my grandfather's things and drove away.

On my way out of town, I stopped by the house on Crescent Row to see Maria. She was happy to see me, and I was just glad to see someone familiar and sane. We shared a small meal together in the kitchen, talking nonstop about the past, about me and my brother, about the years we spent in the house, and about my grandfather. We talked quite a bit about my grandfather, what the last few years had been like for him, how they had changed him in quiet little ways, and how he had finally gone to his rest. He had died quietly, Maria told me, fully dressed in suit and tie and sitting in his chair in the study, as though he was ready to go out for the night. He had faced death ready and willing, she said, all of his affairs in order, all of his things packed and organized.

She asked me about the two things I'd received from him, the box and the case. She'd had no idea what was in them, just that they were treasured by the old man, and that his final wish was that I have them. I think Maria was more than a little disappointed that I hadn't made the funeral, but she didn't mention it, and when I finally apologized, awkwardly and sincere, her eyes brimmed with tears and she hugged me until I almost passed out from lack of breath.

I told her a little about the cardboard box and its content, leaving out the more confusing details, and all of the craziness of the past few days. Maria had always been a strong woman, and still was, but the chances that she'd believe anything I had to tell her about what I'd learned were nil, and I didn't want her thinking the old man had gone crazy, or that I had lost my mind on drugs.

The wooden case, I told her, I had been unable to open, as I had received it locked and without the key. Maria jumped from her chair immediately and, waving me to follow, raced through the house to the study. I trailed along behind, taking in the smells of the old house, pausing only at the door to the study.

It was exactly as I'd remembered from all those years before. The papers were gone now and the books all up on the shelves, but the prints and paintings still hung the walls and the leather chair still sat behind the huge wooden desk, just as the old man had left it.

Maria was behind the desk, rummaging in the drawers, but I found I was reluctant to enter the room. It felt as though I'd be stepping on someone's grave to do so, tampering with the dead. I hung back at the door, waiting for her to finish.

She came up smiling, a small iron key in her hand, and bounced back to where I stood. Of course, I realized, the old man would always have kept a spare.

Finally, it was time for Maria to go of to bed and time for me to head back home. We said our tearful goodbye at the back door, Maria making me promise to visit again, and I answered with all sincerity that I would as soon as I could. I got back in the car and drove the hour north to home.

Back in Austin I found things just as I'd left them a few days before. Hot, dark, and empty of food. I left the cardboard box with the book and my grandfather's things by the door, tossed my suitcase over onto the couch, and headed for the kitchen. There, on the table where I'd left it, was the wooden case, the other half of my inheritance, the remainder of my grandfather's life's work. Pulling the iron key from my pocket, I sat down at the table and pulled the case over in front of me.

The key turned easily in the lock, oiled to perfection, which hardly surprised me. My grandfather always insisted everything in the house be in perfect working order, no matter how old. Or how young, for that matter, considering how he had worked my brother and me. But that was long ago, and all sins forgotten.

I hesitated before opening the case, wondering what might be inside and almost afraid to find out. Finally, curiosity got the better of me, and I carefully lifted the lid up.

There, in precisely shaped indentions on black velvet, sat twin .45 Colt automatics, with a small envelope resting on top. The pistols, like the lock, looked oiled and flawless, as new as they'd looked fifty years before. Fifty years before, I realized, when my grandfather had used them, fighting crime and injustice under the hood of the Black Hand. It was all true, every word of it.

With shaking hands, I lifted up the envelope and

managed to get it open. There was a single sheet of parchment paper inside, the close lines of my grandfather's hand filling one page.

To my beloved grandson, Spencer Tracy Finch,

These were to have been my gift to you on the occasion of your graduation from high school and entry into the world of adults. I had anticipated, and hoped, that you would choose to follow in my footsteps, and in the footsteps of my ancestors, and take up the mantle of the Black Hand. If you have opened this article prior to your other inheritance, the contents of that box should adequately explain what I mean, and what significance that name has had for our family.

I have said that I had hoped you would follow in my footsteps, and I am a foolish enough old man that when you chose your own road in life I allowed myself to feel slighted by it. To feel that you had somehow betrayed me. I apologize for that, and regret now that we have not been closer over the years. However, I have always kept a watchful eye on your progress, both those years you spent with the thief in Louisiana (whom I know all too well; ask him about San Francisco in the Spring of 1949), and your later efforts as a journalist throughout these United States. I want you to know that I could not have been prouder of you, even had you taken on the mantle I wore so many years ago. Through your actions, by following the path of your choosing, you have proven to me that you are upholding, in your own way, the high ideals to which our family has always dedicated itself, and that the Taylor family line is proudly carried forward in you.

I regret, my grandson, that I am not able to tell you these things myself, but I am an old man, too set in my ways, and not long for this world. I will be gone by the time you read these words, so I ask only this. Continue to strive, always strive, for what is good and best, and remember me.

Yours,
Richmond Taylor, the Black Hand

It was some time later that I put the paper down, and sometime after that when I climbed out of the chair and crossed the room. My most cherished angers, my long-held petty grievances, had all been taken from me, and in their place was an overwhelming feeling of loss. And, inexplicably, of satisfaction and accomplishment. I was confused, but then realized that for the first time in a long time, if not ever, I was proud of myself. The validation from my grandfather I had never thought I wanted or needed, when finally given, suddenly put my whole life in another perspective.

I stood thinking for a long while, standing still in the kitchen, before I went back to the living room to get the cardboard box. Returning to the kitchen, I laid out the book I had been given by the angel, and the papers of my grandfather, and started to work.

I turned to the blank pages in the back of the book, where the last member of the Cult of the Lightbringer had left off, before the book had been lost to pirates and found by my seafaring great-grandmother many times removed. The history of the Order of the Black Hand ended there, and that's where I would begin. The papers and articles I would staple in as I went.

I picked up my pen, and wrote, *"My brother and I once met at a bar..."*

ACKNOWLEDGMENTS

Perhaps more than any of my other books, this one in particular would not have been possible without the love, support, and encouragement of my wife, partner, and friend, Allison Baker.

I am also endlessly grateful to Mark Finn, Matthew Sturges, and Bill Willingham, who helped bring this story into focus.

ABOUT THE AUTHOR

Chris Roberson's books include the novels *Here, There & Everywhere, The Voyage of Night Shining White, Paragaea: A Planetary Romance, Set the Seas on Fire, End of the Century, Iron Jaw and Hummingbird, The Dragon's Nine Sons* and *Three Unbroken*, and the comicbook mini-series *Cinderella: From Fabletown With Love*. His short stories have appeared in such magazines as *Asimov's Science Fiction, PostScripts*, and *Subterranean*. Along with his business partner and spouse Allison Baker, he is the publisher of MonkeyBrain Books, an independent publishing house specializing in genre fiction and non-fiction genre studies.

He has been a finalist for the World Fantasy Award four times – twice for publishing, and once each for writing and editing – twice a finalist for the John W. Campbell Award for Best New Writer, and three times for the Sidewise Award for Best Alternate History Short Form (winning in 2004 with his story "O One").

More recently Chris has been writing the acclaimed comic book, *I Zombie*. He lives, with wife and daughter, in Austin, Texas. Read more of his work or just find out what he thinks at ***chrisroberson.net***

Extras...

AUTHOR'S NOTES

Readers of my previous novels may recall that I am the type of person who feels cheated when "The End" are the last words in a book, and who never buys a DVD if the "Special Features" are nothing more than theatrical trailers. While I feel that stories should explain themselves, I nevertheless like a little extra material to explore when I finish the story itself, a bit of behind-the-scenes business that I can dig into after the credits roll.

With that in mind, I offer the following notes.

On the Text

A somewhat different version of this novel was originally published under the title *Voices of Thunder* in a print-on-demand edition by Clockwork Storybook, a short-lived writers' collective in Texas. The present volume represents the author's preferred text.

On the Origins of BOOK OF SECRETS

Like my novel *End of the Century,* with which it shares more than a few points of connection, this story is one that lived in my head for years. The earliest notes on the characters and ideas can be found in notebooks dating back more than twenty years, to when I was an undergraduate at the University of Texas at Austin. I tinkered with the various pieces for years, and by the spring of 1993 I had figured out the basic plot, worked up the back-stories of the various characters, and sketched in the rough outline of the secret history of the world that Spencer's searches would gradually reveal. I did research for the next year or two, filling notebook after notebook with entries on secret societies, mythologies, and other historical minutiae.

By the time I turned twenty-five in 1995, I had the whole story mapped out. But while I had the *plot* figured out, I didn't yet have the structure. But more importantly, I knew I wasn't yet a good enough writer to tell the story I wanted to tell. I started writing the novel at least a half-dozen times, but each time was defeated by it.

By the decade's end I was *almost* ready. As part of the Clockwork Storybook writers' group, I had the constant encouragement (and more importantly, criticism) of the other members – Mark Finn, Matthew Sturges and Bill Willingham – to help me improve my craft. And inspired by Michael

Moorcock's *Fabulous Harbours*, I'd finally worked out the structure that the story demanded.

The version of the story that was published as *Voices of Thunder* was not a first draft – or even a fifteenth – but still in many ways I consider it an unfinished work, bread that wasn't yet fully baked. After a brief life as a print-on-demand edition (that sold only a handful of copies), I continued to tinker with the manuscript, revising it again and again over the years since. The end result is the present volume, now rechristened *Book of Secrets* – perhaps ironically, the title I'd originally given the story back in 1993, which is only fitting, as this is the story that I set out to tell, all those years ago.

On the Black Hand

The notion of a family of heroes is one that has obsessed me since childhood. Not an extended family of adventurers and explorers like the Bonaventure-Carmody family featured in much of my other work (the inspiration for which was found in the works of the late Philip José Farmer), but a *lineage* of masked avengers, a mantle passed down from one generation to the next.

It's an idea I encountered again and again growing up – the masked avenger who carries on the work of their forebears. On the radio and in the pulps, Fran Striker's Green Hornet was the nephew of his Lone Ranger, carrying on in the then modern era the fight begun by his uncle in the Old West.

And in the comic strips, Lee Falk's Phantom was merely the most recent in a long line of Ghosts that Walk, waging a never-ending war against piracy. In the comics, Gray Morrow's re-envisioning of the Black Hood was the modern-day scion of a similar heroic tradition, while Tim Truman's Prowler was a retired hero who spent his twilight years training his successor. Matt Wagner's Grendel was a dark inversion of the model, a masked avenger like the others but far from a hero, and not merely a mantle passed from generation to generation but a demonic spirit of aggression that possesses one host after another.

The work of these talented writers and artists was originally responsible for planting the seed in my fevered young brain that eventually became the Taylor family and the mantle of the Black Hand, and so it is with humble thanks that the present volume is dedicated to them.

Chris Roberson
Austin, TX, USA

CHRIS ROBERSON IN CONVERSATION

Writing is said to be something that people are afflicted with rather than gifted and that it's something you have to do rather than want. What is your opinion of this statement and how true is it to you?

I've always said that anyone who can stop writing should – if you're really a writer, you don't have a choice in the matter. I'm certainly one of those who has written compulsively since childhood, and I couldn't stop if I wanted to. Luckily, I love writing, so it's not any kind of burden. But definitely, even if no one was paying me to write, I'd still be doing it.

When did you realise that you wanted to be a writer?

Very early on. I wrote my first "novel" when I was nine years old. It ran to 426 words on three and a half handwritten pages, and it was entitled *Space Crash*. And it in no way resembled *Star Wars*, which had been released two years before. I kept writing through high school, short stories and poems mostly, all of them horrible. In college I started writing novels, and just didn't stop.

It has been said that if you can write a short story you can write anything. How true do you think this is?

It's certainly true that the skills and discipline involved in crafting a successful short story are the basis for all good writing, and I think anyone who can write a good short story has it within them to write a good novel. Novels just take longer!

If someone were to enter a bookshop, how would you persuade them to try your novel over someone else's and how would you define it?

Book of Secrets is a murder mystery combined with a secret history of mankind, wrapped up in a story about a man coming to terms with his heritage. Oh, and there are gangsters, masked avengers, highwaymen, mythological beings, cat burglars, and more! I quite like the tagline cooked up by someone in the Angry Robot offices: "It's almost like *Angels & Demons* but with real angels and demons." It's not quite accurate, but it captures the flavor nicely.

Who is a must-have on your bookshelf and whose latest release will find you on the bookshop's doorstep waiting for it to open?

Anything by Alan Moore I will sit down and read the minute it appears, and deadlines be damned. Also high on my list are people like Kim Newman, Michael Moorcock, Kage Baker, Terry Pratchett, Michael Chabon, Grant Morrison, and many others.

When you sit down to write, do you know how the story will end or do you just let the pen take you? Do you develop character profiles and outlines for your novels before writing them or do you let your ideas develop as you write?

I outline compulsively, and write incredibly in-depth character profiles and such before ever typing word one. I keep a wiki database for all of my research and worldbuilding, a personal encyclopaedia that gets bigger and bigger as time goes on.

My outlines are closer in some cases to extremely rough drafts, describing the content of each bit of narration and dialogue, but written quickly and without any concern over how they will read. Then, when it comes time to write, I just rewrite that outline into prose form bit by bit, and when I've rewritten the last of the outline I've got a complete story.

What do you do to relax and what have you read recently?

To relax I watch cartoons with my daughter, read comic books, and noodle around with writing projects other than whatever I'm supposed to be working on at the time. At the moment I'm a judge for the World Fantasy Awards, so I'm having to read everything published in 2008 that might conceivably be called fantasy.

The most recent book I finished and enjoyed was Jeffrey Ford's *The Shadow Year*, which is just a tour-de-force of a writer working at the height of his powers.

What is your guiltiest pleasure that few know about?

I have no guilty pleasures, or rather I don't keep any of my pleasures private. I'm proud to admit to all of my strange obsessions, from kids' cartoons to puppetry to superhero comics, and so on.

Lots of writers tend to have pets. What do you have and what are their key traits – and do they appear in your novel in certain character attributes?

We have a cat, or rather a cat has us. But he has not yet appeared in any of my stories, at least not so far as I'm aware…

Which character within your latest book was the most fun to write and why?

Most likely the most fun to write was Tan Perrin, the Fagin of cat-burglars.

How similar to your principal protagonist are you?

Spencer Finch is very much an overly idealized self-portrait of myself at a younger age. I was never much like Finch, but I think I very much wanted to be. He is, however, much cooler than I am.

What hobbies do you have and how do they influence your work?

My hobby *is* my work. That's the real advantage of getting to do the thing you love for a living.

Where do you get your ideas from?

Everywhere!

Do you ever encounter writer's block and if so how do you overcome it?

If I get bogged down in one project, I just switch to another for a while.

Certain authors are renowned for writing at what many would call uncivilised times. When do you write and how do the others in your household feel about it?

I'm very boring in this regard. I write during banker's hours, you could probably say, in the time that my daughter is away at pre-school. Usually it's from nine in the morning to three in the afternoon these days.

Sometimes pieces of music seem to influence certain scenes within novels. Do you have a

soundtrack for your tale or is it a case of writing in silence with perhaps the odd musical break in-between scenes?

I know some writers listen to music when they write to get them into the mood, but I can't manage it. I have to have silence, as complete as possible.

What misconceptions, if any, did you have about the writing and publishing field when you were first getting started?

I had the impression, as many writers do when starting out and meeting rejection, that the publishing industry was this giant monolithic thing that was designed to keep new writers out, a closed and hermetic system that only those with connections could enter. And I was completely wrong. It wasn't that the editors couldn't recognize my genius, it was that my stories were mostly crap. Continue to write, improve, and keep submitting, and sooner or later you'll get published.

What can you tell us about the next novel?

Um, it depends on whether you meant the next one out, or the next one I'm writing.

Well, if you mean the next thing of mine to come out after *Book of Secrets*, it's actually a comic book mini-series I'm doing with Shawn McManus for Vertigo Comics, a spin off of Bill Willingham's *Fables,* entitled *Cinderella: From Fabletown With Love*. It features the reimagined fairy-tale character, who is now "Cinderella, Super Spy," and is *Sex in the City* meets *On Her Majesty's Secret Service*.

What are the last five internet sites that you've visited?

Google Mail, Google Reader, Facebook, Blogger, and of course I should mention my own blog at *www.chrisroberson.net*.

Did you ever take any writing classes or specific instructions to learn the craft?

I took a few creative writing classes, but I don't really recommend them. The best of them I took basically involved the professor assigning us novels to read, some of which were genius and some of which were crap, and asking us to figure out what worked in didn't in each of them. I think the best training in writing comes in reading.

How did you get past the initial barriers of criticism and rejection?

Dogged determination, you could say, if you were being kind. An obsessive compulsion, though, would probably be a better term for it.

In your opinion, what are the best and worst aspects of writing for a living?

The worst aspects are probably the interminable wait between finishing a book or story and readers actually getting a chance to read it.

The best part is that you get to write for a living…

Interview reprinted courtesy of The Falcata Times (http://falcatatimes.blogspot.com)

ANGRY
ROBOT

"A SPECTACULAR WRITER" – ROBERT J SAWYER

LIVE TONIGHT
ON ANGRY ROBOT
TWO MEN. TWO
KNIVES. ONE DUEL.
ONE DEATH IN A
BURST OF BLOOD.
JOIN US EVERY
NIGHT AS WE FIND
OUT WHO HAS THE
EDGE

THOMAS
BLACKTHORNE

angryrobotbooks.com